ONE NIGHT
WITH THE
BILLIONAIRE BOSS

by

SERENITY WOODS

ISBN: 9798374229783

CONTENTS

Chapter One

Elizabeth

Oliver Huxley is well-oiled tonight. I'm not surprised. He's been drinking whisky since the party started at seven, and it's now almost one a.m. Fortunately nobody else can tell, as he's always been able to hold his drink. He's one of those guys who just becomes progressively funnier with each shot he puts away.

I go to put my glass on the table, miss, and nearly fall off my chair. Hmm, maybe it's me who's well-oiled. I've tried to pace myself this evening, but it's tough to refuse Huxley when he's at his most charming, and he's been sending over doubles of the most expensive whiskies all evening. Earlier I complained that he was trying to get me drunk, and he replied that he was hoping I'd fall over to entertain the guests. It's not beyond the realms of possibility considering I'm wearing my usual three-inch stilettos. Being five-foot-one in my bare feet means I nearly always wear high heels—not that it brings me much closer to Huxley's six-two frame. He's always teasing me about being 'vertically-challenged'.

I should go home really. But my dog, Nymph, is at my brother's tonight, and I won't pick her up until the morning, so the apartment is going to be dark and quiet.

Plus, the main reason I've been drinking is to summon the courage to talk to Huxley about a Very Important Matter.

I don't know whether I'm going to get the chance now, though. He's standing at the bar with a group of clients that our friend, Titus, brought with him, and Huxley is in full swing, telling some joke or anecdote that's made them all burst out laughing. He looks gorgeous tonight. It's Valentine's Day and the height of summer in New Zealand, so he discarded the jacket of his three-piece dark-gray suit some time ago, but he's still wearing his waistcoat over his white shirt, and his light-blue tie. His dark-brown hair is ruffled sexily in a way I'm never sure is contrived or natural.

The one woman in the group, a redhead who happens to be wearing a gold lamé shirt that's unbuttoned almost to her navel, has been making eyes at him all evening. She's been stuck to him like cling wrap, so I doubt I'll be able to get him on his own now.

"Hux is in good form," Victoria says. As his business partner and second-in-command, she's been busy making her rounds through the various rooms in the club, ensuring the Valentine's Day party is running smoothly. A while ago she came in claiming she needed a break, so we started chatting, and she hasn't yet left.

"He's always in good form," I reply. "I'd be annoyed if I could summon the energy. He said he only had four hours' sleep last night. I don't know how he does it."

"He might regret his lack of sleep if the redhead gets her way."

"I know what you mean. Her tongue rolled out like a carpet when she met him."

The two of us chuckle. It's not spiteful. We're well used to the effect he has on women.

Huxley bought this club eighteen months ago, and he spent months refitting it before opening it around this time last year. Private clubs are hardly a new idea, but Huxley wanted to replace the men's-only port and smoking rooms with something that catered for the young entrepreneurs of Auckland. Trust in business is essential, especially in our current economic climate, and he recognizes that networking builds relationships that can be nurtured over time. He wanted a place that focused on business but also had the luxuries of some of the more social clubs. And so Huxley's was born.

It's always tough starting off a new enterprise, and so I, Mack, Titus, Victoria, and some of our other friends have spent a lot of time at the club, holding meetings here, bringing our clients, and introducing as many new faces as we can. And it seems to be working; Huxley's won second place on the list of top New Zealand business venues in the last issue of the prestigious *Kaipakihi* trade magazine, so word is definitely spreading.

Situated on five floors, the building has fully serviced offices, nine high spec meeting rooms, a stunning restaurant, lounges and workspaces, a gym, and a range of personal suites. It also has a main function room and several smaller bars, each boasting a different vibe.

The one we're currently in is called the Churchill Lounge. It's a bit old boys' school, which I moan about, but secretly I love all the dark-brown wood, the red leather seats, and the bottles of whisky and brandy above the bar. The whole building is non-smoking, but there's a great painting of Winston Churchill on the wall, complete with cigar. Tonight, Victoria and Huxley have decorated everywhere with strings of red hearts and white Cupids complete with bows and arrows, which is rather adorable.

The club has been busy this evening, many of the young businessmen and women apparently relieved to escape the Valentine's Day craziness, pretending to spend their time talking stocks and shares rather than sweet nothings over their champagne, although I suspect romance has flowed beneath the surface, as it often does when people get together. But it's quietening down now, and Titus has obviously decided to call it a night, and is escorting his guests out. Huxley's going with them, the redhead attached to his arm, so I guess that's it.

I'm sitting with my chair turned sideways, my back against the wall. I sigh, stretch out my legs and lift my feet onto the chair opposite, then carefully peel off my false eyelashes as they're annoying me. I'm ashamed to say I made an extra effort on my appearance this evening, knowing he finds it harder to say no to me when I use my womanly wiles. Clearly, though, it was a waste of time. I finish off my whisky moodily. I'm never going to win over a redhead who's obviously interested in some serious sex.

"It's a shame Mack didn't make it tonight," Victoria says, referring to one of our other closest friends. "I wonder where he got to?"

I smile. "Didn't you hear? He proposed to Sidnie, and she said yes."

Her face lights up with genuine pleasure. "Oh, no, I didn't. That's fantastic."

"Yeah. He seemed terrified she'd say no. As if that was going to happen. She's clearly nuts about him."

"And he about her," Victoria adds with a grin. "I've never seen him so obsessed about a girl."

"I didn't think any woman would be able to distract him from his research. But somehow she managed it."

"The magical power of the pussy. Guaranteed to keep even billionaire geniuses from their work."

I snort. "They're all the same. Obsessed with sex."

"There speaks a woman who isn't getting any."

"I don't need a man to satisfy my urges, thank you very much. Battery-powered devices are much less trouble."

"This sounds like a conversation I definitely want to be involved in." Huxley appears out of nowhere, knocks my feet off the chair in front of me, and pulls it around so he's sitting like me, with his back against the wall. "I'm always interested when women start talking about their—Jesus!" He slams his hand on the table, making us all jump as the glasses rattle. He lifts his hand to inspect his palm, then glares at me as he peels my false eyelashes off his skin. "I thought they were spiders."

I start laughing, pleased he's joined us. "You're such a wuss."

"Any person who isn't scared of spiders needs their head tested."

"Just how drunk are you?"

"I'm not drunk," he protests. "I'm… relaxed."

"So relaxed you'll be under the table in five minutes."

Victoria rolls her eyes. "That's my cue to retire for the night. See you guys tomorrow. Great party, Hux."

"Yeah, thanks for all your hard work."

"No worries. Goodnight." She nods at me, then heads out of the door.

Huxley hooks his foot around the chair she's vacated and pulls it toward us, and we both stretch out our legs and rest our feet on it. I glance across at him, unable to hide a smile. I've known this guy for ten years, and he never fails to make my heart skip a beat. He's tall, and the fact that he took up the unusual sport of archery at school and has practiced it ever since is reflected in his well-muscled shoulders. He has brown hair that's short up the back and longer on the top, and a tiny mole on his left cheekbone that always makes me want to kiss it. He's gorgeous and irresistible, and he knows it, which makes it so much harder for me to keep him at arm's length.

He catches the eye of Ian behind the bar, and holds up two fingers.

"Not for me," I protest. "I should be heading off soon, too."

"If you do that, I'll be drinking alone, and that's just sad."

"What happened to Ms. Gold-lamé? I thought you'd have been balls-deep by now."

He gives me an amused look. "She wasn't my type."

"She was breathing, wasn't she?"

"Haha. She was a very sweet girl. But it's Valentine's Day. Why would I want to spend that with anyone else but you?"

I give him a wry smile. "Technically, it's the fifteenth now."

"Even so." He grins at Ian as he brings two whiskies over. "Cheers."

I sigh and take one of the glasses. "You're trying to destroy my liver," I grumble.

"I like you drunk," Huxley says. "It files off your sharp edges."

"What sharp edges? I don't have any."

He laughs. "Yeah, of course you don't." He holds up his glass, and I tap mine to it. "I always drink to world peace," he says. It's a quote from *Groundhog Day*.

"To world peace."

We both have a mouthful of the amber liquid and sigh.

"Did you like your flowers?" he asks.

Today, he had three dozen pink roses delivered to my office at MediTech.

"They were absolutely gorgeous, and thank you very much. But you've got to stop doing that," I scold.

"Buying my best friend presents?"

"Asking me out."

"I told you ten years ago that I'd ask you out every month until you said yes."

"You did," I murmur, remembering the moment well. Unfortunately, he'd already broken my heart by then, which I'm sure he knows, although we've never openly discussed it. "I thought you'd get bored after the first four or five times I turned you down."

"Nope," he says cheerfully. He just sips his drink, his gorgeous light-gray eyes on mine. Then, lowering his glass, he says, mischievously, "Go on a date with me."

"No," I admonish. "Stop it."

"Why not?"

"Because we're best friends, and I don't want to spoil that."

"Friends to lovers? Isn't that the best romance trope?"

"Hux…"

"How about friends with benefits?"

"Jesus."

"You've got to give me points for trying."

"You don't get any points. Stop nagging me."

"It's your fault for talking about battery-powered devices. It's got me all hot and bothered."

"Your temperature is permanently a hundred degrees. It's your default setting."

"Slanderous talk."

"Yeah, like you hate the fact that you have a reputation in the bedroom," I say sarcastically.

He studies me for a moment. "So do you," he replies.

I stare at him, my jaw dropping, and sit up, livid. "The guys have been talking about me in the locker room? Hux, seriously?"

"So let me get this right—you're indignant at the thought of us guys discussing what you're like in bed, but I'm supposed to be flattered? Where does that fit into your definition of equality, exactly?"

I meet his eyes and slowly close my mouth. "All right," I say sulkily. "Fair enough."

He sips his whisky. "I am a little bit flattered," he concedes, "but that's not the point."

I give a short laugh. "What do they say about me?"

"Nothing," he states. "You know I'd shut down a conversation like that in seconds."

Impishly, I say, "You're not interested?"

"I don't need to listen to gossip to know you'd be amazing in bed."

I nudge him with my elbow. He nudges me back, harder, and I nearly fall off my chair. Luckily, he catches my arm and pulls me back up.

"Jesus," I berate him, "don't do that."

He grins. "Maybe this should be your last whisky."

"You think?"

I'm flustered. I can't believe we're talking about sex. The two of us have a strange relationship. With other women, Huxley prides himself on being a gentleman. He's respectful and polite, and even when he likes a woman, he'll never openly let the conversation turn sexual, not in front of me anyway.

Despite what happened ten years ago, or maybe because of that, we've become best friends. I think both of us feel safe within our relationship, knowing that despite his monthly enquiry, it won't progress beyond platonic, and because of that we tease each other almost continuously. But although sometimes our teasing gets near the knuckle, we very rarely discuss intimate details about the bedroom. Maybe it's because normally Mack or Victoria or Titus is around, and it's unusual for us to be alone together.

"So tell me about my reputation," he says. "I hope it doesn't involve detailed discussion of length and girth."

That makes me giggle. "Maybe."

"Seriously?"

"A man who's as generously endowed as you are—allegedly—shouldn't worry too much about locker-room chat."

"Jesus."

"Don't act like you're not pleased."

"I'm thrilled. And a tad embarrassed."

"No you're not," I scoff.

"Well, it's better than hearing you're all laughing because it's so small, but yeah, it's a little mortifying."

"Well, then, maybe you need to keep it in your pants a bit more, and we wouldn't have so much to talk about."

He drops his gaze to his glass and swirls the whisky over the ice. "I probably deserved that," he says before taking a sip.

I close my eyes for a moment before turning toward him a little. The last thing I meant to do was hurt his feelings. He's still my best friend when it comes to it.

"No, I apologize. That came out sharper than I meant. You're a gorgeous guy. Good looking, funny, and warm-hearted. Women are going to clamber over each other to get you. And why shouldn't you make the most of that?"

He holds my gaze for a long while. I lean my head on a hand and study his light-gray eyes. I've been in love with this guy since the moment I met him. It was at a party, halfway through our first year at university. He turned up with Mack, who I'd met through some extra-curricular computer science lecture I'd attended. Mack introduced us, and as I felt as if I'd been hit between the eyes with a cricket ball. Even back then, Huxley was tall and gorgeous, but it was his manner that won me over—he was funny, warm, and attentive, and right from the start I knew he liked me. We went on a couple of dates—the first to the cinema, and for the second he took me to dinner. Both times we parted with a long, passionate kiss. I wanted to ask him to come up to my room, but I was still a virgin, and shy, and not quite ready for that final step. But the third date, I told myself, that was when it would happen. And I already knew it was going to be amazing.

Unfortunately, though, the third date never materialized. Huxley mysteriously disappeared for two weeks, and I didn't hear from him. Even Mack and Victoria didn't know where he was.

And then one day he reappeared. I was in the library, studying, and I looked up from my laptop to see him standing there, leaning against one of the bookcases, his hands in his pockets, watching me. I felt my face light up, but he didn't smile back.

Heart racing, I packed up my stuff, and we walked over to the coffee shop. He bought me a latte and sat me down, and then he told me what had happened. A girl he'd slept with a few months ago, Brandy Rowland, had told him she was two months pregnant, and he was the father.

It had happened before we'd started dating, which was something, I guess. But even so, it shocked me deeply.

I sat there stiffly, my heart banging on my ribs. "You fucking idiot. Why didn't you use a condom?"

"I did. No contraception is one hundred percent perfect. Shit happens, unfortunately." He seemed very calm about it. But then he'd had a couple of weeks to work off his frustration.

"Are you getting back with her?" I asked.

He shook his head. "It was a one-night stand. Neither of us wants a relationship. But obviously I have to take responsibility."

Of course he did. I'd never met a more honorable guy. There was no alternate universe in which he refused to accept he was the father.

But it still stung. Maybe because they'd had a one-night stand, and I'd held out for the third date. Surely it was better that I hadn't slept with him? But as I sat there, looking into his gorgeous eyes, I'd felt my heart splintering like a log split with an ax.

"Right," I said.

"Things are going to be difficult," he said. "Her parents are very strict, and she's absolutely terrified of telling them. So we're going to say we're an item for now. I'll have to see a lot more of her, and I want to be there when she has the baby. I don't want her to have to go through it on her own. I fucked up, and I have to pay the price for that."

I nodded, swallowing hard.

"I'm so sorry," he said.

I knew then that he was saying we were over. We hadn't even got off the starting blocks, and we were done.

"One day," he said, "when the baby's born, and things have settled down, I'll ask you out again. But I don't expect you to wait for me."

"That's good of you." Disappointed and hurt, I got to my feet.

"Elizabeth." He got up too. "I don't blame you for being angry. I know I've blown it with you. And I'm absolutely gutted. But I hope we can still be friends."

"I don't know." I shoved my chair under the table. "I don't think I'm that big a person, Hux." And I turned and walked out.

I went back to my flat and cried for two days straight, then pulled myself together and realized the sky wasn't falling down. I'd been on two dates with the guy. It wasn't as if we were engaged or anything. I was nineteen years old, and I wasn't going to let this destroy me. It wasn't his fault. Well, technically it was, but he was right—shit happened, and he'd been big enough to come and tell me about it himself. We'd be mixing in the same circles, and I liked him, and I didn't want to shut him out of my life.

And so, in the end, on the surface, not much changed. He wasn't around so much, but when he was, we remained friends. When his daughter was born, I went out with all our mates and celebrated with him. I attended the christening, held the baby, and told Brandy how beautiful her daughter was.

I tried to be the bigger person. I really did. But inside, the fractures in my poor heart refused to heal. Watching him with Brandy, putting his arm around her, being sweet to her, taking care of her, broke me every time. He'd told me it was all pretend, an act for her parents, and I was glad for the baby's sake that he was such a sweetheart toward her, but it still crushed me.

Then, six months to the day after Joanna was born, he asked me out.

I told him I'd think about it. And I did. I thought about nothing else for several days. But, in the end, I said no.

It was too complicated, and I was too young. I didn't want to date a guy who had ties to another woman. He must have had feelings for Brandy to have slept with her, and every time I saw them together, he was gentle and affectionate toward her. Deep down I couldn't shake the notion that they had feelings for each other, and I couldn't have coped with that if we'd been dating. It made me a small person. I knew that. But at least I was honest with myself. I didn't want to date him and ruin it by being jealous. I liked him too much.

And so instead, we stayed good friends.

I began dating someone else shortly afterward—Tim Fanshaw, another chemistry student. I was four months into that relationship before Huxley also finally started dating someone else. His relationship was more short-lived than mine. When I eventually broke up with Tim, Huxley asked me out the day after. And then every month after that, unless I was going out with someone else.

We've continued like that over the last ten years. I know it's just a joke now. We're the best of friends, and there's far too much water under the bridge for us to make a go of things. I've had three failed—no, let's be honest and call them what they are: disastrous—relationships. And Huxley's friendship means far too much to me for me to blow it now just because I'm curious about what he's like in bed.

It's because we're such good friends that I came here tonight to ask him something very special. I didn't think I was going to get a chance. But it's late, and quiet. Ian the bartender has just gone out with a crate of empty glasses, and there are only the two of us in the bar. And I guess there's no better time to ask than when you've both been drinking whisky all evening.

I gather my courage with both hands and take a deep breath. "I wonder if I could ask you something."

He swirls his whisky over the ice. "Of course." I nibble my bottom lip, and he gives me a curious look. "What?"

"I'm nervous," I admit.

"Why?" He looks puzzled.

I blow out a breath. "Okay. Here goes. I'll be twenty-nine soon. And I'm done with men." I watch his eyes flicker with pity. "And that's all right, I've come to terms with that. I don't want another relationship. I have my work, and my dogs, and a great social life. But there is one thing missing. I want a baby."

His eyebrows rise. He hadn't expected that.

"I've been to a fertility clinic," I explain, speeding up a little now I've finally got the words out. "And I've talked to them about having a sperm donor. But there's a three-year wait for clinic-recruited donors for single women. Three years!"

"Jesus."

"Yeah. So… they suggested I find a personal donor. And so… um… I wanted to ask you. Would you help me out?"

Chapter Two

Huxley

Holy fuck. I did not expect that.

Silence falls between us. It's not particularly uncomfortable. We've known each other long enough that we can allow the other time to think.

She rests her head on her hand again, watching me. Her brown eyes are hopeful. It's an unusual expression for her. Over the years, she's become quite cynical, the last person to express belief in notions like true love or soulmates. I know I played a big part in that, and it crushes me every time. But there's not much I can do about it now.

Instead, I try to force my whisky-addled brain to focus on what she's asked me. She wants me to get her pregnant.

I blink and grab onto the balloon of pleasure that floats up inside me. No, Huxley. She doesn't want you to get her pregnant. She wants you to ejaculate into a cup so she can use it to fertilize her eggs. There's a huge difference.

She has a mouthful of whisky. "Say something," she says. "You're making me nervous."

"I'm not ready to answer yet."

"Oh." She sucks her bottom lip.

She was gorgeous when I met her ten years ago, and since then she's grown into a beautiful, confident woman. Tonight, she's wearing a mid-gray trouser suit with a pale pink shirt, and as always, black high-heeled stilettos. When she was younger, she used to have longer wavy hair, but about a year ago she had it cut for the first time into a long bob that brushes her shoulders, which makes her look sophisticated, and suits her professional image much more. Her makeup is immaculate, and I've always loved her French-manicured nails.

She owns her own pharmaceutical company now, working with Mack and Titus at times, using their technology to develop new drugs to combat diseases. She has a large staff, and she runs them with a firm hand. She's one of the most professional and savvy businesspeople I know, and she's been absolutely invaluable in establishing the club. She's also a wonderful auntie to my daughter, Joanna, which is more than I could have hoped for.

And now she wants me to get her pregnant.

Huxley! To fertilize her eggs.

I feel a tug of resentment, deep inside. She won't go on a date with me. She refuses to accept that a relationship might work. But she has the cheek to ask for my sperm. Fucking hell. I made a mistake ten years ago, and for that she's determined to make me pay forever.

And then I look at her big brown eyes, and all my exasperation vanishes. I know I broke her heart back then. She could easily have walked away and refused to talk to me again, but she didn't. When she first met Brandy, I'd been certain that Elizabeth would be cool and dismissive, but she hadn't, she'd been friendly and warm. And when Joanna had been born, Elizabeth had been the first of my friends to visit Brandy, and she'd held Joanna and said how beautiful she was with such graciousness that I'd had to walk out to compose myself.

I broke her heart, and yet she became my best friend. Now, she wants a baby, and out of every man she knows, she's asked me to help. If there's a greater compliment a woman can pay a man, I can't think of it.

"First of all," I say softly, "I'm immensely flattered. Unless you've already asked every other guy you know, and I'm your last resort."

Her lips twitch. "You're the first," she murmurs. "Of course you are. You're a fantastic guy, and you're an amazing dad."

I have a mouthful of whisky to cover my emotion. "Thank you," I say, my voice husky.

"I didn't even have to think about it," she says. "When they said try asking a friend, you were the first and only person I considered." She takes a shaky breath—this has taken her some courage to ask. "I know it's a bit weird, though. Of course I'll be happy to talk it through at length. But first I should say that you would have as much input as you wanted. Legally, when a man donates sperm to a clinic, neither the child nor the donor has rights or liabilities in relation to each other. After saying that, men who donate sperm are required to be identifiable, and a child can ask the clinic for the identity of the man who donated. Because of this, apparently it's common for parents to let their child know about the donor, and sometimes the child and donor stay in contact. I'd… I'd like that. But equally, I'd understand completely if you'd rather not. Especially because you have Joanna. If you were to donate, and would rather me keep it a secret, particularly from our friends or family, I would do that, at least until the child got to an age where they started asking questions. I'd do whatever you wanted."

She stops, and even in the dim light of the room, I can see her cheeks flush.

I tip my head back, inhale deeply, and slowly release the breath. This wasn't how I'd hoped I'd have my next child. Having a relationship and a family hasn't been a big priority for me over the past few years. I've thrown myself into setting up the club, working twelve to fourteen hours most days, and I've been careful not to let any brief fling I've had develop into anything more.

But I'd assumed it would happen one day. I'd like to meet someone and settle down, and I'd hoped for the proper experience of having a family, where you try for a baby, take a test together, celebrate when it's positive, watch your partner's bump grow, and be there for the birth knowing you'll be there for every developmental step. That's how I wanted it to go. Why am I doomed to miss out?

"Hux," Elizabeth says, "I'm dying here. Please say something. Be honest with me."

"Be honest?"

She nods. And at that moment, I know I can't give any other answer.

"Honey, I don't think I can do anything in a cup. I'm so sorry."

The light slowly fades from her eyes. "Oh." Her expression turns from hopeful to disappointed, and her eyes glimmer with tears. It's so unusual for her to show emotion that it's like someone's stabbed me. I've let her down. Ouch.

"Let me explain," I say, hoping she doesn't just get up and walk out. Luckily, she gives a short nod. "I've done the distant father thing already. And it's been so hard."

She runs a hand through her hair and sighs. "I know."

"And to do it with you? The one girl I've always wanted? The one who got away? Jesus. It would fucking kill me."

She blinks, her gaze fixed on mine. Then her bottom lip quivers, and she presses her fingers to her lips.

"You asked me to be honest," I say helplessly.

"I know," she squeaks. She waves a hand at her eyes. "Don't worry, it's the whisky."

I smile and hold up an arm. She presses her lips together, then exhales in a rush and leans against me.

Hugging her, I press my lips to her hair, inhaling the scent of coconut. She has such a big personality that most of the time I forget how tiny she is.

I've only kissed her on the mouth twice, and both of those times were on our two dates ten years ago. I wish I could kiss her again. But I can't. I ask her out every month, and every month she turns me down. I know she's never going to say yes.

It's not all about me, I think. She has a terrible taste in men—I'm including myself in that—and I haven't liked any of her previous partners, although I acknowledge it might say more about me than them. But she's been hurt so badly that she's like a wounded she-wolf who's retreated into her den, and she's refusing to come out.

I'm sure she doesn't think I'm serious when I ask her. I'd sell my soul for a chance to convince her how good we'd be together.

And then an idea strikes me like a hammer on a bell.

I loosen my tie a little. Then I pick up my whisky glass.

"There is an addendum to my decision," I tell her. "Or is pudendum?"

She snorts and pushes me away. "What sort of addendum?"

"I said I wouldn't do anything in a cup. But I am prepared to get you pregnant the old-fashioned way."

"Hux, come on, this isn't a laughing matter."

"I'm not laughing. Look at my face." I point to it. "I'm deadly serious."

She rolls her eyes. "Jesus."

I lift a hand to cup her chin and turn her face so she's looking at me. "I'm serious," I repeat. I release her chin, but her gaze remains fixed on mine.

We study each other for about twenty seconds.

Then, eventually, she says, "Nope."

I'd expected that, and I've prepared my argument. "Okay. Let's look at it this way. From what I understand, at the clinic you'd have two choices of insemination, right? Intra Uterine Insemination and In Vitro Fertilization?"

She narrows her eyes. "How do you know that?"

"I'm a man of the world. I know stuff. So, what's the success rate of IUI?"

"Seven to ten percent per cycle," she says. I knew she'd have all the stats in her head. Not only will she have read up on the process because that's what she does, she's also developing some kind of fertility drug at her company, so she'll be well aware of the facts and figures.

"And of IVF?"

"Fifty-five percent on the first try."

"But there are risks, right?"

"Yeah… multiple births, premature delivery, low birth weight. A few others. And it does involve taking fertility drugs, which I'm wary of."

"So… what's the success rate of getting pregnant the old-fashioned way? If you have sex around ovulation?"

Her lips start to curve up. "Around thirty percent."

"And the risks?"

"All right, smart arse. I know what you're saying. But it's not going to happen."

"Why?"

"Because I don't want another relationship."

"Why?" I ask again, softly. "I know you've never forgiven me for what I did, but what happened with the others that's made you so anti-men?"

"I'm not anti-men," she protests. "I happen to like them very much. And I have forgiven you. It's purely a self-defense mechanism." She looks at her glass and turns it in her fingers. "Do you know what a non-healing fracture is?"

"No."

"It's when the pieces of a broken bone don't grow back together. Bones usually start rebuilding after they've been set. But sometimes bones don't produce new tissue, leaving an aching pain and weakness." She presses her hand to her chest. "That's my heart, Hux. It's been broken so many times that it has a non-healing fracture."

Something twists inside me at her description. "I'm so sorry," I whisper.

She places her hand on mine for a moment and squeezes before releasing it. "It wasn't all you," she confirms.

"You've had, what, three serious relationships? You're so strong, Elizabeth. So resilient. They can't all have broken your heart?"

She looks around. Ian has come back into the bar, and he's currently collecting more glasses. He'll stay until I go home unless I say otherwise.

"Ian," I call out, and he looks around. "Call it a night and finish off tomorrow."

"You're sure?"

"Yeah. Thanks for all your hard work."

"You're welcome." He grabs his jacket, then selects a whisky bottle from the row. He brings it over and puts it on the table, grins, then heads out the door. Now it's just me and Elizabeth.

She takes off her shoes and rests her bare feet on the edge of the chair, knees bent. I look down at her toes as she wiggles them. They also have a French polish.

"Jesus." I close my eyes for a moment.

When I open them again, she's giving me a wry look. "Want me to put my shoes back on?"

"Definitely not. As long as you don't mind wiping the drool from my chin."

She laughs and leans back against the wall. I unscrew the bottle and splash a little whisky in our glasses. She sighs.

"Come on," I say. "Spill the beans." Even though I've seen her most days over the past ten years, I know very little about her love life. She's a private person, and as far as I know, she hasn't told any of our friends about why her relationships ended.

"Let's see," she says. She blinks slowly. She's been drinking all evening, and she must be pretty tipsy to open up like this. "Tim cheated on me. Rich had issues in the bedroom. And Steve…" She hesitates, then says, "Steve hit me. So yeah. Not a great track record."

I stare at her. I don't know where to start.

Actually, yes I do. "He hit you?"

"Yeah."

"Where?"

"In the living room."

"Where on your body, Elizabeth?"

"Ah, across the face."

"Holy fucking shit, that motherfucker."

"Yeah. Don't worry. He only did it once. I pushed him through a plate-glass window for it, and they spent a fortnight picking glass out of his hair."

She wants me to laugh, because that's what we do—we turn our personal disasters into comedy moments—but I'm not laughing. The thought of a man raising his fist to Elizabeth—to any woman—makes me see scarlet.

"Don't burst a blood vessel," she says. "But maybe you can see why I ended that one."

I reel off another string of swear words, down the whisky in one, and pour myself another shot. She does the same, coughs, then gestures for me to refill hers.

I'm quiet for a moment as I battle my fury. I wish she'd told me at the time. I'd have shoved the guy's teeth so far down his throat he'd be shitting molars for a fortnight. But Elizabeth's not the kind of girl who appreciates displays of testosterone, so I keep it under, for now.

"And Tim cheated on you?" I say when I finally feel I can speak.

"Yeah. I came home one night and found him in bed with Patsy Landingham. Do you remember her?"

"Tits bigger than her IQ?"

"That's the one. I wouldn't have minded so much if she'd been a rocket scientist. But to be passed over for a giant pair of knockers." She looks down at her breasts. "I always thought I had nice boobs."

"You have exceptional boobs."

"Thank you. I knew you'd appreciate them."

We clink glasses and have another mouthful of whisky. I wipe my mouth with the back of my hand. "I can't believe he cheated on you. What an imbecile."

"I thought so."

"Did he get the plate-glass window treatment too?"

"No. I just turned and walked out."

"That's a shame."

"Yeah, part of me wishes I'd kicked him in the family jewels, but hey. It's done."

"So what about Rich then?" I ask. "What were the issues in the bedroom?"

"You know I'm only telling you this because I'm drunk."

"Why d'you think I'm pouring the whisky?"

She sighs. "He suffered from premature ejaculation." She glares at me as I start laughing. "It's not funny."

"I know. There but by the grace of God and all that. It's every guy's worst nightmare."

"So why are you laughing?"

"I honestly don't know. Christ, Elizabeth."

"Me and sex don't go together well," she says somewhat gloomily.

"I think you're a perfect match."

"Yeah, yeah. Between you and me, I think sex is vastly overrated. I get far more enjoyment out of my vibrator than I've ever done with any guy," she says, a little sulkily.

"Ah, man." She's determined to torture me tonight. The thought of her preferring to pleasure herself is both an incredible turn-on, and a little bit sad at the same time. "Please don't say that."

"Men are high maintenance. They're so selfish."

"We are, it's true."

"No, not you. Well, maybe, I don't know, I can't think about you and sex in the same sentence." She waves a hand. "But generally, you know, guys just want to get to the finish line. So it's like, five minutes of foreplay max, which involves one erogenous zone, or two if you're lucky, and speaking of which, why do guys think it's a turn on to touch you as if they're stuffing a chicken?"

I give a short, humorless laugh. "Jesus."

"And then they're like, hey, what do you mean you're not ready for me? So they have at it anyway, then they're shocked when you don't come. And then afterward when they leave you unfulfilled and you ask them for some help, you're the selfish one for keeping them awake when they want to doze off. So you lie there while they're pressing buttons knowing they're thinking for fuck's sake, come on, and if anything's going to kill your passion, it's that…" Her diatribe trails off as she looks up at me.

I'm resting my forehead on a hand. "Please don't tell me any more. You're killing me."

"I'm sorry. I'm just telling it how it is."

"Elizabeth… please go to bed with me."

That makes her laugh. "We are so drunk."

"Go to bed with me. Let's have some amazing sex, and get you pregnant in the process."

"I told you, I don't want a relationship."

"Fine. Give me one night, then."

She blinks, and her gaze slowly focuses on me. "You're serious."

"I'm deadly fucking serious."

"I'm not going to sleep with you."

"Why? I can't be any worse than Rich-oh-fuck-I've-come-already-Halcome."

She giggles. Then she lifts a hand to my face. Her gaze is filled with longing.

"We'd make the most beautiful baby," I say.

She brushes a thumb across my bottom lip. "I thought you didn't want to be a distant father again? Why would that be any different?"

"Because I think if you give me one night, I'll be so irresistible that you'll want two. And then three. And we'll never look back. And we'll have a dozen beautiful children and be happily married until the end of time."

She lowers her hand and gives a short laugh. "It's a nice fantasy."

"We could make it a reality."

"I don't think so."

"Why not?"

"You remember the story I just told you about having a non-healing fracture?"

"That was ten years ago. We were kids back then. We're grown-ups now. We'd make it work."

"I don't want that, Hux."

"You're just scared."

"Maybe."

"And it's understandable. But if you give me time, I'll prove to you that I'm serious about you."

She looks at her glass. Then she has another mouthful of whisky.

"Let's start with one night," I tell her. "When you're ovulating. I'll make love to you as many times as I can manage it. And if, after that, you want to call it a day, I won't argue."

She gives me a mischievous look. "How many times do you think you could... ah... arrive in one night?"

"Arrive?"

"It means come."

"Funnily enough, I was able to decrypt your Enigma code. So, with you? Ah... Fourteen, fifteen?" My lips curve up as she giggles. "All right, that might be an overestimation. Um…" I think about it. "In one night? I'm not as young as I used to be."

"Ballpark."

"Ah… okay… if I don't self-administer for a few days before…"

She gives a short laugh, and her eyes dance.

"Four?" I suggest. "Five if you paint your toenails red?"

She snorts. "Five? Seriously?"

"Yeah. After that the well might run dry for a day or so."

Her gaze drops to my mouth. "How often do you self-administer? Loving these euphemisms, by the way."

"Most mornings." I sip my whisky. "You?"

She sucks her bottom lip for a moment. "Most mornings."

We both smile.

"We are really, really drunk," she says.

"Yeah, I know."

"I'm so going to regret this conversation in the morning."

"It's the most honest we've ever been," I tell her. "I'm loving it."

She leans forward and rests her forehead on my shoulder for a moment. "Don't tell anyone."

"Which bit? The self-administering bit, or about Rich Halcome?"

"All of it." She sighs. "Especially the bit about Steve hitting me. Mack and Titus will get all riled up and then the Magnificent Three will go off to teach him a lesson, and I don't want that."

"Why not?"

"I dealt with it. Plate-glass window, remember? The fucker will have scars on his face for life. He won't ever forget the day he gave me a fucking backhander."

I kiss the top of her head. "That's my girl."

"I love you," she says.

I sigh. "You are plastered, aren't you?"

"I mean it."

"I know."

"Why aren't you drunk?" she demands.

"I am."

"You never seem it."

"Well I'm about three foot taller than you, so I can hold it more. And I know how to disguise it better."

She turns her head and rests her cheek on my shoulder. "I'm sorry."

"For what?"

"For asking you to inseminate me."

I sigh. "Oh, Elizabeth. I think that's the sexiest thing a woman has ever said to me."

"Ah, don't make me laugh."

"I'm so glad you asked me. And I do want to help. I just think it'll be a lot more fun to do it properly. Don't you think?"

"Mmm," she says, noncommittally.

"I'm not bad in bed," I say.

"I'm sure you're not."

"I even got a gold star once."

She laughs.

"I'd give you as many orgasms as you could stand," I tell her.

She groans. "I'd be glad with just one."

"Let's reach for the sky and go for two."

"Hux…"

"Two really, really good ones."

She sighs.

"Thirty percent," I remind her. "That's all I'm saying. If we had sex three months running, that's a ninety percent chance of getting pregnant."

"I don't think probability works like that."

"Maths was never my strong point."

"Wasn't it part of your business and economics degree?"

"I bribed the examiner to give me a pass."

"You know, that wouldn't shock me."

I rest my lips on the top of her head. "One night. That's all I'm asking."

"Did you just sniff my hair?"

"It smells of coconut. It makes my mouth water."

She lifts her head, rests it back on the wall, and looks up at me with hazy eyes. "I know I'm going to regret this in the morning, but I don't care. I want to kiss you. Will you let me?"

"I'll think about it." I wait a second, my heart racing. "All right, I've thought about it. Yes. You may kiss me."

She puts down her drink, and then, to my surprise, she takes her feet off the chair and gets up. She sways a little and laughs, then turns to face me. I inhale as she lifts a leg over where mine are stretched out and sits on my lap, straddling me.

Ohhh… we are obviously both very drunk. Neither of us would suggest anything like this if we were sober. But no way am I going to turn down the opportunity to kiss a tipsy Elizabeth Tremblay.

She leans on the back of my chair and studies my face. "You have a nice mouth," she murmurs.

I chuckle, lift a hand and slide it into her hair, and pull her head down to kiss her.

Her mouth is incredibly soft. Her lipstick has worn off, and her lips are warm and dry. I press mine to them a couple of times, trying to stay calm, as if she's a deer in the woods, and I'm afraid of frightening her away.

Not wanting to push my luck, I'm about to release her when she tilts her head to the side and opens her mouth to me.

I don't need any further encouragement. I brush my tongue against her bottom lip, and then when I slide my tongue against hers, they indulge in a sensual dance that gives me a hard-on and leaves me tingling all over in seconds.

We kiss for a long time, slowly, languidly, and I wonder whether she's feeling the same as me—wanting the magic to go on forever. I don't ever want to stop. I want to lift her and carry her up to my room, take off all her clothes, kiss her all over, and then make love to her until she screams my name into the night.

She lifts her head, and her eyes glitter in the light from the bar as she rocks her hips, obviously feeling my erection. "We could go back to your room," she whispers.

Ahhh… I'm so fucking tempted.

But I can't. In the morning we'll be embarrassed, but we can dismiss the kiss. If we go all the way, though… I know she'll regret it, and then I'll feel like a heel for not being the gentleman. She won't blame me openly, because she's a big proponent of equality and the theory that it takes two to tango, but even so, I'm not so drunk that I don't know what I'm doing, and that means I need to stay in control.

I lift my head, sigh, and kiss her forehead. "Don't tempt me, Frodo."

She blows out a breath. "You and your fucking principles."

I laugh and lift her off me. "I'm calling you an Uber."

She finishes off her whisky, then bends carefully to pick up her shoes and purse. I take her hand and lead her to the door. I very rarely see her without her heels, and she's so tiny without them. For some reason I find it a huge turn on.

"I don't have much willpower at the best of times," I tell her. "If we have sex now, you'll hate me tomorrow."

"I wouldn't."

"You would, and I'd hate that. Come on, Tremblay."

I lead her along the corridor, through the double doors, and then out through the lobby. Gail, the daytime receptionist, has gone home. Will, who's on the night shift tonight, smiles at us.

I look at Elizabeth. She's practically asleep. I'm not sure I trust her to get out of the Uber and up to her apartment.

I sigh and look back at Will. "What suites are free?"

"Eleven and twelve, sir."

"Give me a key for eleven."

Will programs the key card and passes it to me. "It sounds like it was a great party, sir."

"Yeah. It went very well. I'm going to put Ms. Tremblay to bed. Can you do me a favor and have a look for my jacket? It might be in the Chess Room, or maybe in Churchill's? I can't remember where I left it."

"Yes, of course."

"Can you bring it to my room if you find it?"

The height of professionalism and discretion, Will doesn't bat an eyelid as he asks, "Which room will you be in, sir?"

I give him a wry look. "My room."

"Of course, sir."

I bend, slide an arm beneath Elizabeth's legs, and pick her up. Then I carry her into the elevator, and carefully press for the next floor.

The doors slide shut, and the elevator goes up silently. I look down at the sleeping girl in my arms. Well, she's not a girl, she's very much a woman now. Although she looks a lot younger asleep. She's incredibly beautiful. I know that tomorrow she's going to regret everything she said tonight. It's a shame, because I've had such fun.

The elevator doors part, and I carry her along the corridor to room eleven. I touch the card to the door, open it, and go inside.

Carefully, I lower her onto the bed. I place her shoes on the carpet, and put her purse on the bed beside her. I get a bottle of water from the fridge and leave it next to the bed with a couple of Panadol from the box in the cupboard. Then I bring the waste-paper bin over and leave it by the side of the bed, just in case.

She's going to regret sleeping in her expensive suit, but I'm not so drunk that I think helping her out of it is a good idea.

She's out for the count. I look down at her. *I love you*, she said. I have no doubt that's true. I love her too. She's my best friend, and the last thing I'd ever want to do is take advantage of her.

I blow out a breath, turn out the light, and leave the room. Sometimes, having principles sucks.

Chapter Three

Elizabeth

I open my eyes. It's pitch black in the room, the only light coming from a small red dot of a TV on standby. I'm confused, because I don't have a TV in my room at home. The red display on the alarm clock on the bedside table reads 03:11.

I lift my head and groan as the room spins. Ahhh… why do I do this to myself? I love alcohol, but I detest this part of being drunk.

My stomach churns, and I groan again and push myself up to a sitting position. I recognize the layout of the room—I'm in one of the suites at Huxley's. I'm shoeless but fully dressed, and lying on top of the covers.

Nausea rises inside me, and I get up and stumble into the bathroom, where I vomit into the toilet. When I'm done, I lurch back into the bedroom, taking off my jacket, trousers, and shirt as I go, leaving them where they drop. In just my underwear, I pull back the duvet, collapse into bed, pull the duvet over my head, and fall asleep.

At 04:16, and again at 05:27, I rise and vomit again. The third time, I force myself to drink half the bottle of water that was sitting on the bedside table before I fall back asleep.

The next time I wake, there's light coming through the crack in the curtains. The clock reads 06:39.

My head's still spinning, but I feel a bit clearer. Gradually, memories of the night before bloom in my mind.

Cautiously, I look to my right. The bed's empty. I lift my head and look around the room. It's the kind of standard suite I've slept in at Huxley's many times before when I couldn't be bothered to go home.

How did I get here? I honestly don't recall. Why didn't I go back to my apartment?

What's the last thing I do remember? My brain is like a rusty machine, the cogs squeaking as the mechanism clicks into gear. I was in the Churchill Bar, talking to Victoria. Then Huxley came in, and Victoria left. I remember Huxley dismissing Ian, who brought a bottle of whisky over before he left. Hux and I had a few more drinks while we talked…

I asked him if he'd donate for me.

And then, gradually, the rest of the conversation filters back.

Pulling a pillow over my head, I press my hands on it as if I could suffocate myself.

I asked him to donate for me. And he said no. But he did clarify it with *I said I wouldn't do anything in a cup. But I am prepared to get you pregnant the old-fashioned way.*

I breathe slowly, trying to calm my racing heart.

Slowly, I lift the pillow and drop it onto the bed.

I told him about Tim, and Rich, and that Steve hit me. I remember the twenty or thirty swear words he used, one or two I hadn't even heard of. His quiet outrage. Sweet, sweet Huxley, riding in on his white charger.

I think I rambled on about how sex was overrated. Jesus, that would be like a red rag to a bull to a guy like Huxley. And it's why he said *Go to bed with me. Let's have some amazing sex, and get you pregnant in the process.*

Covering my face with my hands, I try to keep calm.

I think we kissed. Yep, he definitely gave me a long, luscious smooch. Oh my.

We'd make the most beautiful baby.

Tears prick my eyes. It's the after-effects of the whisky, I tell myself, but I know it's not. I want to cry because more than anything in the world I want to say yes. But I can't.

I meant it when I told him I had a non-healing fracture in my heart. Disappointment after disappointment in love have made me determined not to date ever again. I've cried too much over men. After my failed relationships, I can only conclude there must be something seriously wrong with me. I'm too demanding, too prickly, too unwilling to settle. My standards must be too high. And yet I can't bear to lower them. What is it that Bill Pullman says to Meg Ryan in *Sleepless in Seattle*? Something about marriage being difficult enough without bringing such low expectations into it?

Do I ask too much? I expect monogamy in a relationship. I understand that some people are happy to play around at the beginning as they try different partners on, but I've never done that. I've never had a one-night stand. Never done the Tinder thing. When I've met a guy I've liked, I've gone on a few dates and then we've mutually agreed to be exclusive. Tim slept with someone else while we were a couple. Is it wrong of me to have dumped him for that?

I do like sex, whatever I said to Huxley. I like sharing myself with someone in a physical way. But I understand that the body doesn't always work the way you want it to. I didn't leave Rich because he sometimes suffered from premature ejaculation. I would have been prepared to work with him, if he'd been willing, and to find ways to deal with it. But he was embarrassed, furious even, every time it happened. It came out as resentment and anger toward me, and I couldn't deal with that.

Steve was the most difficult one in many ways, because mostly we were a good fit. He didn't cheat. He was okay in bed, although the issues I told Huxley about were mostly connected with him. But we liked the same music and movies. He was smart and good looking and funny—not in Huxley's league by any means—but not bad. He had a terrible temper, though, and lost his rag all the time about stupid things like computers going wrong or missing a program on TV. It was impossible for me not to compare him to Huxley, who gets angry, of course, but never about small things, only when it matters: to defend someone who's been bullied or mistreated, or over unfairness, or injustice.

The day Steve hit me, he'd lost his temper because something had gone wrong with the oven and it burned the dinner. Usually when he started shouting, I'd walk out or try to defuse it by solving whatever had wound him up, but that night I'd been tired, and frustration had made me yell that I wished he was more of a man like Huxley. Steve was already jealous of our friendship, and he'd accused me of cheating on him with Hux, and then hit me.

I didn't tell Huxley that bit.

I look up at the ceiling. Huxley is tall and handsome—the best-looking guy I know. He's incredibly clever—his crack last night about bribing the examination officer for a pass in mathematics was amusing because he was top of all his mathematics and economics classes. The guy's a fucking smart arse. He's honorable and fair. Very funny.

Extremely affable and a great host, seeing it as his calling in life to put everyone at ease. And because of all that I wouldn't be surprised if he's great in bed. He sounds perfect.

But he's not of course. I can overlook the fact that he's afraid of spiders, heights, thunderstorms, needles, clowns, dolls, the sight of blood, and probably a dozen other things. I can forgive him for being incredibly ambitious, a tad arrogant, squeamish, for only eating his food one item at a time without mixing them on his plate, for liking practical jokes, and for being stubborn and prideful and even Mr. Darcy-like at times, refusing to admit he's wrong.

I can forget all that. But when it comes down to it, I can't forget that he's a player, a tomcat who's never been out with a girl for more than six months, in my knowledge. That's not to say he uses women. I don't think he's ever had to talk a girl into his bed, and I doubt he's ever had to promise a wedding ring to get them to sleep with him. But I've had to console girls when they've come to find him and he's conveniently disappeared. I've watched them cry, and I've been determined never to put myself in the same position.

Mack and Titus are the same—or Mack was until he met Sidnie—and I guess it might have something to do with the guys being so rich; I think they're all wary about women being after their money. Which, as a woman, I'd get resentful about, except I've actually overheard women they've dated joke about hooking a billionaire, so I know it's a factor.

I understand why he's been reluctant to commit in the past. And I accept that he might have changed, because he's older now, and his business is relatively stable, and he might be looking to settle down at last. He did promise me, *If you give me one night, I'll be so irresistible that you'll want two. And then three. And we'll never look back.*

But am I willing to bet my heart on it?

No. I am not.

I know he's fond of me. Maybe that he even loves me, as a friend. But it's impossible not to think that he only wants me because he hasn't had me. And that once the novelty's worn off, he'll be looking elsewhere for entertainment. If that were to happen; if we were to date, and then he either cheated on me or broke it off because he was bored… I cover my face with my hands at the thought, my insides twisting. I would never, ever recover.

I blow out a long, slow breath and lower my hands. I feel better now I've thought it all through. Last night was an amusing diversion, and I enjoyed flirting with him, and kissing him. But the crux of it is that I asked him to donate, and he said no. Forget all the jokes about doing it the old-fashioned way. He doesn't want to be a distant father, and that's fair enough. I shouldn't have asked him, I guess, but it's done, and now I can move on.

So... what's next? Do I ask one of the other guys I know?

My face flushes at the thought. A few months ago I might have asked Mack, because we're good friends and I like and admire him, even though we argue a lot. But I can't ask now he's with Sidnie; that would just be weird. Wouldn't it? At the clinic, they said it's relatively common for men who have partners to donate, and the partners are asked to sign the consent form so they're aware of the issue around the donor being identifiable. But I can't help but think that if I was Sidnie, I wouldn't want my man fathering other women's children.

What about Titus? I've known him as long as the others. He's lovely—taller and bigger even than Hux and good looking with it. I've given him several nicknames over the years—the Incredible Hunk and the Striking Viking jumping to mind, because of his Scandinavian heritage. But we've never had that connection that I have with Huxley. Perhaps that's a good thing, though? Maybe it would be better to have a baby with someone like that?

I rest a hand on my tummy beneath the covers. I don't know. The thought of getting pregnant by Titus feels bizarre. The whole process is a bit freaky, actually. I'm beginning to think I'd rather not know the donor. So what does that mean? That I have to wait three years for a clinic donor?

I'll only be thirty-two. Hardly old to have my first child. But it feels like such a long time. I'm at a good point in my life right now. My company is well-established and doing great. I have a fantastic apartment, a beautiful dog, lots of friends, and a blossoming bank account. I feel as if I'm in the perfect place for a baby. I want one so badly. I didn't think I was the sort of woman who'd get broody, but I am, terribly so. And now I have to wait three years?

I look at the clock. It's now 7:05. I need to get home, shower and change, and go to the office. I have two meetings this morning, then I'm supposed to be coming back to Huxley's for a one p.m. meeting with the Auckland Business Consortium. Which, of course, Huxley will be at. I groan. I'm going to have to face him at some point. I'm not ashamed that I asked him to be a donor—I like to think it's a flattering thing if a woman likes you enough to father her child. And I'm not embarrassed that I opened up a bit. I don't even mind that we kissed— we were drunk, and we're both single. Nobody was hurt in the process.

Okay, I'm a little mortified to have discussed self-administering and vibrators. But hey, I'm a woman of the world. Fuck it. It's done. If that's the only thing I have to worry about, my life isn't going too badly.

I get up, groan as I open the curtains, and pull on my suit. I could shower here, but I don't have all my toiletries or a change of clothes, and I'd rather go home.

I tidy my hair, wipe away the worst of the black smudges under my eyes, and pick up my purse. Then I frown as I see the waste-paper bin beside the bed, and the two Panadol and the bottle of water on the bedside table. Did I leave them there? I don't remember. That was very smart of me considering I was out of my tree. Shrugging, I take the Panadol, put my shoes on, a little unsteadily, and then quietly leave the room.

I'm relieved to get to reception without bumping into Huxley. I hand Gail my key card with a smile, then head over to the elevator and call the carriage.

It's only as I walk in and press the button for the ground floor that something filters into my memory. As the doors close, I stare ahead, not seeing the mirror, but instead a flicker of an image from last night. Huxley's waistcoat and shirt collar from close up. His strong arms around me. Holy shit—he carried me in here and took me up to the room. He was the one who left the bin and the Panadol.

I lean against the wall and let my head fall back with a thud. He could so easily have taken advantage of me. But instead he took me up to a spare suite, put me to bed, and left.

Oh my God, Huxley. What am I going to do with you?

*

At 1:10 p.m., I arrive back at the club. I feel a lot better than I did earlier. I went home, picked up Nymph from my brother, took her for a run, showered and changed, and ate breakfast, even though my stomach was still a bit uneasy. By eighty-thirty I was in the office, and

I've had a busy and productive morning. I've just dropped Nymph off home, and now I feel ready to face the music.

I'm a little late because my last meeting ran over, but it won't matter—everyone in the Consortium runs a business, and we all know the pressures we're under, and make allowances accordingly.

I have to admit, though, to feeling butterflies in my stomach as the elevator rises to the third floor. Will Huxley have told any of the others what we talked about last night? I can't imagine he would have. Even so, I have to take several deep breaths as I walk out of the elevator and along the corridor to the board room where the meeting is always held.

As I approach the room, I can see the shape of the other eleven members of the Consortium behind the frosted glass, and then the muffled sound of laughter. I sigh, put my hand on the door, and push it open.

"Hey," I say, "Sorry I'm late."

"Hey, Elizabeth." Mack, Titus, and the other members call out as I walk in. I run my gaze along the table and see the one available chair near the far end of the table. Opposite Huxley.

Eyes down, I walk to the chair, pull it out, and sit. The head of the Consortium, Marvin Law, says, "We were just talking about the postal strikes in the U.K."

"Right," I say, getting my laptop out of my briefcase. I put it on the table and open it up as one of the guys asks the others about what courier services they use. Pulling up the notes I'd prepared for the meeting, I type the date and press return a few times to leave a space.

Then, finally, I look up.

Huxley's leaning back in his seat, his arm over the back of his chair, watching me. As I meet his eyes, his lips curve up for a moment before he turns his gaze back to Marvin.

I let mine linger on him for a second. He's showered, shaved, and changed into a navy suit. He looks fresh as a daisy, as if he's had ten hours' uninterrupted sleep.

Gritting my teeth, I drop my gaze back to the laptop and force myself to concentrate on the meeting.

After half an hour, there's a knock at the door, and he leaps up to open it for the catering assistants, who bring in several platters of sandwiches and nibbles for a working lunch. As usual, he moves around in the background while the meeting continues, getting people coffees, handing out serviettes and plates, and directing the caterers quietly so the meeting can continue.

The guys tuck into the sandwiches with gusto, never failing to amaze me with how much food they can put away and still remain trim. I and the other two women at the table nibble more sedately, me mostly because my stomach still feels uneasy.

Toward the end of the lunch, Huxley chooses a small chocolate éclair filled with fresh cream, puts it on a plate, then offers it to me. He knows they're my favorite. And I also think it's some kind of peace offering, maybe him saying he's sorry for what happened last night. I give a small smile and take it. No doubt he's also having regrets about our conversation. I'm sure he doesn't want to lose my friendship any more than I want to lose his.

Eventually the meeting comes to a close, and everyone starts putting away their laptops and getting to their feet.

Mack comes over to me and says to me, "Hang on a minute, will you?"

"Sure." I sit back down and watch him go over and ask Titus and Victoria, too. Huxley obviously realizes something's going on because he stays sitting. Titus and Victoria move up to sit next to us, and Mack takes the seat at the top of the table.

When the others have gone out and the door swings shut, he smiles. "You might have heard already, but I just wanted to tell you personally that I asked Sidnie to marry me last night, and she said yes."

I knew because I played a small part in his proposal, and I vaguely remember telling Victoria last night. But Huxley and Titus obviously haven't heard because their eyebrows rise in surprise, and they get up to congratulate him.

Mack and Titus exchange a bearhug, and then Mack faces Huxley. "I'm hoping you'll be my best man," he says.

Huxley's eyebrows rise. "What about Jamie, and Kai?" he asks, naming Mack's younger brother, and his business partner at Koru Technology.

I'm not surprised Mack has chosen Huxley. Both Jamie and Kai are quiet men who dislike the limelight, whereas Huxley was born for the role.

But Mack just says, "It was always going to be you, bro," and Huxley nods and they exchange a bearhug, holding it a little longer than normal. It brings a lump to my throat, and Victoria says, "Aw, you two."

"So when's the big day?" I ask.

They break apart, and Mack says, "Well, we talked about it last night and decided that we don't want to wait long. Neither of us wants a big wedding, and Sidnie especially would prefer to keep it quiet as her dad's still having treatment. So we've decided to have a relatively quiet wedding on April the second. I hope you can make it."

We all stare at him, delighted. "Where?" I ask.

"Do you know Cameron Brown?"

"The CEO of Panther Enterprises?"

"Yeah. He owns a luxury yacht, and he's a celebrant. I spoke to him this morning, and I've hired his yacht for two nights. We'll set sail on the first in the afternoon, go up to the Bay of Islands, and stop at one of the islands overnight. Then the next day we'll pick up my family, do a day tour of the islands, and he'll marry us. We'll drop my family off next morning and then head back to Auckland."

"Oh Mack," I say with pleasure, "that sounds amazing. Of course we'll be there." I look around for confirmation, and everyone nods.

"Wedding bells," Huxley says. "We're all growing up, aren't we?"

Mack grins. "Yeah. Just a bit."

"I have to say," Victoria says, "I'm not sure she's good for you. You have dark rings under your eyes."

"I'm not getting a lot of sleep," he concedes, lips twisting as we all laugh. "She's young," he says, "and energetic. She's wearing me out."

"I'm going to have to get myself one of those," Titus says. "Has she got a sister?"

"No, but Huxley's got four," Mack replies. "And only one of them is married."

"How about Evie?" She's a police officer. "She'll have access to handcuffs."

"She frightens the shit out of me," Titus says, and we all laugh.

"Plus you have the X-Y chromosome thing going," Huxley adds.

"Oh yeah," I say, "I forgot she was gay."

"Chrissie?" Victoria suggests. She partnered Titus in a mixed doubles tennis tournament back in January.

"She's sweet," he says. "But she's dating an accountant."

"That leaves Heidi," I say, somewhat mischievously. Heidi Huxley is twenty-four and gorgeous, with blonde hair that's so long it reaches past her bottom. When Huxley was twenty-one, he had a party at their parents' house, and Heidi, who was all of sixteen at the time, was there. She had a couple of dances with Titus, and afterward I walked into the kitchen to get a drink and caught them kissing. They broke apart, and Titus's first words were, "Don't tell Huxley." Nothing came of it, I don't think, because she left shortly afterward to travel around Europe, and she now lives and teaches in England.

Titus opens his mouth to reply, then catches Huxley's gaze. Huxley raises his eyebrows, amused. Oh… he knows. I guess Heidi must have told him.

Titus clears his throat. "Er… yeah, lovely girl. Bit of a drawback that she lives on the other side of the world."

Huxley chuckles. "She's coming home during her summer holidays for a visit."

"There you go," I say. "Looks like a holiday fling is in order."

Titus gives me a wry look, then stands and picks up his briefcase. "And on that note, time for me to go. Congratulations, Mack. See you guys later." He heads out.

"Yeah, I'd better be off," Mack says, and the rest of us get to our feet.

"Elizabeth," Huxley says, "can I have a word before you go, please?"

It's not at all unusual for any of the guys to make such a request, so I have no idea why my face grows hot. I see Mack glance at me, obviously spot the blush, and watch his eyebrows rise and a smile spread before he sees my glare, hastily wipes the smile away, and leaves the room. Jesus. I concentrate on finishing off my notes and packing up my briefcase as the others file out after him before finally getting to my feet.

Huxley has walked around the table, and now he rests his butt on it and leans his hands on the edge as he waits for me to walk toward him.

"Afternoon," he says.

I stand in front of him, holding my briefcase like a shield. "Hey," I say quietly.

He tips his head to the side as he studies me. "You okay? How are you feeling?"

"Delicate. Not surprisingly. You?"

"Yeah, a bit fragile."

"You don't look it."

"Neither do you. You gorgeous young thing." He smiles.

I study my shoes for a moment, liking the compliment, although I would never admit it. Then I lift my gaze to his. "Thank you for taking me to the suite last night."

His light-gray eyes crinkle at the corners. "You're welcome."

"I appreciate it. You know. What you did. Not... um... taking advantage of me, at the risk of sounding like a character from a Jane Austen novel."

He gives a short laugh and then sighs. "I did kiss you though. I'm sorry about that."

"I asked you to, if I remember correctly."

"Yeah, well." His lips twist. Of course, I was the one who suggested we go back to his room, too. Fuck. I really shouldn't go near alcohol.

"I'm... sorry," I say.

His eyebrows rise. "For what?"

"For everything. I shouldn't have started the conversation. About being a donor."

"Of course you should. I was extremely honored that you asked me." His eyes are open and honest—he means it.

"Yeah, well, I should have thought more about the fact that you'd already had to go through being a distant father once. I should really have spoken to Mack or Titus first."

He stiffens, and his eyes flare. Ohhh... he doesn't like that.

There's a long silence.

"Are you going to ask them?" he says eventually.

"I'm thinking about it."

His jaw knots. He's gritting his teeth. I'm enough of a woman to feel a touch of smugness that I've made him jealous. Then I think how ridiculous that is and feel a wave of tiredness. I'm going to bed at seven tonight and I'm going to sleep for twelve hours.

He inhales, then breathes out slowly. Finally, he says, "Before you do that, I want you to think about my offer."

"Which offer was that?"

"The one to do it the old-fashioned way."

It's my turn to look surprised. I'd assumed that conversation had been provoked by the whisky.

I frown. "I said no, remember?"

"Yeah. I happen to recall every detail of what happened last night." His eyes gleam. Is he talking about the kiss? Or my diatribe about sex?

"I'm not sleeping with you," I say with some exasperation.

"One night," he says. "And I'll get you pregnant."

"For a start, as you pointed out, there's only a thirty percent chance."

"Okay, but one in three is pretty good odds."

"That may be, but it's not going to happen."

"Why?"

"Because Reasons, Hux. I described them all last night in great detail."

"I remember."

"This is about sex," I say impatiently. "Because I said it's overrated, and you feel this ridiculous testosterone-fueled desire to put me to rights."

"Not at all. Okay, a little bit. Can you blame me?"

"You only want me because you haven't had me. Deny it."

"I do deny it. But let's pretend you're right. Give me one night and you'll cure my obsession and have a one-in-three chance of walking away with a bun in the oven at the same time. Win-win, right?"

"Jesus. Romantic, much. And I thought you didn't want to be a distant father? I still don't understand how this is any different to jerking off into a cup. You do that every morning anyway, as I recall."

He gives me a wry look, then says again, "Give me one night. If after that I haven't convinced you to give me—us—a chance, I'll walk away. I swear."

His sheer arrogance infuriates me. "You're that confident of your abilities in the bedroom that you think one fuck will make me put my broken heart into your noncommitting hands?"

"Well, a) I promised you four fucks, possibly five depending on the color of your toenail polish, b) technically I'm not sure that hands can commit one way or the other, and c) you're not going to provoke me into a shouting match. Go and see Mack if that's what you want."

"Maybe I will. I'm betting he'll jerk off into a fucking cup to impregnate his best friend."

He gets up from the table and walks toward me. I back away and meet the wall with a bump.

He stops in front of me. Even with my high heels, I'm still about ten inches shorter than him, and I have to crane my neck to look up at him.

He gives me a look that's hot and sultry. "Are you trying to turn me on?" he murmurs.

I blink. "What the…?"

He shrugs. "I dunno. The word impregnate gets me all hot and bothered."

"Jesus."

"Say inseminate."

"No."

"Fertilize?"

"Hux!"

He laughs. Damn him, he's so incredibly charismatic. "You're not going to win this argument," he says, amused. "I don't care how much you stamp your feet."

I glare at him. "I'm not stamping, not in these heels."

For a moment I think he's going to kiss me, but he doesn't. Instead, his gaze turns gentle, affectionate. "Look, ten years ago I did something stupid. I know that, and you were right to tell me to get lost."

"I didn't—"

"Let me speak. You were right, and so I convinced myself you were better off without me, and I let you go."

"You call asking me out every month letting me go?"

"I wanted to let you know that if you ever changed your mind, I'd be there for you. But you didn't, and that's fair enough." His gaze drops to my mouth. "Then, last night, something changed."

"Yeah, I got drunk."

"Alcohol is a truth serum. It removes your inhibitions and makes you say what you're really feeling." His eyes are very intense. "You wanted me to kiss you, and you wanted to go back to my room with me."

I moisten my lips with the tip of my tongue. "It was the whisky talking."

"I don't believe that." He stabs a finger into my left shoulder. "I think your brain is in charge of your heart, and I understand why because you've been hurt so much, but you can't lock your heart up in a cage forever."

"Just watch me."

"Is that supposed to make me less interested in you? You're my friend. Even if I didn't fancy the pants off you, I'd want to do everything I could to convince you to love again."

"Like a very annoying, altruistic Cupid?"

He laughs. "Maybe. All I can say is that since I left you in that room, all I've thought about is kissing you again. I've done my penance, Elizabeth. And now I'm going to take my reward."

"Which is?"

"You." He smiles.

My jaw drops. "Do I get a say in this?"

"Not really. Sorry about that."

"So, what, you're going to browbeat me into having sex with you?"

He gives me an impatient look. "I won't be doing anything to you that you don't want done. I'm going to seduce you until you beg me to make love to you."

"Beg you? Ha! I've been turning you down since I was twenty. I think I'll be able to resist you."

"You think that was seduction? Girl, you have no idea. You are going to be the full focus of my attention from now on. I'm going to use all my manly wiles on you."

Despite my frustration, that makes me laugh. "Your what?"

"It's the opposite of womanly wiles, except I get to wrestle a bear afterward."

He always manages to disarm me with humor. I lean forward and rest my forehead on his chest, and he presses his lips to the top of my head. "Coconut," he murmurs. "You make me think of Bounty bars. Sweet and somehow exotic at the same time."

I inhale the scent of his aftershave, huff a sigh, then straighten. He smiles.

"Are you still coming to Joanna's birthday party on Saturday?" he asks.

"Yeah, of course."

"You've got four days to think about it, then. I'll expect your answer on Saturday."

"I've given you my answer."

"Thirty percent," he says, ignoring me. "Plus orgasms." He opens the door and gestures for me to precede him out.

I leave the room, scowling as I walk back to the elevator. The man's insufferable. There's no way I'm going to agree to sleep with him.

Even if now, I can't think about anything else.

Chapter Four

Elizabeth

On Saturday, I arrive at Huxley's parents' place around 3:30 p.m. They live in a huge house on Shore Road with a gorgeous view across Hobson Bay. I have to wait for the white double gates to slowly swing open before I ease my Mazda MX5 convertible down the drive.

Several cars are parked out the front, including my own parents' Ford Ranger, as they're good friends with Huxley's parents. Huxley's beloved obsidian Mercedes AMG GT is also already here, snoozing like a panther in the afternoon sunshine. I slide the Mazda into the space next to it and turn off the engine. After unclipping Nymph's safety harness from the seatbelt, I get out, and she leaps across my seat, out the door, and sprints around the side of the house toward the back garden.

Smiling, I retrieve the wrapped present from the boot and follow the poodle.

Huxley's mum, Helene, is an artist, a very good one, and sells her paintings at a local gallery. I doubt she makes a fortune, though, and most of their fortune has come through his father. Peter is in banking and, like his son, has a flair for mathematics and economics, and an astute business sense that I'm pretty sure can't be taught. Thirty years of clever investment in stocks and shares have obviously resulted in a very generous bank balance, and even the fact that they've had six kids hasn't noticeably drained it.

"Elizabeth!" Helene has come around the side of the house to meet me, and she holds out her arms as I walk toward her. "Thank you so much for coming!"

"Hey." I give her a big hug. She's taller than me, not that that means much because most people are, with shoulder-length blonde hair that's still not showing any gray. Her figure reflects the fact that she's had six children, but she always dresses beautifully, and I love that she clearly doesn't care. "How's the birthday girl?" I ask.

"In her element." She links arms with me as we head for the garden. "I'd forgotten what it was like to have a dozen children in the house. Girls are so much easier than boys, though. I remember Oliver's thirteenth birthday party. It poured down, and it was absolute chaos with them playing rugby indoors. Oliver fell down the stairs and gave himself a bump on his forehead the size of a walnut, Mack broke a lamp, and Victoria ate too much birthday cake and vomited all over my favorite Persian rug."

I laugh and give her an affectionate squeeze. Victoria is a transgender woman and went to the same boys' school as Mack and Huxley when she was young. Both my and Huxley's parents have been extremely supportive of her over the years, which we've all appreciated.

"Was Huxley as cute as a boy as he is now?" I ask.

"He was adorable. His hair was a lot curlier and blonder then."

"He was blond?" I laugh.

"He looked like an angel. I always said I should have called him Gabriel."

"He's not very angelic now," I grumble.

"Oh, I don't know." She smiles as we round the corner, and the view opens up. "He's not bad."

In the middle of the large lawn in front of us, Huxley is currently walking on his hands to the cheers of a dozen nine-year-old girls. He's wearing swim shorts and nothing else. His legs and feet are bare and brown, and his shoulders are all taut and muscular where they're supporting his body.

We stop walking and laugh, and I feel a tug of something deep inside as he eventually tips back onto his feet and Joanna runs up to give him a hug.

"Nymph!" she says then as the poodle bounds up to her, and the other girls cheer and immediately fuss the dog.

I watch Huxley turn and look for me, and then he heads up the lawn toward the deck as I walk over to it with Helene.

"Hey," I say to everyone already sitting there, trying to ignore my racing heart.

"Elizabeth!" Peter stands and comes over to hug me. He's tall like his son, and just as good looking, but there's a harder edge to him that his son doesn't seem to possess. I've always been a little scared of Peter Huxley, although he's never been anything but nice to me.

I go around and hug everyone else. First my dad, Neville, lying on a lounger with a beer, and then my mum, Raewyn, who's sitting in the shade, looking flaky as usual in a floor-length terracotta-colored skirt with an olive-green vest, bangles on her arms, and a scarf holding back her brown hair. She's very alternative. I have no idea why she and Helene are friends, but they've been close ever since they met when Huxley and I first introduced them.

Next is Brandy—Joanna's mum. She gets up and we have a big hug.

"Thank you so much for coming," she says. "I really appreciate it."

"Of course." I release her and smile. "I wasn't going to miss Joanna's birthday."

Huxley's had a lot of girlfriends over the years, and they've all been a certain type. I joked about him going off with the redhead in the gold lamé top at the club, but the truth is that he likes smart women—those who are going to challenge him and hold their own in a conversation. Brandy is not his type at all. She's lovely, very girl-next-door, with curly dark-blonde hair, but by her own admission she's not academic at all. She didn't go to university—I don't actually know where they met; at a club, I guess. She's arty, so she gets on with Helene and my mum, and in her spare time she makes jewelry out of tiny glass beads and wire that's really quite beautiful. But by day she works in the local supermarket, which isn't anything to be ashamed of by any means, don't get me wrong, it's just that I'd never have put the two of them together.

She's also flat-chested, and he does like a big pair of boobs.

But they both insist it was a one-night stand, and I think maybe alcohol was involved, and when you're a nineteen-year-old guy who's desperate for sex, I suppose you don't always need to discuss the national economy to get it on with a girl.

"You look nice," she says. "I don't see you in a dress very often."

I look down at myself. I'm wearing a knee-length summer dress that's a light-blue color with small pink flowers, which sounds awful but is actually really pretty. "Well, it's a party," I say. "I wanted to dress up a bit, and I'm always in suits, so…" I flush. Huxley likes the dress, and I know that's why I wore it.

"Hey you," he says, running up the steps of the deck and coming over. "Thanks for coming." His gaze skims down me, soft and light. "You look gorgeous."

Flustered, I say, "I caught the performance. Didn't know you could do a handstand."

"I have many talents you don't know about." He lifts his eyebrows briefly, telling me that he's thinking something naughty, gives me an impish smile, then turns to the drinks table. "What can I get you?"

"Just a Coke Zero," I reply. I mustn't get flustered. Everyone's used to us talking like this. If I start looking discombobulated, they're going to know something's up.

He pours a can into a glass and hands it to me. "Nympho!" he says as the poodle runs up to him, and he drops to his haunches to fuss her.

"I wish you wouldn't call her that," I say as our parents laugh.

"Sorry."

"No, you're not."

"No, I'm not."

"I can see you two are on good form," Helene says wryly. "Leave the girl alone, Oliver. She doesn't get much time off and she needs a rest."

"I'm not stopping her."

"Daddy!" Joanna runs up the steps, her friends hot on her heels. "You promised you'd play Just Dance with us."

He looks at me and pulls an eek face. "I did. Later, maybe. You should make the most of the sunshine for now. Why don't you take Nymph in the pool? She loves a swim."

"Will you come in?"

"Yeah," he says good-naturedly, putting one arm around her and hugging her. "Hey, have you said hello to Auntie Elizabeth?"

"No, hello!" She comes up and hugs me.

"Hello, you." I give her a big cuddle. She's only a few inches shorter than me. "You want your prezzie now?"

"Ooh, yes please!" She sees the parcel I brought on the table and rushes over to it. "Can I open it now?"

"Of course."

She rips off the paper as her friends crowd around, and they all squeal. It's a nail stamper kit with kid-safe polish, over a hundred icons, and five design pods.

"I thought you could all give yourself mani-pedis at your sleepover tonight," I tell them.

"I love it! Thank you so much!" She comes up and hugs me again and then runs off with her friends to investigate the different icons.

Huxley gives me a wry look.

"What?" I ask.

"You know they're going to want to give me a manicure."

"Why do you think I bought it?"

He meets my gaze, and his eyes are hot, bright. "Don't think I didn't notice," he says.

"Notice what?"

He drops his gaze to my feet, then looks back up at me. "I presume that's a good sign."

I look down at my toenails. I painted them red last night.

"I forgot," I say.

"Yeah. Right."

"Seriously!"

"What's going on?" Helene asks with amusement.

"Nothing," we both say, and laugh.

Joanna's finished looking at her new present, and she comes up to him again. "Dad. Show everyone how you do the nine times table."

"It's the hardest one," one of the girls complains.

"No it's not," he says. "It's one of the easiest, if you know the trick." He makes them all stand in a row. Then he nudges his way into the middle of the line so he's facing the same way as them. "Hold up your hands like this," he instructs, lifting his hands up so his palms are facing him. All the girls follow. It's like watching the Pied Piper.

I glance at Brandy, and she grins at me. I have no idea what he's doing.

"You're going to use them to count to ten like this. One, two, three…" He continues, going from the thumb of his left hand all the way to his little finger for five, then the little finger of his right hand for six, all the way to his right thumb for ten.

"Let's say you want to work out what four nines are," he says. "Fold your fourth finger down." He bends his ring finger and looks along the line. "Fourth finger," he corrects the girl next to him, tapping them. "One, two, three, four." He folds it down for her, and she giggles. "The fingers on the left of the folded down one are tens. The fingers on the right of the folded down one are units. So how many tens do you have?"

"Three…" They all say doubtfully.

"And how many units?"

"Six?"

"Exactly! Four nines are thirty-six!"

The girls all stare at him as the penny drops.

"Do this one," he says. "Eight times nine."

They all stare at their fingers and count to eight, which turns out to be the middle finger of their right hand. They fold it down, looking at each other to make sure they've got the right one.

"How many tens?" he asks.

"Seven!"

"And units?"

"Two!"

"So what are eight nines?"

"Seventy-two!" they all call, and laugh.

He grins. "Told you it was easy. Now it's pool time! Go and get your togs on, and we'll bring you some drinks and snacks down to the pool."

They all run off giggling. He smiles at the rest of us who've been sitting enjoying the show.

"You should have been a teacher," Mum tells him. "You have a lovely way with children."

"Thank you," he says graciously, pouring himself a Sprite Zero.

"His head's big enough," I scold. "Don't give him any more compliments or he won't be able to get in the door."

"Credit where credit's due," Mum says. "He's a great dad."

"He's very popular with all the girls' mums," Brandy says mischievously.

"Of course he is," I reply. "I bet they all think he's a DILF."

He coughs and then reaches for a serviette. "You made Sprite go up my nose."

I chuckle, then smile as a woman comes out of the house carrying a baby. Huxley has four sisters: Abigail, Chrissie, Evie, and Heidi. Abigail is the oldest, and she gave birth to baby Robin only three months ago.

He also has an older brother, Guy. He's in the South Island. That's all I know about him. The family never mentions him. When I asked

Huxley about him, unusually for him, he replied that he'd rather not talk about it. It's a strange blight on an otherwise idyllic family.

"Hello, Elizabeth!" Abigail—tall, athletic, pretty in a sporty kind of way—gives me a big smile, then turns to her brother, who's still standing. "Can you hold Robin for a minute? I've fed him and he should doze off in a minute. I just need to visit the bathroom."

"Yeah, give him here." Huxley takes the baby from her and holds him up in the air. "Hello, my little ray of sunshine! Why don't we go and watch those girls splashing in the pool? You never know, dude, you might pull, although they're probably a year or two too old for you yet." Still talking to the baby, he goes down the steps and walks across the lawn.

I blow out a breath.

"You all right?" Mum asks.

"Yeah. He makes my ovaries ache."

They all chuckle, and Brandy giggles.

"Sorry," I say to her, suddenly remembering she's the mother of his child.

"No, you're right," she says cheerfully. "He's a gorgeous daddy."

I smile, but it makes me wonder why the two of them have never gotten together, as far as I know. It can't just be that she has a flat chest.

"I'd better take some drinks down for the girls," Helene says, "now Oliver's been diverted."

"I'll give you a hand," I say. I kick off my sandals, then get up and help her put the large jugs of iced water with chopped fruit and homemade lemonade on trays, along with a dozen paper cups. Together, we walk across the lawn with them, and let ourselves through the gate to the poolside.

It's a large pool built in an interesting shape with steps down to a shallow section, a central area that's about four feet deep, and one part that's over six feet deep. Huxley's sitting on a chair under one of the umbrellas in the shade, cuddling Robin, and with one eye on the girls, who are screaming and laughing as they poke each other with noodles and fall off the various blown-up animals that are floating around in the pool. Nymph is also in the water, swimming between them, which they think is the best thing ever.

"Drinks," Helene calls, putting her tray down on the tiles, and I put mine beside it.

The girls start swimming over. "Are you coming in, Dad?" Joanna calls.

"I'll take Robin, if you like," Helene says.

"All right." He kisses the baby's head, then hands him over to his mum. Helene sits next to him under the umbrella, enjoying a sneaky cuddle with her grandson.

Huxley gets up and gestures with his head for me to join him over by the barrier. A little nervously, I walk over and lean on the railing next to him. In the distance, Hobson Bay reflects the cornflower-blue sky, busy with sailboats. It's the nineteenth of February, and it's still hot and humid, the only sign of autumn's approach visible in the early mornings, which are often cool and misty.

"Joanna seems to be having a nice time," I say.

"Yeah. Give kids a pool and you're guaranteed at least an hour of peace." He winces as one of the girls screams.

"You were saying?"

He grins and studies me for a moment. "So?" he asks softly. "Have you been thinking about my offer?"

I sigh and watch the fantails jumping about in the branches of the jacaranda tree across the lawn. "Yes, of course. And I'm afraid the answer is still no."

He doesn't say anything, and I look up at him, expecting to see him looking disappointed.

He isn't. His eyes are gleaming. "You're kidding me," he says.

"I can't," I whisper. "I'm sorry. I understand why you offered, and I want to say thank you for being kind and trying to help, but you're my best friend, and I really don't want to lose you."

"Lose me?"

"When it all goes wrong."

He rolls his eyes. "Why would it go wrong?"

"Because it always does."

"That doesn't mean it would this time."

"It's called extrapolation."

"It's called fear, Elizabeth."

"Says the man who's afraid of spiders, needles, heights, and a hundred other things."

He ignores that. "You can't refuse to have a relationship ever again because it might go wrong."

"I can do whatever I like."

"Don't bristle."

"I'm not bristling."

"Yes, you are. We were meant to be together, and all you're doing is delaying the inevitable."

"You reckon," I say sarcastically.

"I do. One day, when we're lying in bed having had fantastic sex, you're going to say to me, 'We should have done this years ago.'"

I push off the railing. "That's not going to happen. The answer's no, Hux, and I need you to accept that and stop badgering me."

I turn away. Then, a few seconds later, I squeal as he picks me up and puts me over his shoulder in a firefighter's lift.

"Huxley!" Furious, upside down, I smack his butt, but he just laughs.

"Oliver," his mother scolds, "what do you think you're doing? Put her down!"

The girls obviously notice then, because they all whoop and cheer, and Nymph barks.

"Put me down," I yell, embarrassed that all those young women have seen me at the mercy of a guy.

As easily as if I was a rolled-up blanket, he tosses me up, then catches me in his arms. I kick my legs, but he holds me tightly to his chest.

"Give me one night," he says, turning so his back is to the pool.

"No! Put me down!"

He takes a few steps back. "Give me one night, or you're going in."

I glare at him. His eyes are full of frustration.

Something inside me softens, and I reach up and touch his face. "I know this is difficult for you, honey. I know it's not what you want, and you're not used to being told no. But you can't bully me into it. That's not fair."

He looks into my eyes. There's a line between his brows, as if he's understanding for the first time that I'm really not going to give in.

Then the line disappears. "Fair enough," he says.

My eyes widen in alarm. "Oliver Huxley, don't you d—"

But it's too late—he tips backward, and we both fall into the pool.

Chapter Five

Elizabeth

I squelch back up to the deck, ignoring Huxley, who walks beside me, trying not to laugh.

"Come on," he says, "don't be mad."

"I'm not talking to you." I mount the steps, while everyone who's sitting there stares at me as I drip all over the deck.

"Oh my God," my mother says, "what happened?"

I glare at Huxley. "He threw me in."

"Oliver," his father scolds. "Seriously?"

"She asked for it," he says, picking up a towel from the pile on the side and tossing it to me.

I take it and rub my hair, knowing I must look a sight. I'm not wearing waterproof mascara for a start. "That wasn't very gentlemanly, *Ollie.*"

"Then maybe you should have said yes, *Liz.*"

"Yes to what?" Brandy asks.

"Yes," I say, "why don't you explain?"

"If you want me to," he replies, amused.

I glare at him. His gaze dips down, and his smile widens. I follow it and discover that my dress is plastered to my body. It's now very obvious that I'm not wearing a bra.

"Jesus." I clutch the towel to me.

He chuckles, comes over, and gives me a hug. "I'm sorry," he murmurs. "That was a bit mean."

"You're an arsehole."

"Yeah, I know." He kisses my forehead, then lets me go. "I'm going to play with the girls for a bit." He heads off toward the pool.

I blow out a breath and turn my glare on my father, who's chuckling away as he drinks his beer. "Thanks for leaping to my defense," I say irritably.

"You've never needed a white knight before," he says. "You're perfectly capable of defending yourself."

"Not against a six-foot-two maniac. He's stronger than the Hulk."

"Don't give me that," Dad says, "you learned years ago that women fight with their heads, not their muscles. Something tells me you're enjoying this, so stop pretending to be mad."

I poke my tongue out at him. He crosses his eyes at me.

Brandy laughs. "I've got a spare summer dress in my room, Elizabeth, if you want to get changed."

"Yes, please, I'd appreciate that."

"Come on." She gets up, and I follow her into the house.

We walk along the wide corridor with its light-gray carpets and high windows, pass the tall urn with its Greek figures, and go up the stairs, holding on to the white banister. At the top, she turns toward the bedrooms, counts three doors, then goes inside.

The same carpet that runs through the house makes this room feel big and spacious. The king-size bed in the middle has a pretty pink-and-purple duvet, and Helene has coordinated that with some of her gorgeous abstract artwork.

"Lovely room," I say, trying to towel-dry myself so I don't drip on the carpet.

"It is. I'm very lucky." Brandy goes over to the wardrobe and extracts a long red maxi dress. "Here you go. Although it might be a bit long for you."

"It's okay, it's better than nothing, thank you."

"Want some spare underwear?" She opens a drawer and offers a pair of white cotton knickers.

"If that's okay, thanks." I take them from her.

She chuckles and closes the drawer. "I can't believe he did that."

"Yeah, well, I did provoke him."

"What did you say?" I hesitate, and she smiles. "It's okay, you don't have to tell me. I know what the two of you are like."

My face warms. "There's nothing going on between us," I protest.

"I know," she says. "I don't know why. You obviously like each other."

We study each other for a moment. Her smile spreads. Her eyes are astute. I think I've underestimated her. She's smarter than I thought.

"Brandy…" I say softly, "you're the mother of his child. I wouldn't—"

"We're not an item," she says. "I don't have any claim on him."

"The two of you have never thought about getting together permanently?"

"No. I'm not his type."

"You were at least once," I point out, puzzled.

She studies her hands. "Yeah, well, that was different."

I guess she knows that Huxley and I were dating when she found out she was pregnant. Has he ever told her? I've certainly never discussed it with her, so maybe she doesn't. We weren't dating when he slept with her. I'm not sure I'd have been able to stay friends with him if that was the case.

"Does Joanna ever ask if the two of you will get together?" I ask.

"No, never. I'm very open with her. She knows Hux and I were never an item. I'll always be grateful for what he did for me. Supporting me, I mean. I know how lucky I am." She gestures around the room. I know what she means. I've met her parents. Her mother serves behind the till in a petrol station, and her father works in a building firm. She could have picked a lot worse men to sleep with than Huxley, who I'm guessing is a multi-millionaire, if not a billionaire by now. He takes after his father with his business acumen, and I know he invests in stocks and shares, and has made a lot of money over the years.

It's funny to think he slept with her. I know it was ten years ago, and he's had a lot of girlfriends since then, but Brandy was different. They made a baby. She's carried it inside her. She'll always have that piece of him, that connection that's so different from any other woman he's been with.

"I asked him if he'd be a sperm donor for me," I blurt out. Shit. Why did I say that? I think I just want to talk about it to someone, and most of my friends are guys. Plus, I realize part of me needs to know how she'd feel about it.

Her eyebrows rise. "Oh…" she says, and her face lights up. "How lovely."

"I'm twenty-nine soon and I don't want another relationship. But I really want a baby."

Her expression softens. "That's understandable."

"But he said no."

She blinks and her jaw drops. Clearly the thought of Huxley turning down a woman in need is as surprising to her as it was to me. "Seriously?"

"He… he says he'll do it the old-fashioned way, though."

She gives a short laugh. "Cheeky bastard."

"Yeah."

"But you said no," she says slowly. "That's why he threw you in the pool."

"He broke my heart once," I murmur. "I wouldn't be able to cope if he did it again."

She meets my eyes, and I can see that she understands. He did tell her about me.

"I've never said I'm sorry about that," she whispers. "But I am."

I inhale deeply and exhale slowly. "As you said, it was a long time ago."

"I didn't ask him to stop seeing you," she says. "It's important to me that you know that. It was his choice. He said it wouldn't be fair to you or to me, and you know what he's like about fairness."

"I do." We smile at each other. Actually, it does make me feel better to know she didn't demand he not see me.

"He wouldn't break your heart again," she says. "You know he's crazy about you, right?"

I sigh. "You know what he's like. He doesn't have a great track record with women."

"Only because he's not dated the right one."

"You don't know that. He's a great guy. He's intelligent and smart, but that also means he gets bored quickly. He's interested in me because I'm Moby-Dick and he's Ahab. I'm the one who got away— he actually called me that. He's a completionist—have you seen him play on the PlayStation? He has to finish every trophy in the game."

"Yeah, I know what you mean. You could also argue that he's been interested in you for ten years. That's not a crush or an infatuation. He felt he had to stop seeing you because of what happened between us, but he didn't stop liking you. You don't see the way he watches you when you're not looking. He always has, right from when we were first together. The time's never been right, that's all. He needed to make something of himself, to prove to his father that he was 'worthwhile'." She puts air quotes around the word. "And he's a guy, and he doesn't take much notice of the passing of time. But I guess something happened recently, and now he's decided he's ready."

I think about Valentine's Day, and the fact that we kissed. *You wanted me to kiss you, and you wanted to go back to my room with me.* He's right, and we both know it.

But there's more to it than that.

"He might be ready, but I'm not," I whisper. "My heart's been broken too many times and I… I can't risk it again. I told him, but he won't listen."

"He's very persistent."

"Stubborn is the word I'd use."

"That works, too. I don't envy you."

My eyebrows lift. "Why?"

"When Huxley makes his mind up about something, he doesn't let go of it easily."

"Like a mutt with a bone."

"There's definitely a bone involved somewhere."

We both laugh.

"Actually," she says, her cheeks flushing a little, "I've got something to tell you. I'm seeing someone."

"Oh!" I didn't expect that. "Who?"

"His name's Billy. He's an accountant. Hux introduced us, funnily enough. He's a year younger than me. I call him my toy boy." She laughs.

"How long have you been seeing each other?"

"Only a few weeks. I asked him to come today but he's not quite ready to meet everyone yet. But I think he will soon. He seems… serious." Her blush deepens.

"Has he met Joanna?"

She nods. "She likes him, which is good. I've put off dating for a long time because I've worried what she might think, but when I told her she was really happy for me, which was lovely."

"And you've told Huxley?"

"Of course—he was the first person I told. He said 'about fucking time'." She laughs.

I can't explain why, but the whole story warms me right through. I smooth my wet hair off my face. "I should get changed."

"Yeah. I'm glad we had this chat."

"Me, too."

I walk off to her ensuite with the dress and underwear.

"Elizabeth," she calls, and I stop and turn. "He's one of the good guys," she says.

"Yeah, I know." I sigh, go into the bathroom, and shut the door.

*

Huxley

When I finally get out of the pool, having been dunked by a dozen girls about a hundred times, I make my way up to the deck and discover Elizabeth stretched out on a sunbed, drying her hair in the sunshine. She's wearing a dress that I think is Brandy's, which is of course far too long for her, but she's pulled it up a little to let the sun get to her legs.

I stand over her and shake myself like Nymph. She puts a hand up to shade her eyes and glares at me.

"I've just got dry," she says.

I laugh and pick up a towel. "Dress a bit long, is it?"

I can see her about to tell me to fuck off, but then Joanna comes up on the deck, so she leans back and closes her eyes again.

Chuckling, I go inside, grab my shorts and tee from the bag I left by the door, and head to the bathroom to change. When I come out, Mum and Raewyn are in the kitchen, starting to get the food ready for the girls' tea.

"Are they ever getting out of the pool?" Raewyn asks. "They're going to look like prunes."

"They'll have to—there's not enough water left. I think I drank half of it."

"You did seem to spend more time beneath the surface than above it," Mum says, amused.

I lean past Raewyn to grab one of the sandwiches she's putting on the plate. She lets me with a smile. "Take two," she says.

"Thanks."

"You've always spoiled him," Mum complains.

"That's because he's such a sweet boy." Raewyn kisses my shoulder, and I smile. I like her a lot. On the surface, Elizabeth isn't much like either of her parents—she's not as laid back as Neville, and she doesn't possess Raewyn's flakiness. She's not particularly arty either. But when you get to know her, you realize she got her love of chemistry and her plain-spokenness from her father, and her kind heart and generosity from her mother.

"Will you take these out to the table on the deck?" Mum gestures at the plates.

"Yeah, sure." I collect two and head out into the sunshine.

The girls are just getting out of the pool, and I spend the next fifteen minutes handing out towels, directing them to the bathrooms, then collecting wet swimming costumes and spreading them out along the deck to dry. By the time they're all changed, the food is ready, and I hand out plates and make sure everyone has a drink and a seat before finally helping myself.

Elizabeth joins me at the table and eyes my plate, which is piled high. "Eating for two?" she asks.

"I feel as if I've swum the Ditch," I say, referring to the Tasman Sea between Australia and New Zealand. "Anyway, you know I have a healthy appetite."

She snorts and chooses another couple of sandwiches. I hold out a small fresh-cream donut. She studies it, then takes it and adds it to her plate.

I lick my fingers free of sugar. "Come for a walk with me?"

"Don't you want to eat your tea?"

"I can multitask."

She hesitates. "I don't think that's a good idea."

I study her face for a moment. She's had to cleanse her face of most of her smudged makeup, and now she looks fresh-faced and youthful. Her wet brown hair is drying with a touch of a wave, which I didn't expect.

"Give me five minutes," I say. "I want to apologize."

She gestures for me to pass her another donut. "All right. Hold on a minute."

She takes a moment to tuck the skirt of her dress up in her knickers so it doesn't trail on the ground. "Don't say a word," she scolds as I smirk.

With our plates full and a cup of soda in the other hand, we walk down the steps. There's a bench under the jacaranda tree, and we head there and sit, putting our drinks on the ground. We lean back, and for a little while we eat our food, listening to the girls laughing up on the deck, and the song of the fantails above our heads.

I look down at her sitting beside me. "I'm sorry I threw you in the pool."

"Did your mother make you apologize?"

I laugh. "No. This is all me. I shouldn't have done it. It was very childish."

"It was."

"Are you mad at me?"

She smiles. "I can never be mad at you for long."

"Good, I'm glad."

She has a bite of a sandwich, and lifts a crumb from her lip with a finger. "But Hux, you have to realize that you can't keep harassing me. I've given you my answer. And I haven't changed my mind."

"I am sorry. I just find it unbelievable that you're saying no to some really, really good sex."

She huffs. "I don't know how you can be so sure of yourself. Where do you get all that confidence?"

"I'm not talking about me. I'm talking about us. Sex is just a series of physical instructions—put tab a) into slot b). Or c). Or possibly d) if you're really lucky. And then move up and down a bit."

She gives a short laugh.

"Well, it is," I continue. "And orgasms are the same. You've seen that Friends episode where they talk about erogenous zones."

"Seven, seven, seven!"

I grin. "Yeah. But Monica was right—it's about pressing a woman's buttons in the right order. It's not complicated."

"It is for a lot of guys, I'm telling you."

"And for women. Apparently ten to fifteen percent of women have never had an orgasm."

She blinks. "Jesus. Really?"

"Apparently."

She looks puzzled. "I don't get that. Don't they… you know…"

"Self-administer?" I smile. "Not everyone's as open about sex as you, Elizabeth. A lot of people are told it's wrong to touch yourself. Dirty, somehow. And some people have issues with abuse or other psychological problems."

"I guess. I hadn't thought about it."

"We're digressing. My point is that sex is just a bodily function. It's the person you have it with that makes it special. That makes it amazing."

She looks up at me then. Her brown eyes are the color of polished mahogany, and they contain flecks of gold at the center. Her lips, free from lipstick or gloss, are pale pink and look incredibly soft.

"I want to kiss you," I say. "So fucking badly."

Her lips curve up, and she looks away.

"Tell me you don't want to kiss me."

"Hux…"

"Tell me."

"That's not the point."

"So you do?"

Her gaze comes back to my mouth. "What woman wouldn't?"

It's a nice compliment, but it's not what I asked. "Do you remember our kiss on Valentine's Day?"

"Yes."

"Do you remember how you slid your hand into my hair? How you opened your mouth to me?"

She sucks her bottom lip and nods.

"Don't you want to do it again?"

She puts her plate on the bench beside her, leans forward, and puts her face in her hands for a moment. I watch her, my smile fading. I wish I'd known how much her previous boyfriends had hurt her. She kept it so quiet; I had no idea. I'm guessing she didn't tell any of our other friends, not even Victoria, who I'm sure would have mentioned it to me. I feel a surge of anger toward those guys who have damaged her for me. And toward the world, or Fate, or whoever else is to blame, for the fact that I didn't get to date her properly right at the beginning.

I shouldn't have left it this long. I should have been more persistent much earlier. But I honestly thought she'd never go out with me again. She was so insistent, and I thought I'd missed my chance. It was only when she kissed me on Valentine's Day that I realized she was still into me.

She sits back and lowers her hands. "I think I'll go back to the house."

"Wait. I'm going to ask one more time. Give me one night. Pretty please. With a cherry on top."

"There's as much chance of me having a one-night stand with you as there is of you jumping off the Sky Tower," she states. "Does that make it clearer?"

I look at her brown eyes, her soft mouth.

"What?" she says, frowning.

I run my tongue across my teeth. Am I really about to say this?

I think about the way she kissed me on Valentine's Day, and the feel of her soft body beneath my hands.

I guess I am.

"How about we have a bet?" I ask.

"A what?"

"A bet."

"What kind of bet?"

"Come to the Sky Tower with me and watch me jump off. If I back out, I'll do it in a cup for you, and you can have all the semen you want. But if I jump, you give me one night."

She stares at me. Then she laughs. "You'd never jump off in a million years."

"So what have you got to lose?"

"Huxley, do you remember that time we went into the restaurant at the top of the Sky Tower? You couldn't even sit near the window. You spent the whole evening with your back to the view, practically glued to the column. We had to peel you off it."

"Yeah…"

"So how, exactly, do you think you're going to jump off?"

"I don't know. I'm already beginning to doubt my sanity."

"I've done it myself, remember? For charity a couple of years ago. It's over six hundred feet—a hundred and ninety-two meters. Fifty-three floors. You fall at eighty-five kilometers per hour."

"Jesus, enough already." My heart's racing at the thought. "I don't need to know all the ins and outs."

"I'm just saying, you'll never do it."

"So, like I said, what do you have to lose?"

She gives me a bewildered look. "You don't have to put yourself through that. Why don't you just go to the clinic, look at a girlie mag, and do your thing?"

"Because I want you. I want you so badly, I'm prepared to do this to get you. Doesn't that tell you something about how I feel?"

She looks at me like I'm crazy. She could have a point.

"When?" she asks.

"I'll book it for next weekend."

"You'd really put yourself through seven whole days of panic?"

"To get you in my bed? Hell, yeah."

I can see she's flattered. Equally, I can see she doesn't believe I'll go through with it.

I've been afraid of heights since I was a kid. I can't go up a ladder without having palpitations.

But she's severely underestimating my desire for her. And how stubborn I am. I'm absolutely determined to get this girl in my bed. And if it means I have to conquer one of my greatest fears, I'm absolutely going to do it.

Chapter Six

Huxley

Victoria, Mack, and I are in one of the club meeting rooms and have just started our weekly Friday lunch when Titus rolls in around 1:15 p.m.

"Sorry I'm late," he says, taking a seat next to Mack at the table.

"No worries," I say. "Coffee?"

"Actually, can I have water, please? I've just had a coffee with Elizabeth. If I have any more, I'll have tachycardia all afternoon."

"Elizabeth?" I pass him a bottle of cold water from the fridge. "Is she coming today?"

"No, she asked me to send her apologies. She's got some Japanese investors over—I think she brought them here yesterday?"

"Oh yeah, that's right. I forgot they were staying until Friday." My heart sinks a little. I was hoping to see her today.

I think she's avoiding me. I've only seen her a couple of times this week—two lunchtime meetings and once yesterday when she brought the investors in for a karaoke evening in one of our bars. I had the misfortune of catching her performance of Adele's *Someone Like You*. The lady has many talents, but unfortunately singing isn't one of them.

"How is she?" Victoria asks, taking one of the chicken salads on the table. "I thought she looked tired last night."

"She's okay." Titus somehow manages to fit a whole sausage roll in his mouth in one go. "Mind you, we had a very strange conversation," he says in a muffled voice.

Mack takes a stack of sandwiches and a handful of potato chips. "About what?"

Titus gives him an amused look. "I think you know."

Mack meets his gaze and grins. "Oh... that."

"Yeah. Could've knocked me down with a feather." He looks at me. "She must have asked you, surely?"

"Asked me what?"

"About donating."

My heart shudders to a stop. My gaze slides to Victoria, who's giving us a puzzled look. "Donating?" she asks. "Are you talking about the SPCA raffle?"

"Not quite," Mack says. "Elizabeth wants a baby."

Victoria's eyes nearly fall out of her head. "What?"

"She's been to the fertility clinic," Titus says. "She asked them about a clinic donor, but there's a three-year wait, can you believe it?"

"Jesus," Victoria says.

"Yeah," Mack said, "so they suggested she ask a friend to donate."

"What did you say?" Titus asks him.

Mack shrugs. "I said I'd discuss it with Sidnie. We chatted about it last night, and she's okay about it, so I'll probably say yes. You?"

"Yeah, I said why not?"

"How's she going to choose which of you to use?" Victoria asks.

"She's talking about letting the clinic decide," Titus says. He picks up a sandwich, realizes it's vegetarian, and puts it back with a grimace before choosing a roast beef one. "So she won't actually know which of us will father the baby. She said she likes the idea of it being random."

I've gone completely cold inside. She actually asked them? I'm shocked by how hurt I feel. It's my own fault for saying no to doing it in a cup for her. Fuck. I love the two guys here but the thought of them fathering Elizabeth's baby makes me want to attack them with a chainsaw.

"I'm donating on Monday," Mack says. "She says if we can all give samples over the next week or so, she'll be inseminated the week after, and…" His voice trails off, and his brows draw together as he looks at me. "Aw," he says, "I can't do it, guys. Look at his face."

Titus and Victoria glance at me and start laughing, and Mack grins.

"Jesus." I tip my head back and look at the ceiling for a moment before throwing them all a glare. "You actually had me for a moment."

"Don't blame us," Titus says. "It was Elizabeth's idea."

"That little… She put you up to this?"

"She said she wanted to mess with you," Victoria says. "Something to do with being thrown in the pool?"

"Ah. Yeah. Okay, fair enough."

Mack chuckles. "I can't believe you did that and survived."

"Eh," I say, "she was only mad for a few minutes."

"So." Mack smiles. "She really has asked you to donate?"

"Yeah. I said no."

They all look surprised. "Seriously?" Titus says.

I give them a mischievous look. "I told her I want to do it the old-fashioned way."

They all stare at me. Then, as one, they all start laughing.

"Hand it over," Mack says to Titus and Victoria.

Titus rolls his eyes. "Jesus, seriously? After all this time?"

Mack just flicks his fingers up.

I frown. "What's going on?"

Titus and Victoria both fish ten bucks out of their pockets. "Mack bet us ten bucks at university that the two of you would end up in bed together," Titus says, handing his note over.

"Well, you should keep your money for now," I say. "We're not there yet. She said no."

Victoria and Titus take their notes out of Mack's hand, and he glares at them as he says, "What do you mean?"

"She said there was as much likelihood of her sleeping with me as of me jumping off the Sky Tower. So we made a bet. I'm going up there tomorrow. If I don't jump, I'll donate for her. If I do… she gives me one night." I smile.

They all stare at me.

"What?" Titus says.

"Hux." Victoria looks baffled. "You get a nosebleed if you stand on a chair."

"Slight exaggeration." I scratch the back of my neck. "But I appreciate that I might have painted myself into a corner."

Titus gives a slow whistle. "Dude, you really have got it bad."

"It's kinda romantic," Victoria says. "And fucking stupid at the same time."

I glower. "I've asked her out pretty much every month for ten years. She won't go out with me. What was I supposed to do?"

"Give up?" Victoria suggests. "Accept you've lost?"

"Yeah, that sounds like something I'd do."

"How are you feeling?" Mack asks.

"Fucking terrified."

"But you're still going through with it?"

I shrug and give him a helpless look. "I can't think what else to do."

He meets my eyes for a moment, and then we both smile. Now he's got Sidnie, he understands the stupid things you do for the woman you love.

"So if you jump, she's agreed to give you one night?" Victoria asks. "What happens after that?"

"I'll be so absolutely amazing in bed that she'll beg to see me again."

She lifts an eyebrow.

"Yeah," I say, "it's a stretch, I know. I'm going to have to pull out all the stops."

"You mean you'll actually have to do some foreplay for a change?"

"And pay for the pizza at the end."

They all snort.

Mack leans back, stretching out his legs. "I don't quite know why she's so reluctant to date you. Obviously, what happened back at uni was difficult for her, but the two of you have remained such good friends. Clearly, she's still attracted to you."

I turn my pen in my fingers. She asked me not to tell the others what she told me on Valentine's Day, but we're a close-knit group, and I know they won't spread it any further. "She's had three long-term relationships, and the guys have all broken her heart. Did you know Tim cheated on her?"

"Fuck! Seriously?" Titus says it, but they're all shocked.

"With Patsy Landingham."

Victoria holds her hands in front of her chest. "She with the big knockers?"

"That's the one."

"Bastard," Mack says. "I didn't know."

"That's not all. She had problems with Rich," I won't go into detail there, "and he sort of turned it all on her, blamed her for everything. And Steve…" I shift in my chair.

"What?" Victoria asks.

I lean forward and glare at the sandwiches. "He hit her."

Titus puts his legs down and sits up. Victoria stares at me. "What the fuck?"

"Across the face."

Her jaw drops. Mack gives a short, humorless laugh. "Jesus."

"Apparently she pushed him through a plate-glass window and put him in hospital. I guess that's a suitable punishment. I still want to break the bastard's legs, though."

"Too obvious," Titus says. "Let's tamper with his brakes."

"Poison for me," Victoria adds. "We should put cyanide in his whisky."

"Fucker," Mack says. "What is it with men who hurt women? They should be fucking castrated."

"Yeah, I'm with you there. So anyway, that's why she's reluctant to date again—not just me, anyone. But I'm working on it."

Mack meets my eyes, and for a moment I think he's going to berate me for being so dumb, but he just says, "Okay, let's move on. I want to talk about the calendar in March—Victoria, can I book a table for ten in the restaurant on the fifteenth? I've got an Australian company coming over and I thought I'd bring them for dinner here."

The conversation moves on, and I listen and type notes and add my two cents, although inside my heart's still beating faster than normal. I can't think what else to do. The words ring in my ears. I know this is my last chance to get with Elizabeth. If I don't jump tomorrow, it's over. She's right—I can't turn my monthly request into harassment. If she's determined to say no, however much I think she's wrong, I'm going to have to accept that's her decision and bow out.

Two o'clock approaches, and Victoria closes her laptop. "All right, I've got to get back to work."

"Yep. Thanks, guys." Titus gets up. "Good luck tomorrow, Hux. Let me know how it goes."

"Will do."

Titus and Victoria head out, and the door swings shut.

Mack rises and puts his laptop back in his bag. We head toward the door together, but as we reach it, he puts a hand on it, stopping me from opening it.

"You're really going to do this?" he says.

"I have to." I study my shoes. "She's been saying no to me for years. I didn't think she was interested. But we kissed on Valentine's Day. And she asked me to take her back to my room."

I lift my gaze back up at him. He looks surprised. "Shit."

"I didn't. We were both drunk. But she definitely wanted me to. I didn't realize... All this time I thought she wasn't into me. She's terrified of getting hurt again though. I get it, after what happened with

Tim and Steve. But I know I contributed to her broken heart. I put the first crack in it."

He sighs.

"She doesn't think I'm serious," I continue, "and I need to make a grand gesture."

His lips curve up. "By jumping off the Sky Tower?"

I give him a pained look. "It seemed like a good idea at the time."

He chuckles. Then he says, "You want me to come with you?"

I hesitate. "Does it make me a wuss if I say yes?"

"Elizabeth can wait at the bottom to celebrate with you when you land. Best she's not at the top while you're waiting, eh?"

He knows how hard this is going to be for me. "Yeah."

"What time?"

"Ten a.m. I made it early because I couldn't bear to wait all day."

He grins. "You're meeting Elizabeth there?"

"Yeah."

"I'll pick you up at nine thirty."

I blow out a breath. "All right. Thanks, man."

He claps me on the shoulder. "We'll get you the girl, don't worry." He opens the door and goes out.

I watch him walk down the corridor, feeling an odd sense of relief to have his support. I'm going to need it.

*

Saturday, 9.40 a.m.

Jamie pulls up in Federal Street, just down from the Sky Tower, and parks the car.

"Ready?" Mack says to me as Jamie turns off the engine.

I look across at him. I'm in a cold sweat, and I'm trembling. "Yep," I say. "Can't wait."

His brows draw together, and he exchanges a look with Jamie. "You got a minute?" he asks him. When Jamie nods, he adds, "Can you come with us?"

"Sure."

"Come on then." Mack and Jamie get out of the car.

I open the back passenger door and swing my legs around, then sit there for a moment, elbows on my knees, head bowed. I'm not sure my legs will hold me up. Jesus, I really didn't think this through. I'm not going to be able to go through with it.

Mack's legs appear in front of me. Then he bends forward and puts a hand on my back. "Deep breaths."

"I need a minute."

"I can see Elizabeth."

"Fuck." I close my eyes for a moment. I can't back out now, with her watching. "All right." I push myself up.

"Come on." Mack walks with me across the pedestrian area to the place where the Sky Jump ends. And there's Elizabeth, leaning on the railing, smiling.

"Wow," she says, "you turned up! That's more than I thought you'd do."

"Oh ye of little faith." My heart's racing so fast now that I feel faint, but I'm not going to let her know that.

"Hux, why don't you and Jamie go over to the entrance," Mack says. "I want to have a quick word with Elizabeth."

"Okay." When he first said about her waiting at the bottom, I wasn't sure that was the right decision, but now I'm glad she's not going to be there. I'm enough of a guy not to want her to see me cry.

"Chin up," she says. "You did well just by getting here. I'm proud of you."

I give her a wry look. "I'll see you in a few minutes. Vertically."

She laughs. "Yeah, right. Via the elevator."

I don't have a quick comeback. I turn away and let Jamie lead me over to the building, needing every ounce of concentration I own to keep myself in one piece.

*

Elizabeth

I watch Huxley walk off and chuckle. "He's positively green. Bless him. I meant it though. I'm proud of him for turning up. I was convinced I'd get a call on the way here to say he'd chickened out."

I look back at Mack. He's standing there with his hands on his hips. Whoa. That's not a good sign.

"I need a word with you," he says.

"Okay…"

"That guy," and he points briefly at the disappearing Huxley, "is so in love with you that he's prepared to jump off a fucking building. He's absolutely terrified. And I'm not going to let him put himself through this unless you tell me right now that you're prepared to follow through with the bet. If he does, if he jumps, are you going to do it?"

I'm so shocked that I can only stare at him. "He told you about our bet?"

"Yeah. And I think it's fucking crazy, but hey, whatever makes the two of you pull your heads out of your arses and get your act together."

I glare at him. "He's not in love with me. He just wants to get in my knickers."

"Elizabeth, for fuck's sake, stop it. You've led him on for ten years. It's time you brought this to an end, one way or another."

Fury blows through me like a Saharan wind. "What are you talking about? I didn't tell him to ask me out every month! I've repeatedly turned him down, but he's so fucking stubborn that he won't give up."

"He won't give up because he's crazy about you. He always has been. And I know you feel the same way. Shut up—you're going to listen to this. At any point you could have taken him to one side and told him to stop. But you haven't—you've teased him and flirted with him, and kept him hanging on."

A sudden rush of emotion tightens my throat. "That's not true." But it stings because it is true, of course.

"I understand why you're frightened," he says, a bit more gently. "Hux explained what Tim and Steve did."

My face burns. "I told him not to tell you."

"He told us because he knew we'd understand. He loves you, and he's furious that a guy would dare to treat you like that. So yeah, I get why you're reluctant to get involved with anyone. You know what he told me yesterday? He said he knows he contributed to your broken heart, that he put the first crack in it."

I swallow hard.

"Elizabeth… what happened ten years ago… Do you think yours was the only heart that was broken?"

I stare at him.

"He was devastated to lose you," Mack says. "The night before he told you, we went out to a bar, and he spent the whole evening talking about you while he slowly emptied a bottle of whisky."

"I didn't know," I whisper.

"He felt that he didn't have a choice." He looks over at the building, then back at me. "Look, I need to get in there with him. But like I said, I'm not going to let him put himself through this if at the last minute you say no. You have every right to turn him down, of course you do. It's a stupid bet, and it's your prerogative to say you've changed your mind. But if you're going to do it, do it now. Because I swear, if he does this, if he faces his fear and does the fucking jump, and then you refuse to carry it through, I'm never going to talk to you again."

"He won't do it, Mack. He hyperventilates if he stands up too quickly. He's never going to jump off the Sky Tower."

His eyes gleam. "He will, because I'm going to fucking push him off, if it comes to it. So tell me, are you in? Or are you out?"

My mind has gone blank. He really thinks Huxley will go through with this? I can't believe it. But I suppose there is a miniscule chance. So, if he were to do it, what would I do?

"He won't jump," I say. "Which means he'll donate for me. It's a risk I'm willing to take."

"That's not an answer. If he does, will you give him the one night he wants?"

I meet his eyes. His right is blue—his left is a peculiar mix of blue, green, and brown, like the planet Earth. They're slightly feverish. He has ADHD, and he's always like this when he's feeling hyper.

"Of course," I say, surprising myself. "I wouldn't back out if he did it. That wouldn't be fair. I do know what he's putting himself through. I just don't believe he wants me that much. I think he's going to get up there and realize he's made a huge mistake, and it was all for show, and he'll back out and come down all sheepish."

"I'd ask for it in writing," he says, "but there's not enough time."

"All right." I'm annoyed now. "Let's get this over with, one way or another."

He backs away. "I'm holding you to it," he says, pointing at me. Then he turns and strides across to the building.

I glare at his back, then lean on the railing and huff moodily. There's absolutely no way Huxley will ever jump off this building. He's been afraid of heights ever since I met him. Not just reluctant, but absolutely terrified. I love the guy dearly, but he's a showman—he performs on a daily basis, like a gorilla beating his chest. He's done this because he thinks I'll be impressed and sleep with him even if he backs out. Well, I won't. He has to keep his side of the bet, too.

I look up at the side of the Sky Tower. Fifty-three floors. Over six hundred feet.

He's never going to do it.

Not in a million years.

Chapter Seven

Huxley

The elevator doors open, and Mack and I step out into the spacious room. Jamie has stayed down with Elizabeth.

I catch a glimpse of tiled floors, large pillars, big fans, and a waiting area with seats. Then all I can focus on are the huge panes of glass, looking out at the cloudless blue sky.

"You okay?" Mack asks. "You've lost all color in your face."

"I might need the bathroom."

"Over here." He steers me toward the Gents'. I push open the door, go into one of the cubicles, and promptly vomit up the contents of my stomach into the toilet.

"Ah, Jesus." I wait to make sure I'm done, then flush it and go out.

Mack's leaning against the wall, hands in his pockets. He watches as I wash my hands and splash my face with cold water. I wait for him to say *You don't have to do this, Hux.*

He doesn't. When I eventually straighten and take a couple of paper towels, he smiles and hands me a mint from the box in his pocket, then says, "You ready now?"

I toss the paper towels in the bin, pop the mint in my mouth, and lean on the wall opposite. "I don't think I can do this."

His unusual eyes are very light. He's in one of his energetic moods. "I told Elizabeth you were going to do it if I have to push you out." He grins as my eyes widen in alarm. "It was a joke, don't worry. They don't allow spectators in the jump zone."

I stuff my hands in the pockets of my jeans and hunch my shoulders. "What did you talk to her about?"

"I wanted to make sure that when you do it, she'll keep her side of the bet."

"Seriously?"

"Yeah."

I hold his gaze for a moment. His lips curve up.

"What did she say?" I whisper.

"She said of course she will. She just doesn't believe you'll do it, because she doesn't think you want her that much."

"I do."

"Of course you do. Why else would you be jumping off a fucking building?"

"I really want to do it," I say meekly. "I just don't think my legs will let me walk over there."

"I know it's not easy," he says, reminding me that he did this with Elizabeth, Titus, and a few others a couple of years ago for charity. "The key is to focus on something else. Like your reward."

"My reward?"

"In about ten minutes' time, it'll be all over. Ten minutes of fear in return for what I'm sure will be really fantastic sex."

I blow out a long breath. "It's not a bad deal."

"It's an incredible deal. Focus on Elizabeth. The five-foot-one fireball."

I chuckle. "That about sums her up."

"Think about how you're going to ruffle up that neat hairdo and smudge her lipstick."

I close my eyes, thinking about sinking my hands into her soft brown hair. "Okay."

"Picture what clothes she's going to be wearing. And then imagine taking them all off."

I breathe deeply. "Yeah, that's working."

"She's all yours, dude. She wants to make a baby with you. You're not going to let a little thing like this stand in the way, are you?"

I think about how it's going to feel when I make love to her without a condom. How I'll be able to look into her eyes as I come and know I could have made her pregnant. I want to do that for her.

And for myself, obviously.

I open my eyes. "All right, I'm ready."

"Come on, then. Let's do it."

We go out, and Mack leads me over to the check-in point. Luckily I'm kept busy then—I have to take a breath alcohol test, and they weigh me to make sure I'm within the maximum limit. I think I make a joke about looking like Jabba the Hutt and make them all laugh, but

I can't be sure as my brain's not firing properly at the moment. They give me a flying suit, like a jumpsuit that zips up the front. Finally, I have to step into the harness, which they tighten all over until it's snug enough so I can't slip out of it.

Despite saying spectators aren't allowed in the jump zone, Mack's obviously slipped the guy a few bucks because he comes through the barrier with me, right up to the point where the path leads out of the door onto the metal walkway.

I turn and face him.

He smiles. "She's waiting for you, Hux."

"I have literally never been this scared in my life." Oh God, please don't let me vomit all over the assistant.

"Being courageous doesn't mean that you aren't afraid, it means acting *despite* being afraid. I have absolute faith in you, Oliver Huxley. You came up here and you're going to do this even though you're terrified. That's how much you love this girl. Go and show her."

I swallow hard. "Think about the sex."

"Think about the sex. I'll see you at the bottom."

I blow out a breath, nod, turn, and walk along the path and out onto the metal platform. I feel as if I'm walking on a planet with intense gravity, as it seems to take more effort than usual to move my feet.

The assistants there stop me and check my harness several times, then finally clip the huge wire to the back. They talk me through what's going to happen, which I don't really take in because now my brain has completely shut down.

I'm trembling all over. Why on earth did I think I could do this? I'd rather have fallen into a box of spiders. Or maybe not. Don't think about spiders. Or clowns. Or needles.

Think about Elizabeth. I close my eyes as the cool breeze blows across my face. I'm doing this for her. To show her how serious I am about being with her. Mack says she'll definitely go through with it. A few seconds to jump, for a whole night with her.

She just doesn't believe you'll do it, because she doesn't think you want her that much.

I open my eyes and look over my shoulder at the assistant who's holding onto the harness behind me.

"Ready?" he asks.

I nod.

"Go for it," he says.

For a second I can't let go of the railing. It's like my hands have been Superglued to it. I peel them off and grip hold of my harness.

"Think of the sex," Mack yells from behind me.

I give a short, somewhat hysterical laugh. Then I run down the short platform and leap off the end.

I think I scream, but luckily there's nobody to hear it except the seagulls. For a long moment my stomach's in my mouth and there's just blue sky, and I'm falling like a stone, and oh my God this fucking wire is never going to be able to hold me, I'm going to hit the fucking ground and die instantly, and I turn a little in the air and see the floors of the Sky Tower flying by, and oh Jesus I actually did it, I jumped off the fucking Sky Tower! Even though I'm not yet down, sheer exultance replaces the fear. I yell loudly as the wire kicks in and I feel resistance, and then it's lowering me slowly to the ground, where I land gently on both feet on the blue safety mat.

*

Elizabeth

I stare in shock as Huxley lands on the mat near the assistant. Oh my God. He actually did it.

"Wooooooo!" he yells, fists pumping the air. The assistant unclips him from the wire, then helps him out of the harness, laughing as Huxley bounces all over the place, refusing to stand still.

"He fucking did it," Jamie says beside me, "Jesus! I really didn't think he'd go through with it."

"Me neither," I whisper.

I know what it's taken for him to do this. I've been with him many times when he's been faced with heights. He can't go up ladders or outside stairs even if they have a railing, and he won't look out of airplane windows, or any window in a building that's more than a few floors off the ground.

So for him to jump off a tiny platform six hundred feet in the air, with only a wire to keep him safe, will have taken immense courage.

Did he really do it for me?

He thanks the assistant and shakes his hand, then leaves the landing area and walks over to us.

"Dude!" Jamie runs up and claps him on the arm. "You did it!"

"I did. I really did. I jumped off the Sky Tower." He looks up at the platform, swallows, then bends forward with his hands on his knees. "Holy shit."

The poor guy's shaking like a leaf. My heart goes out to him, and I put a hand on his back and rub it.

"You're okay, sweetheart. You're back on terra firma. Just take deep breaths."

He inhales and blows it out slowly. "I'll be all right in a minute."

"Take as long as you need. Are you going to throw up?"

"Already done it."

"Aw, Hux!" I bend and kiss his hair.

He doesn't reply, breathing deeply, and I think he's fighting nausea.

"I'll get him some water," Jamie says.

"Okay, thanks." My hands are cool, and I put one on the nape of his neck, my thumb stroking up the short hair on the back of his head. "I'm not going anywhere. I've got you. You're all right."

"Sorry."

"Hey, you've earned five minutes of recovery." I bend to hug his back and kiss his hair again. "I can't believe you actually went through with it. I was convinced you wouldn't."

"I know." He stares at the ground as if he's afraid it's going to disappear.

"I'm so proud of you," I tell him. "I'm going to kiss you when you feel better."

He glances up at me for the first time with a touch of humor. "There's an incentive if ever I heard one."

"Hux!" It's Mack, emerging from the Tower and running across the pedestrian area toward me. "Hey, you fucking legend!"

Huxley laughs and straightens, and Mack runs up and envelops him in a bearhug.

"You did it!" he says. "I knew you would."

"Thanks, man. I couldn't have done it without you."

Huxley goes to release Mack, but Mack doesn't let go, and Huxley laughs and hugs him again. My throat tightens, and I press my fingers to my mouth.

Our group of friends is pretty close-knit. Huxley and Victoria took the same courses at university, and decided early on that they were going to run a business together, even though it took them a few years to get there. When they were setting it up, we all did what we could to help, but Titus probably worked the hardest as his father is a politician and has a lot of connections in the Auckland business community, and Titus worked his socks off to introduce them to Huxley and get them to visit the club. And of course I've known them all since I was nineteen, and I'm as close to them as I am to my own siblings.

But Huxley and Mack have always been the best of friends. Huxley is Mack's wingman, his confidante, the Robin to Mack's Batman, although he'd probably say it was the other way around. The two of them know each other's strengths and weaknesses, and they've helped each other through all the ups and downs that life brings. Seeing Mack now, so thrilled for his friend, makes tears prick my eyes.

"Jesus, you two," I say, "are you trying to make me cry?"

They break apart with a laugh. Jamie comes up with a bottle of water, and Huxley unscrews the cap and has a few mouthfuls. "Oh, that's better."

"Did you really throw up?" I ask.

"Yep," he says cheerfully. "Legs like jelly. I've never been so fucking scared. I tell you, if I ever talk about doing anything like this again, shoot me."

"The assistant said he'd never seen anyone turn the color you did," Mack says. "You went from a whiter shade of pale to the color of that sign." He points to a sign over a shop—it's lime green.

I giggle. "And yet you still went ahead and did it."

"Mack shared a good technique," he reveals.

I raise my eyebrows. "What was that?"

"Something private," Mack says, and Huxley grins.

I glance at Mack and Jamie. "Do you think you could give us a minute?"

"We'll get us all a coffee," Mack says, and he and Jamie head across to the nearby café.

Huxley watches them go, then looks back at me with a smile.

"How are you doing?" I ask.

"I think my soul has finally caught up with my body."

I chuckle. "You have a bit more color in your cheeks, anyway."

He gives a rueful smile and runs a hand through his hair. "I'm so glad it's over. I still can't believe it." He looks at the landing area and shakes his head.

"What was the technique?" I tease. "I'm guessing it had something to do with thinking about my boobs."

He smiles. "Mack told me to think about you. About ruffling up your hair and smudging your lipstick."

"Seriously?"

"He knows how to incentivize me." His gaze is warm.

I take a deep breath. "And now I suppose I have to follow through with the bet. Mack didn't quite manage to make me sign a contract, but it was as near as dammit. He told me he wouldn't speak to me again if I didn't hold up my end of the bargain." I smile.

He doesn't return it, and studies me thoughtfully. He's wearing jeans and Converses, and a blue polo shirt that I'm pretty sure I bought him for his birthday last year. He's so incredibly gorgeous. And the way his biceps stretching the sleeves of his top makes me quiver. How come he's even more sexy now than he was at nineteen? It makes all this so much more complicated.

"Forget Mack," he says eventually, putting his hands on his hips exactly the way Mack did about twenty minutes ago when he berated me. "I appreciate his help, but I'm not going to make you do anything you don't want to do. I don't force women to sleep with me."

My face flushes. "I know."

"And I don't want to have to draw up a contract to get you in my bed. I did that—" And he points up at the platform—"one hundred percent for you. I threw myself off a building because I needed to make you understand how I feel about you. It's called a grand gesture. And if it doesn't convince you to give me a chance, then, well, I'll have to deal with the fact that we're just not meant to be, I guess, even though that will be harder than doing the jump." He looks up at the platform, then back at me. "Probably."

I swallow hard. "I don't know how you do it."

"Do what?"

"How you manage to reach inside me and tug at my heart strings every damn time."

He huffs a sigh. He's just faced his worst fear—other than maybe covering himself in tarantulas. Am I really going to tell him it hasn't worked? That he's not going to get the girl?

I'm not going to follow through with the bet because I promised Mack, or because I don't like to think I'm the kind of person who doesn't hold up her end of a bargain.

I'm going to do it because the guy standing before me threw himself off a building for me, and he's the most gorgeous man I've ever met, and I'm totally in love with him, and even though I know it's madness to let myself sleep with him, I want to do it more than anything in the world.

I pull my phone out of my back pocket. "Hold on."

"You're choosing this moment to check your texts?"

"Keep your knickers on." I scroll through to the app I want and check the calendar.

"I need to get my phone back off Mack," he says. "I should call Joanna. It would be nice for her to know they're not scraping her father off the ground with a trowel. And that I didn't embarrass myself. Too much, anyway. Jesus. I feel like Alexander the Great—as if I could conquer the world. Maybe I should go and invade Persia."

"Will you stop talking, just for a moment?"

"I can't control my mouth, sorry. It's the fear. It hasn't quite left the building. Jesus, that platform is a long way up. I don't remember anything about the fall except the seagulls. Did I tell you I think I screamed?"

I tuck my phone back into my pocket. "March the eighth," I say. "It's a Tuesday. Do you think you would be able to take the evening off?"

"Uh… yeah, probably. I'll have to check with Victoria. I don't think we've got anything big on that week. Why?"

I press my lips together for a moment. Am I really going to say this? I take a deep breath. "That's apparently the best day for me to get pregnant. The day before I ovulate."

His eyes widen. "Oh."

"I have an app," I say unnecessarily.

"Right."

We study each other for a moment. He looks speechless. Aw. He didn't really expect me to go through with it.

"Shall we go away somewhere for the night?" I say softly.

"Really?"

"Yeah. Where do you fancy?"

He gives me a beautiful smile. "Leave it with me. I'll book somewhere nice."

"Okay." I move a bit closer to him. "I can't believe you went through with it."

"I really like you, you know," he says, somewhat helplessly.

"You mean you really want to have sex with me," I tease.

"That too."

I laugh and lean my hands on his chest. "I'm extremely flattered."

He rests his hands on my hips. "Then it was worth it."

"Would you like a celebratory kiss?"

"More than anything in the world."

I lift a hand to the back of his head, slide my fingers into his hair, and bring his head down.

I press my lips to his. "Mm," I murmur as our lips peel apart, "I'm wearing lip gloss, sorry."

"That's so fucking hot," he says, and we both laugh and kiss again. He tilts his head to the side, I open my mouth to him, and we kiss for a long time, my arms rising around his neck, his sliding around my waist.

I've never had a kiss like it, warm and luxurious, bathed in the late-summer sunshine, with the smell of coffee and muffins wafting across us from the café. I can feel him still buzzing from the jump, and his happiness at the thought of going to bed with me. How can I resist him when he wants me so badly? When I want him, too? The thought of being with him… letting him undress me… kiss me all over… slide inside me… ohhhh…

Maybe he was right, and this is the only way we can cure ourselves of our obsession. And have a one-in-three chance of walking away with a bun in the oven at the same time. He's right, it's a win-win, isn't it?

Chapter Eight

Huxley

I'm convinced it's going to be the longest ten days of my life, but in the end the time passes pretty quickly. We're having some renovations carried out on two of the meeting rooms at the club, and we also close the restaurant for two days to have it completely repainted. Even though it's an obvious loss in revenue, the result is stunning, a vast improvement on the original, and Victoria and I are really pleased with it.

Despite the work going on, the club is busy. The available meeting rooms are mostly booked all day, the workrooms are bustling, the bars are packed in the evenings, and the calendar for functions is becoming nicely full. We get a great review on one of the top New Zealand business websites, and the biggest bank in the city contacts us to say they're interested in using us for their international AGM in September, which would mean huge business for us.

Although I'm cautious about jinxing it, I have to admit that the club has been successful, more than I'd hoped, and is continuing to flourish.

But even though I start work at nine and finish late, and I barely have a moment to myself, there's still plenty of time to think about Elizabeth and our coming adventure.

She's busy too, working on a new project with Titus and Mack, something to do with AI and IVF, and although I see her a couple of times in meetings, I don't get any alone time with her.

She texts or Snapchats me several times a day though. This is nothing new—I'm used to my phone buzzing in my jacket pocket announcing a message from her: a query about a meeting room, a fun anecdote, a photo of Nymph covered in mud following a walk, or a brief joke. But this time the messages are a little more intimate, flirty even.

It begins the day after my jump.

Her: *By the way, I feel I should remind you about your promise not to self-administer before our trip. ;-)*

Me: *A No Nut Ten Days?!*

Her: *Ha! Yeah, if you like. You need to build up your army.*

Me: *I'll try if you agree to try with me. It's only fair.*

Her: *Argh! Okay. I can't promise anything though.*

Me: *I foresee lots of long walks and cold showers.*

Her: *Maybe we should wear boxing gloves in bed.*

Me: *LOL! It's not going to be easy. You realize it's going to be like the 1883 eruption of Krakatoa when we eventually get together.*

Her: *That made coffee come out of my nose! Well, I expect a daily report on your success.*

Me: *Will do. We'll compare notes in the morning.*

The next day, I text her as I promised.

Me: *How did you get on last night/this morning?*

Her: *Success! I feel a bit jittery now though. You?*

Me: *Same. I'm going to have sex on the brain until the tenth.*

Her: *No change there, then!*

Me: *LOL. I guess not. Now, no extra-long visit to the Ladies' during the day…*

Her: *I've never done that!*

Me: *Are you fibbing?*

Her: *Maybe. *blushes**

Me: *Ahh that backfired. Now I'm imagining you sneaking off for some personal afternoon delight.*

Her: *Have you ever done it?*

Me: *Of course! So has every other guy in the world, I would think.*

Her: *Seriously? *fans self**

Me: *We're a rabid bunch, especially when we're young. When I was a teenager I only had to sit on a bumpy bus to get a hard on.*

Her: *When have you ever been on a bus?!*

Me: *We used coaches to travel to rugby matches. There was so much testosterone around even the women teachers grew mustaches.*

And so it continues through the week, with both of us checking in each morning to declare we've been good and abstained for yet another day.

I don't know if she's being honest, but I am, and it's not easy, especially because I keep fantasizing about what's going to happen on the tenth. When I'm feeling frisky, I have to get on the treadmill in the gym and spend half an hour running to try to wear it off.

I exercise so much over the week I would have reached the South Island if I'd run in a straight line.

And then finally, Tuesday the eighth of March arrives. I spend most of the day at work, making sure everything's organized. Victoria pushes me out of the door at four p.m., and I go home, have a shower, pack a bag, then get into my Merc and head over to Elizabeth's apartment.

I get there just before five and text her to say I'm outside. Just a few minutes later, I see her exit the building and approach the car. She throws her bag in the boot, and then opens the passenger door and slides in.

"Hey," she says, somewhat shyly.

She's wearing an eau-de-nil-colored wraparound dress that emphasizes her curves and parts to show her tanned bare legs. Her feet are encased in sexy cream high-heeled sandals. I look at her toes for a second, then lift my gaze to hers.

"Red?" I say.

"I'm keen to get five out of you." She gives me an impish smile.

"You don't have to worry about that." I start the engine. "The way I'm feeling you'll be lucky to keep me in single figures."

She gives a beautiful, girlish giggle. "Thank you for this," she says softly as I slide the car into the traffic.

"It's my pleasure. Literally. And I'm just glad you showed up."

"You didn't think I would?"

"Part of me thought you'd back out at the last minute," I say honestly. I've expected a text or a call all week from her saying she couldn't go through with it.

She looks out of the window. Her fingers are clenched tightly around her purse in her lap. She's nervous, and I don't think we're out of the woods yet.

I change the subject and ask her how her new project is going, and she chats for a while, telling me about an English pharmaceutical company that's promising a large investment. Gradually her fingers loosen their grip on her purse, and when I make her laugh a few times, her posture relaxes a little.

Her nervousness amuses me more than anything. We've known each other a long time, so it's not like going on a date with someone new. I know she's attracted to me. So why's she afraid about finally going to bed with me?

It doesn't take long to get to the heliport at Mechanics Bay, and I slot the Merc into a space in the overnight parking area and turn off the engine. "Ready?" I ask.

She sucks her bottom lip and nods.

"You need to relax or you're going to break something," I tell her.

She gives me a wry look. "I'm a bit nervous, that's all."

"Why? It's only me."

Now she looks exasperated. "If you don't understand, I'm not going to tell you." She opens the door and gets out.

Puzzled, I get out too, and retrieve our bags from the boot. We walk over to the office, I sign the paperwork, and then we head over to where the helicopter is waiting for us on the TLOF—the touchdown and lift-off area.

We put our bags in, get into our seats, and buckle ourselves in. Then we both pull on our headsets and adjust the microphones. I run through the safety procedures and standard checks, and then when we're all ready, turn the helicopter on.

Some people might find it strange that I don't mind flying when I'm afraid of heights, but as long as I don't look directly down, for some reason I'm absolutely fine, and I actually enjoy it. Titus, Mack, and I took helicopter flying lessons a couple of years ago, and I fly regularly enough that I'm comfortable doing it now. I open the throttle to increase the speed of the rotor, pull up on the collective, and depress the left foot pedal to counteract the torque as the pitch of the blades changes. When it gets light on its skids, I grip the cyclic and nudge the helicopter forward, and slowly we rise, head out over Waitemata Harbour, and fly east.

"Are we going to Waiheke Island?" Elizabeth asks. I'd kept it a secret up until now.

"Yep."

"Oh…" Her face lights up. I know it's one of her favorite places. It's New Zealand's most densely populated island, roughly twelve miles by six, and very hilly. The eastern part is the remains of a volcano that erupted fifteen million years ago. There are lots of scenic beaches, and it's also a very arty place, with a cinema, a theater, a library, and an art gallery. But today we're heading to one of the isolated ridges, to an exclusive collection of villas I think she's going to love.

"This is such an amazing view," she says as we cross the Pacific, which is a glorious deep blue. It's a beautiful evening, with not a cloud in the cerulean sky, and the sun is summer-warm, even though we're heading into autumn now.

"Oh my God, Hux, look!" She points down to where the huge black fluke of an orca whale appears out of the ocean before sinking down beneath the surface. "Oh how fantastic."

I smile, glad she's enjoying herself. We all work hard, and most of her time is dedicated to helping others, so it's great to treat her for once. This isn't all about sex. Okay, so it's mainly about sex, but I want her to enjoy herself.

I want to enjoy myself, too. It's rare for me to take an afternoon off work, and the fact that I'm out with my favorite girl is a bonus. Whatever happens today, hopefully at the least we'll have a great meal, a swim in the pool, and a few drinks as we watch the sun go down.

And if it ends with the spectacular sex I know the two of us could have, even better.

I head inland, over the dense bush of Whakanewha Regional Park, to a hilltop retreat on a high ridge of land with fantastic views over the island and the Hauraki Gulf.

I land the helicopter on the pad to the rear of the property and turn off the engine.

"Wait a sec." I get out, go around to the passenger side, open the door, and offer her a hand. She climbs out carefully in her high-heeled sandals, but stumbles a little as her feet touch the ground, and she falls against me.

"Careful," I murmur, catching her.

She places both hands on my chest, and her face flushes. "I think you did that on purpose," she scolds as I rest my hands on her hips.

"Any excuse." I kiss her nose. Then, as she looks up at me, I kiss her lips gently, and she sighs.

Unfortunately, we're interrupted as a guy comes over to welcome us and collect our bags. "Mr. Huxley?" he confirms. "And Ms. Tremblay, it's lovely to have you here. I'm the manager, Ralph Inman. Please, follow me."

We cross the helipad toward the main reception. Wow, this place is very swish. A dozen individual villas radiate out from the central block, all angled in such a way as to give them complete privacy. When we go into the building, Ralph tells us there's a gym, a large, heated pool, and a restaurant just five minutes' walk away at the vineyard that borders the property.

We sign in, and then he takes us across to our villa. He tells us as we walk that it's the biggest one, often reserved for celebrities and other important guests—the guy is very proud to name several movie stars who've stayed here. He unlocks the door, and we go inside.

The huge living room contains what looks like a comfortable cream leather sofa and chairs, a huge flat-screen TV, and a desk and chair in case you want to catch up on some work. A good-sized kitchen is tucked into the corner.

We walk out through double sliding doors onto a large private deck. It has an outdoor sofa and chairs, a dining area, and its own giant hot tub that faces the magnificent view.

Lastly, we turn into the bedroom that's set in a separate area at right angles to the living room with its own entrance off the deck. It's beautiful: large and lit by the early evening sun. A circular white rug takes up most of the floor. There's a dressing table with an old-fashioned oval mirror and a chest of drawers, and a sofa to one side. But it's the bed that grabs my attention. It's a huge four-poster, with a sumptuous lavender-colored duvet, pillows that look soft as puffy clouds, and lavender curtains that can be drawn to give the occupants complete privacy.

Elizabeth meets my eyes again. Her lips curve up a little, and I wink at her.

"I hope you enjoy your stay," Ralph says. "Please, don't hesitate to call if you need anything. I booked you a table at the vineyard for six."

"Thank you."

He smiles at us both and heads out of the villa, closing the door behind him.

"Wow." I walk across to the sliding doors that open onto the deck. "Look at that view."

She comes to stand beside me. "It's a gorgeous place. Thank you so much for organizing it."

"My pleasure." I turn and slip my arms around her waist. She rests her hands on my chest again, and she gives a little shiver. "Are you cold?" I ask.

"No."

Aw. I kiss her forehead. Then her nose. Then, finally, her mouth.

She sighs and lifts her face to me, and we exchange a slow, gentle kiss that sends a frisson running down my back. It would be so easy to turn and direct her back into the bedroom, strip off her clothes, and throw her straight onto the bed, but I don't want to do that. Even though that's why we're here, and we're not strictly on a date, I want to romance her a little.

"Come on," I say. "Let's walk slowly down to the vineyard. We can have a drink before we eat."

She blows out what I think is a relieved breath. "Okay."

We lock up the villa and head out into the sunshine. The path leads around the buildings and then along the top of the ridge, with the Pacific sparkling to our left and the vineyards rich and green to our right. The sun is sinking gradually behind the hills of the mainland to the west, and it's still warm. I hold out my hand, and she looks at it for a moment, then slips hers into it.

"How's your day been?" I ask as we walk slowly along the path.

"Yeah, good, thanks. I was talking to Titus today about the new English investment opportunity."

She continues to chat about business for a while, and I'm happy to let her. She tells me about the IVF treatment she's working on, and how Titus is hoping to develop the use of Artificial Intelligence to improve the choice of embryos. I know that her sister, Penelope, is on her third round of IVF after a few years of failing to fall pregnant with her husband, and that's one reason why Elizabeth has chosen it as a project.

I ask lots of questions, and I can feel her relaxing as she explains, using her free hand a lot to gesture. She's the smartest woman I know, and damn, if that isn't the hottest thing ever.

She stops speaking and gives me a wry look. "I'm talking too much."

"Not at all."

"You haven't said anything for, like, five minutes."

"I'm listening. You're very articulate. I like that. It makes me hot."

She laughs. "Only because you haven't self-administered for a whole week."

"I concede that might be a factor." I squeeze her hand. "But I like your brain."

"That's the first time anyone's ever said that to me. Okay, here's a question: brain or boobs?"

That makes me laugh. "Brain," I say.

She blows a raspberry. "Yeah, right."

"I'm being polite."

"Figures." She smiles, though.

We approach the vineyard, which consists of a collection of low brick buildings around a central courtyard paved with flagstones. It looks as if it's been transported straight out of Italy, with hanging baskets filled with a riot of colorful flowers, and vines threaded across a wooden frame above the outdoor seating area, so that the burgeoning grapes hang down in rich clusters.

We walk through to the main restaurant. Only half a dozen tables are occupied as it's still early.

"Good evening," a waiter says with a smile as we walk up to the desk.

"Hi," I say, "we have a reservation for Huxley for six p.m.?"

"Absolutely, sir."

"We're a bit early."

"That's fine, we're not busy yet as you can see. Would you prefer to sit inside or outside?"

"Out?" I suggest to Elizabeth, and she nods.

"Come this way," the waiter says. He leads us to the outdoor seating area, and over to one of the tables that's looking out across the lawn to the gorgeous view.

"Thank you." I hold Elizabeth's chair as she sits, then go around and take my chair.

"Can I get you a drink?" the waiter asks, gesturing at the wine list. "Or would you like to do a tasting?"

"Ooh, yes please," Elizabeth says, and he smiles.

"White and red?" he asks, and I nod.

"I'll go and organize it," he states. "And I'll take your food order when I return." He walks off.

I lean on the table. "It's an amazing view."

"Oh yeah," she says. I glance back at her—she's looking at me with a smile. "You look nice today," she states, a little shyly.

I look down at myself. I'm wearing black jeans, a white shirt with a blue paisley pattern, and a gray blazer. "Thank you. And I like your dress. The color suits you."

"I'm glad you like it," she says. "It's new."

"You bought it for today?"

She nods and flushes.

I hold her gaze, smiling.

She pokes me beneath the table with her toe. "Look at your menu," she scolds.

Chuckling, I lean back and pick it up. "Okay. What are you in the mood for?"

"Nothing too heavy."

"No. Got to make sure we're not too full when we exercise."

She laughs, keeping her gaze on the menu. "Behave."

"I'm trying."

We spend a few minutes discussing the options. The waiter returns with two wooden racks holding six small glasses, each holding a different wine, and places them before us. He gives us a card each that contains a few sentences about each wine and says he'll be happy to expand on any of them if we want more information. Finally he takes our order. We've decided on a platter so we can pick and choose as much as we like, and he tells us that's a great option and goes off to put the order in.

"Right," I say. "Let's start with the white wines."

Gradually, we work our way through the six glasses, reading the explanations and trying to see if we can pick up the tasting notes. We try a Chardonnay, a Pinot Gris, and a Viognier, and then move on to the reds: a Cabernet Sauvignon, a Merlot, and a Syrah. The food comes halfway through: a gorgeous platter of mixed meats, cheese, crackers, homemade dips: hummus, beetroot, and Kiwi onion, and fruits like apricots and figs, all the flavors mixing well with the wines.

We finish the tasting and decide to order a bottle of our favorite: the Merlot, which bursts with dense chocolate and plum flavors.

The sun is sliding behind the hills, and the waiter comes over and lights the candle on our table, then pulls one of the deck heaters closer to make sure we're not too chilled by the evening breeze.

I've deliberately tried to keep the conversation light, because I know she's nervous. We talk about music and movies, and our friends: about Mack and Sidnie's wedding, and how pleased we are that Mack has finally found someone who understands him.

But as the lights dims and the candle flickers on the table, and the wine threads through my veins, I feel the need to turn the conversation more intimate. We both know where we're heading tonight. Elizabeth began the evening tense and professional, but as the wine's done its job, she began leaning on the table, playing with her hair, even though I don't think she's aware she's doing it.

She still looks a bit nervous, and that puzzles me, because she's usually so confident, and I know she's not inexperienced. Perhaps it's the idea of making a baby that's made her anxious, and that's fair enough. She's not going to be the easiest woman to seduce, but I enjoy a challenge, and I'm more than happy to take my time, conscious of the pot of gold at the end of the rainbow.

Chapter Nine

Elizabeth

In the flickering candlelight, Huxley's eyes are filled with the buzz of adventure. He's gorgeous when he's like this—excited and full of energy, no doubt fueled by his self-styled 'no-nut ten days'. The guy could light the whole of the island on his pent-up sexual energy.

He looks young, handsome, and wealthy today in his smart-casual clothes. As always, he carries himself with an attractive insouciance and an inner confidence that gives me goosebumps.

He must have shaved earlier today; his jaw is stubble-free and smooth. During the day, he usually wears a lighter aftershave, but he's wearing his evening fragrance now—dark and sensual, with a mouthwatering touch of blackcurrant and a sensual undertone of jasmine and musk. It smells expensive and sexy.

I have the sudden, irrational thought that he's sprayed himself with pheromones. Maybe that's his secret?

The deck heater is warm, and he slips off his jacket and hangs it on the back of his chair. His shirt emphasizes his shoulders and biceps, which have always been impressive because of his archery training. He's kept trim over the years, and he has a narrow waist and not an ounce of fat on him. I like the way the muscles of his thighs stretch the denim of his jeans.

We've spent the meal talking about everything under the sun except what we came here for: sex. I know he's done that on purpose. I know him well enough to understand that he's trying to relax me. Putting people at ease is his job, and he's very good at it. But we're on a train heading for our destination, and at some point we're going to arrive. I can't avoid it.

"Are you nervous?" he asks. "Because that's okay. I know you're probably quite inexperienced, and I'm happy to show you the ropes."

I give him a wry look.

"If you're a virgin," he adds mischievously, "I promise I'll be gentle."

That makes me laugh. Then I admit, "I was. When we first dated."

He stares at me. He looks genuinely shocked. "Seriously?"

"I was a late bloomer. I was very shy when I was young."

And I was saving myself for the right guy. I think it, but I don't say it out loud. I don't want to harp on about the past and spoil the mood.

"Are you nervous?" I ask.

"No."

"Why not?" I'm a little resentful that he seems so in control.

He tips his head to the side. "Do you remember the Band of Brothers episode where Captain Speirs tells Private Blithe the way to survive the war is to accept you're already dead?"

"Uh, yeah."

"It's kind of like that. If you accept that in a few hours we're definitely going to be having really, really good sex, it'll help a lot."

I think I've turned scarlet, judging by the heat in my face. His lips curve up, so he obviously notices.

"How can you be so confident?" I ask enviously.

"I have great faith in my powers of seduction." He sips his wine, his eyes gleaming over the rim. I blow out a breath, and he chuckles. "I'm teasing. Why are you so anxious? It's only me."

"That's exactly why I'm nervous. We've never crossed that line other than a few kisses. And you're all…" I wave a hand at him. He raises his eyebrows. "Scented and shaved," I say.

That makes him laugh. "I bet you are too," he says, his eyes gleaming. "Waxed and body-creamed and sublime. I can't wait."

"Oh God."

"Will you calm down? I thought you were a self-assured, modern woman. You're acting like a teenager on her first date. I should have brought some weed."

"Why are you mocking me?" I snap.

If I'd hoped to shame him, I'm going to be disappointed. He just grins. "Because it's funny. I didn't expect this. I thought you'd be confident and aggressive in the bedroom. I thought you'd have me tied to the bedpost in the first five minutes and be screwing my brains out."

"Wow."

"Are you into BDSM? I have visions of you in leather with a whip."

"Oh my God."

"I'm just saying, I'm not a natural sub. We might have a bit of an issue if you're expecting me to do as I'm told."

"Hux!"

"What?" He laughs again. "I honestly can't remember the last time I saw you blush." He tips his head to the side as he studies me. "It's kinda sexy."

"You're not helping."

"You've had at least three partners I know of, and I'd be shocked if it wasn't more, because you're so gorgeous. Why are you so hesitant?"

"Like I said, because it's you. I don't know how to act."

"What do you mean?"

"I don't know," I say resentfully. "I mean, should I call you Oliver when we're… you know… at it?"

He gives me a baffled look. "Firstly, 'at it'? And secondly, why?"

"Because it's your name?"

"I don't think you've ever called me Oliver other than when you're annoyed with me. It would just be weird now."

"I can't sleep with you and call you by your surname."

He laughs again. He's thoroughly enjoying himself, the bastard.

"You don't get it," I say, a little irritable. "You're you, and I'm just me. I feel as if I've arrived at the palace and met Prince Charming. I'm out of my depth, and you're mocking me for it. I honestly don't think I'm going to be able to relax. So here's my idea. I think we should just get it over with."

His smile fades. "Get it over with," he repeats flatly.

"Yeah. I don't need foreplay or anything. I have some lube in my purse. We don't even have to kiss. When we get back, let's just have at it and get it done."

"Jesus." Now it's his turn to look exasperated. He glances around to make sure nobody's listening, then leans on the table. "You might not need foreplay, but I do. I'm not a robot. In fact, I don't just require it—I enjoy it. And I like kissing. I've been looking forward to this. Stop spoiling my fun."

My lips curve up. "Don't pout."

"You're teasing me."

"A bit."

"So you're not serious?"

"Maybe twenty percent. Possibly thirty."

"Do you really have lube in your purse?"

"Yeah. Just in case."

"You won't need it." He smirks.

"Depends what we're gonna do."

"If you're talking about what I think you're talking about, I don't think you've got the hang of how a baby's made."

That makes me laugh. He's always known how to disarm me.

We've finished the wine, and the waiter comes over to take our plates. "Can I get you a dessert?" he asks.

I shake my head, and Huxley says, "No, I think we're done with food. Maybe a whisky to finish?"

"Of course."

"What's the best you've got?"

"We have a thirty-two-year-old Bowmore." He names the price of a single shot.

My eyebrows rise, but Huxley just nods. "Oh yeah, we'll have two glasses of that, please. Doubles."

The waiter smiles. "Of course. Are you happy staying here, or would you like to come inside? There's an open fire."

"That sounds great," Huxley says, so we rise and go inside, over to the sofa in front of the log fire. He sits in the right-hand corner, and I sit in the middle next to him. He puts his arm around me, pulling me right up to him, and I lean against him, tingling at the notion of being so close.

Even though I'm still nervous, the wine has done its job. My joints feel loose, and my spine has relaxed. He's right. I should just accept that we're going to end up in bed together. There's no point in fighting it. I can't resist him, and I think he knows it.

I give him a mischievous look. "I've got something to admit."

"Oh?"

"Once, a while ago, I overheard two women talking at a bar in Auckland. I was there with a couple of friends who were unconnected to you guys. I went up to order another round. It was impossible not to overhear their conversation as the bar was crowded and they were standing right next to me. One of them—a blonde—said to the other, who was a brunette, 'So how was it? 'He was amazing,' the brunette said. 'He had incredible stamina. He went on for hours. And he actually knew how to get to my clitoris without a map.'"

His brows draw together. "It'd be funny if it wasn't so sad."

"The blonde said, 'I hope you're seeing him again,' and the brunette replied, 'Yeah, you'll get to meet him if you stay.' The guy walked in about half an hour later."

"I hope you got his number," he says, amused.

I give a small smile. "It was you, Huxley."

His eyebrows rise. He hadn't expected that. "Oh."

"You didn't see me. You left with her five minutes later."

"When was this?"

"A few years ago. I think her name was Rachel?"

"Ah, yeah. I remember. Nice girl. She moved to Australia a few weeks after I'd met her. Not because of me. Well, I don't think it was."

I think about how much her words had affected me at the time. I was convinced I'd never discover for myself what he was like in bed, and I'd burned with jealousy that she'd been with him, and I would never get the chance.

And now I will. Holy moly.

"I couldn't look you in the face for days without blushing," I admit.

He chuckles. "Really?"

I glance at where the material of his shirt is stretched across his shoulders and run a finger down the seam. It's like discovering yourself on a date with a movie star when you've had a poster of him on your wall since you were a kid. I tell myself I'm a confident, sassy woman, but inside I'm still the nineteen-year-old who had a huge crush on him, and whose heart he broke.

"I've tried so hard not to think about what it'd be like to go to bed with you," I murmur. "I'd convinced myself the brunette in the bar must have been exaggerating. But I'm beginning to think she wasn't, and I'm puzzled and terrified and excited all rolled into one."

He opens his mouth to reply, then stops as the waiter comes up with our whiskies. "Thanks," Huxley says, taking them and passing one to me. The waiter withdraws, and we sip the amber liquid. Ooh, that's smooth, warming me all the way down to my stomach. Mind you, it should be good for that price.

He studies me for a while, maybe thinking about what I've said. He's obviously mystified.

Eventually, I smile. "You genuinely don't understand why that girl said what she said, do you?"

"It's a nice compliment. I mean, I don't think I'm bad in bed. What puzzles me is that it's not difficult."

"Maybe technically. But not everyone has your patience or interest in pleasing the girl. Not in my experience anyway. Obviously, Rich suffered from premature ejaculation, so extended foreplay definitely wasn't on the table there. But even with the others… they just couldn't be bothered."

"Did you talk to them about it?"

"Yeah, of course. But the odd thing is that in the movies it's really common to see two people start kissing and then move straight to intercourse. The woman acts like she's ready for it immediately, and then she has an instant orgasm. It's no wonder guys are puzzled when that doesn't happen, or why they think that if the girl's not like that, there's something wrong with her. They don't consider it's partly their fault. Not all, obviously. It's up to us to explain what we want in bed. But they have to be willing to listen and act on it." I give him a curious look. "How did you learn what to do?"

"I minored in gigolo training at uni."

"Hux, seriously…"

"I don't know. Lots of practice?" He looks amused.

He genuinely doesn't realize that he's unusual. Maybe it's just the way he is. Unselfish, always interested in making sure that other people have a good time.

Lots of practice. Something occurs to me then. "Was there someone along the way who helped you… ah… develop your techniques, shall we say?"

"Yeah, because sharing the bedroom antics of past partners is a real turn on."

"You don't have to go into detail. I'm interested. Was there someone?"

He sighs. "Well… When I was in my early twenties, I dated an older woman for a while."

"What was her name?"

"Gillian."

I don't remember her. "When you say older…"

"She was thirty-four. Ten years older than I was at the time. She was a yoga instructor, and I met her at the gym. We had a fling for a few months."

Ten years is quite a bit at that age, and especially when the guy's younger. "So you were her toyboy?"

He gives a wry smile. "I guess."

"And she taught you about foreplay?"

I can see he doesn't like talking about it. He just says, "Kinda."

"Why didn't you stay with her?" I ask softly.

He sips his whisky. "She was separated from her husband when I met her, but in the end she went back to him. She's got two kids now."

That implies he's still in touch with her. And then the penny drops. "Are you talking about Gillian Porter?"

He just smiles.

"Oh…" Her husband is a member of the club. I met her once. I was out with Huxley and the others in a restaurant, and she came up to our table with her husband. Huxley stood and gave her a hug, and seemed genuinely pleased to see her. He introduced her as an old friend. She was small, I remember, and dark-haired.

"She didn't look unlike me," I comment.

"What a shock," he says, rolling his eyes.

Is he saying that's why he went with her? I wonder whether he broke it off, or if she left him to go back to her husband. I remember her introducing her husband at the table, and Huxley shaking hands with him. That must have been hard. "Did she break your heart?" I ask softly.

He gives a rueful smile. "No. You're the only one who's ever done that."

My eyebrows rise. "What do you mean?"

He looks into his glass and doesn't reply.

"Do you mean when we were nineteen?" I ask.

He stretches out his legs, sliding down on the sofa a little. "Six months after Joanna was born, when I asked you out and you said no, I went around Victoria's apartment, and I was so angry I swung one of her golf clubs at a tree and bent it."

"Really?"

"It was a 5-iron, I think. Maybe a 4-iron. Anyway, she called Mack and Titus, and they brought a bottle of Laphroaig around and sat there while I drank a third of it and then passed out on the sofa. Victoria said I snored so hard her flat-mate thought there was a pneumatic drill outside the room."

He's trying to make me laugh, but I'm so shocked I can only stare at him. "I didn't know," I whisper.

His lovely gray eyes observe me. "I stopped seeing you because I had to do right by Brandy and Joanna. But I was devastated when you wouldn't go out with me again. I was crazy about you. I still am."

"Do you think that will change when we've gone to bed?" I ask.

He tips his head to the side. "Nice to hear you say when, and not if."

"You haven't answered the question."

"You think I've only had a *crush* on you for ten years?"

I frown. I'm not sure what the alternative is.

He finishes off his drink. "Come on. I think it's time we went back to the villa." He gets to his feet.

I have the last mouthful of whisky, wincing as it slides down inside me, and let him pull me up. I bump against him, and he slips an arm around my waist. I'm not drunk, but the alcohol is definitely having an effect. He was probably right—it was necessary.

He holds me until he's sure I've got my balance on my high heels. And then he holds me for a little bit longer. His gaze has dropped to my mouth, and right there, in the middle of the room with all the tables filled around us, he lowers his lips to mine.

It's not a long kiss, no tongues or anything, hardly X-rated, but when he eventually lifts his head, my face is burning. I glance around, and I meet the eyes of an older woman who's sitting at a table with a man. She gives me a mischievous smile, and my lips curve up before I look away.

Huxley goes over to the desk, ignores me when I ask if I can pay half, and touches his Apple watch to the card reader. The waiter says goodbye, and we walk out into the night air.

We took a couple of hours over the meal, so it's now nearly eight, and the sun has set. Luckily solar lights mark the path. Huxley takes my hand, and we slowly walk back to the villas.

We don't say anything as we walk. It's not an awkward silence, but I can feel my nerves building again.

"Thank you for a lovely evening," I say, because I can't think of anything else.

He gives a short laugh, then he stops and pulls me into his arms. "You haven't changed a bit since the day I met you," he says. "You're still maddening. Confident and shy in equal measure. Still fucking gorgeous." And then he slides a hand to the back of my neck and crushes his lips to mine.

It's relatively forceful for a guy I've always thought of as gentle, and my heart hammers. I hadn't expected that. I feel as if I went with Pooh Bear into the woods, and I've suddenly discovered he's actually a grizzly bear.

He slides his tongue into my mouth, and his other hand presses against the base of my spine, pulling me against him. Oh my God—he has an erection. The feel of it, long and hard, makes me feel as if someone's thrown a bucket of water over me.

We're really doing this. I'm really going to bed with him.

Elation floods me, and I lift up on my tiptoes and wrap my arms around his neck as I tilt my head and return his kiss a hundred percent. He growls deep in his throat and his fingers clench in my hair. Ooh, I like passionate, sexed-up, grizzly-bear Huxley.

I stroke my tongue against his, thrilled at the invasion, as the wall I've built around me over ten years of longing, yearning, comes crumbling down. I want him so much. I want his hands and mouth on my body; I want him naked; I want him inside me.

He tears his lips away from mine. His chest heaves. Without another word, he takes my hand and marches along the path.

I can barely keep up with him in my high heels, but I totter along as best as I can. Thankfully we're nearly there, and he practically drags me across the drive, unlocks the door to our villa, and pushes me inside.

There's no time for me to gather my wits because the moment the door shuts behind us, Huxley's mouth is on mine, and he's kissing the living daylights out of me once again. He walks me backward, and I meet the wall with a bump and a gasp. He takes advantage of my open mouth to plunge his tongue inside again, and my head spins as he deepens the kiss, firing me up, sending my heart pounding and the blood speeding through my veins.

His mouth leaves mine, and he plants hot kisses up my jaw to my ear. His hot breath whispers across it, and I shiver, unable to stop a muttered exhalation escaping my lips.

In response, he captures my hands and pins them on the wall above my head.

"I've waited a long time for this," he says, his voice husky. "To hear you moan. Say my name."

I don't think he means Oliver somehow. I close my eyes as he kisses down my neck and whisper, "Huxley…"

He closes his mouth over the place where my pulse beats and sucks gently.

"I want you," I whisper. "So much."

"Have me, then," he says. "I've always been yours anyway." And he crushes his mouth to mine once again.

Chapter Ten

Elizabeth

Huxley wasn't joking when he said he likes kissing. His mouth barely leaves mine as he gradually walks me backward through the living room and out onto the deck.

When he does finally lift his head, it's to look out at the view, where he stops for a second and stares. I follow his head and inhale at the sight of the stars popping out on the dark velvet sky. There's little light pollution here, with Auckland behind us, and the celestial sphere is reflected on the vast expanse of the Pacific, making it look like an endless diamond-scattered carpet. The moon is half-full to the west, and with the stars provides more than enough light to see by.

"Normally I'm not a lights-out kind of guy in the bedroom," he says, "but I might make an exception tonight." He looks back at me, cups my face in his hands, and strokes his thumbs across my cheeks. "You're so fucking beautiful."

I've watched Huxley turn his charm—his inner light—on so many people over the years, but I've never been the full focus of it myself, and I feel dazzled. He kisses me again, and all thoughts flee my mind except the feel of his mouth on mine, and his hands touching my face, my hair. Somehow, he shepherds us toward the bedroom, opens the door, and steers us inside. He closes the door, probably so we don't get cold and to keep out the insects, but leaves the curtains open, so the starlight fills the room.

Now I've done what he asked—accepted that tonight is going to end in really, really good sex—my nerves have—mostly—fled. That might also be something to do with the wine and whisky. But I'm glad of it, because it's as if all the barriers, the chains, and the padlocks around my heart are gone, and, just for now, I can give myself to him one hundred percent.

I start pushing the buttons through the holes on his shirt, and he murmurs his approval, still kissing me. When I get to the bottom, I push the sides of the shirt apart, and he shrugs it off his shoulders and lets it fall to the floor.

Placing my hands on his chest, I smooth them across his pecs and up and over his shoulders. "You have a magnificent body," I whisper, tracing his powerful biceps, then coming back to run my fingers down his sternum to his navel and the defined muscles across his chest and stomach. He told me once that he pulls the bow with his whole body, and I can see what he meant now.

He starts lifting the skirt of my dress with his fingers. "I'd like to return the compliment."

I nod shyly, and he peels the dress up, lifts it over my head, and lays it over the nearby chair. He comes back to me, rests his hands on my hips, and lets his gaze drift down me like a silk scarf. "I've waited a long time for this," he says softly.

I shiver, feeling the brush of his gaze like a feather over my skin. I'm wearing a cream lace half-cup bra and matching knickers I bought for the occasion, and his admiration of them fills me with a warm glow.

Sliding my hands down his chest, I stop at his belt and begin to loosen it. He helps me out, undoing the belt, then the button and the zipper. He toes off his shoes and flicks off his socks, then steps out of his trousers and leaves them on the chair.

He's wearing a pair of black boxer-briefs that fit extremely snugly. Wow. As he bends to move his shoes under the table, I get to observe his magnificent butt, and then he straightens and turns, and… whoa. I feel a bit faint.

He follows my gaze down, then smirks and comes up to nuzzle my neck and kiss my ear. "That made your eyes light up."

"It was alarm. I'm only tiny and you're… not."

"We'll have to make sure you're nicely lubricated then, won't we?"

"I'll get my purse."

He laughs. "Not this time. I told you, you won't need it." He kisses me, skimming his fingers around my waist to my back while he walks me back to the bed.

"Can I take my sandals off without you mocking me for being short?" I ask.

He takes my face in his hands. "I'm sorry for every time I've done that. I love that you're small."

I slip my sandals off. He's teased me about my height for as long as I can remember. "Yeah, right."

He pulls me toward him. He's a lot taller than me now, but to my surprise he's not smiling. "I've had to hide my feelings for you behind a veneer of friendship and teasing. But you've always fascinated me. I've watched you talk to a boardroom of people without an ounce of nerves. You handle men with ease. You're sassy and confident and smart. And it's all wrapped up in this gorgeous package." He smooths his hands down my sides, then bends and picks me up in his arms as if I weigh nothing. He kisses me, then walks to the side of the four-poster bed and tosses me onto it.

I bounce, the breath leaving me in a whoosh, and push myself up onto the pillows, but there's no time to recover because he climbs on the bed, tucks a hand under each of my knees, and pulls me down a few inches so I'm lying flat. Before I can exclaim or move back up, he moves over me and lowers himself down, then rolls onto his back, taking me with him, so I'm stretched out on top of him. It's all done in one move, so smoothly that it takes me by surprise.

He strokes his hands down my back to my butt and slowly tilts his hips up, pressing his erection into my soft flesh. "Now we're talking," he murmurs.

I'm breathless with how quickly I've been maneuvered. I prop myself up on my hands and look down into his gorgeous gray eyes that have almost been taken over by his huge pupils.

"You know that gigolo training you said you had…"

He laughs, slides a hand to the back of my head, and kisses me.

Ohhh… the delight of having his arms around me, his fingers brushing over my skin, his hot mouth claiming mine. He's so laid back normally, so relaxed and mellow, even when he's busy—he's like the embers of a fire, eternally warm and comfortable. And so I hadn't expected this fierce heat, like a blow torch singeing me from top to toe.

Despite his obvious desire, he takes his time to kiss me, his tongue playing with mine, his hands roving slowly over my skin, fingers trailing from my shoulders down my back to my bottom, then stroking up my sides. Mmm… it's wonderful, but I want to explore him, too.

I push myself up to a sitting position astride him, and he watches me as I skim my hands down over the impressive muscles of his arms, and over his shoulders and chest. I don't know what's happened tonight, whether it's the gorgeous setting, the delicious meal and the fine wine, the prolonged kissing, the fact that I haven't indulged in any DIY for ten days, or just the thrill of being with him, but I feel *hot as*, my body humming with desire, aching with need.

I take his hands and move them above his head. His lips curve up, but he plays along, pretending I'm able to pin him down, and I hold him there as I slowly rock my hips, arousing myself on him.

"I'm so hot for you," I whisper, bending to touch my lips to his.

He breathes in, then exhales slowly. "You're severely testing my self-control."

I touch my tongue to his bottom lip, pleased that he's not as in control as he looks. As much as I've enjoyed his slow seduction, I want to do the same to him. I want him aching for me. I want to provoke the grizzly bear until he roars.

Releasing his hands, I sit back up. He's not paid much attention to my breasts yet, and I know that's because he's trying to take his time and not rush things.

Time I stepped things up a bit.

I lift my hands behind my back to undo my bra, slide the straps down, and toss it onto the floor.

He gives a deep, helpless sigh.

I know he's a breast man, and I'm happy to give him a moment to admire them. I think my breasts are one of my best assets, and I have a feeling he might think so too.

He lifts his gaze to mine, hot, amused, then cups my breasts and brushes his thumbs across my nipples.

I sigh, tip my head back, and arch my spine, and he groans and tugs my nipples gently. I feel him take my hands, and then he lifts them above his head, pulling me down so my breasts are level with his head, where he closes his mouth over a nipple.

"Aaahhh…" I exhale as he strokes it with his tongue, then sucks. He swaps to the other nipple, teasing the first with his fingers, and his touch on the sensitive wet skin sends shivers down my spine.

I clutch my fingers in his hair and pull his head up, and crush my lips to his. In response he wraps his arms around me and rolls, and now I'm beneath him, his weight pinning me down.

He plants hot kisses down my neck to my breasts and takes each nipple in his mouth in turn, teasing them with his lips, teeth, and tongue.

"Stop wriggling," he scolds when I squirm beneath him.

"Ahhh… you're making me ache," I protest.

He kisses down my belly, dips his tongue in my belly button, then continues to kiss down. "You can expect a lot more where that came from."

I close my eyes and lift my hips as he tucks his fingers in the elastic of my knickers and peels them down my legs. Holy moly, is he heading where I think he's heading?

He is. Oh my God, Huxley's going down on me. How many times have I dreamed about this? Every night in my bed, I think, although I'd never admit it to myself.

He kisses over my hip, trails his tongue across my tummy, making me quiver, then moves between my legs and settles down there. He pushes up my knees, kisses the skin on each inner thigh, then slides his thumb down through my folds. I groan, covering my face as he turns his hand and teases my entrance with a finger.

"Just relax," he says, kissing my thighs again and returning to stroking with his thumb.

"I am relaxed."

"Yeah, that's why you're practically squeezing me to death with your thighs. Which isn't an unpleasant way to go, and you're wet, but you're the size of a pinhole, and I don't want to hurt you." He circles his thumb over my clit. "Let me in. You know you want to."

I roll my eyes, then close them again and blow out a long breath. Slowly, I force my muscles to loosen.

"Mmm," he says. "That's better." He lowers his head and strokes his tongue up through my folds.

I catch my bottom lip between my teeth and suck it as he flicks my clit with the tip of his tongue, then gently sucks. Ohhh… I should have known he'd be fantastic at this. He spends ages licking, sucking, and teasing with his fingers, and I guess I must relax because eventually he turns his hand palm up and slides one, then two fingers inside me.

"Good girl," he murmurs.

I shake my head, not opening my eyes. Oh Jesus, he's curving his fingers up and… ohhh… I didn't think G-spots really existed, is that what this is? Trust Huxley to find mine… holy fuck… It's an unusual sensation, intense and… um… ohhh… absolutely fucking wonderful…

I'm just starting to feel the first flickers of an orgasm when he withdraws his fingers and sits up. I open my eyes, my breath leaving me in a frustrated rush.

"Sorry," he says, removing his underwear before moving up over me. He looks down and kisses my nose. "This first time, I want you to come while I'm inside you."

I look up at him as he nudges my legs apart. He tips his head to the side and watches with interest as he slides the tip of his erection through my folds a few times.

His eyes come up to mine, hot and sexy. "Sensitive without a condom," he says. Of course, I'd forgotten. He looks back down, doing it a few more times, his eyes filled with a hazy desire, and then eventually he parts my folds and presses against my entrance.

Leaning forward, he bends and kisses me. "Try to relax," he murmurs.

It's hard, because my heart is hammering. I'd completely forgotten that we came here to make a baby, and excitement sparks inside me.

Propped on his hands, he pushes his hips forward. I close my hands, feeling him penetrate me, and ohhh... the sensation of him sliding inside me is just exquisite.

He withdraws, teases my entrance a couple of times with small thrusts, then pushes forward again. This time he goes deeper. He does this a couple more times, easing into me gradually, until the fourth or fifth time he's finally buried inside me, his hips flush against the back of my thighs.

"Fuck," he says, just the one word, but it somehow manages to sum up the moment.

I open my eyes and look straight into his, which sends a zing right through me.

He gives me a beautiful smile that's a mixture of triumph, smugness, and pleasure, and I laugh and pull his head down so I can kiss him.

He lowers down to kiss me, then starts moving, and I wrap my legs around him, matching each rock of his hips with one of my own. Mmm... that feels good. It feels like we were made to do this. Oh I'm so glad I came here tonight... This is just amazing... He's lit by starlight, and he's so fucking handsome... I can't believe we actually made it. I was convinced one or other of us—probably me—would change their mind at the last minute. But here we are... and it's delicious and so amazing. I groan with each thrust he gives, embarrassed with myself for being so vocal, but he just says, "Oh yeah," and kisses me, so I guess he doesn't mind.

And hmm… it's not been long, but I can feel my orgasm not far away… ooh, that's embarrassing, I should have been able to wait a bit longer. But I can't help it; it's being with him like this, having him on top of me, inside me after spending so long dreaming about him…

"Hux…"

He kisses me. "Yeah?"

"I'm… um… oh… I think I'm going to come, sorry…"

He slides a hand down my thigh and encourages me to move my legs higher, around his waist. Now he's plunging down into me, and fuck that feels amazing.

"I wanted to make it last," he says, his voice husky, "but I think we'll have to accept that this first time is going to be quick."

Quick? We've spent ages making out.

"Come for me," he says, dipping his tongue into my mouth for a deep, sensual kiss before lifting up onto his hands again.

He starts thrusting hard, each movement of his hips causing him to grind against me. I cry out with every thrust, "Oh fuck, oh fuck," and ohh… I can't hold back any longer, so I let him carry me all the way, closing my eyes as I feel the blissful sensation deep inside as all my muscles tense, and the intense five or six pulses that come straight afterward, so exquisite as I clench around him.

"Oh fuck," he says, and then he shudders and his muscles tense as he pushes forward with a series of jerks that make me feel as if he's trying to impale me on the bed. Oh my, Huxley is coming inside me, and I dig my nails in his back and give him a little scratch to help him along.

Ooh, that was intense. When he eventually opens his eyes, we're both breathing heavily, our gasps filling the semi-darkness.

"Jesus," he says. "Your pelvic floor is fucking amazing." That makes me giggle, and he glares at me. "Laughter doesn't help."

"Sorry."

"Ouch. Wow. Hold on." He withdraws carefully, wincing, then pushes my knees up to my chest. "Stay there. It encourages the little swimmers to reach the finish line." Then he falls onto his back on the bed beside me and lets out a long groan.

I lie there, hugging my knees, and look up at the ceiling. Oh my God. We might have just made a baby.

I roll my head to look at him. He's watching me. We look at each other for a long, long time. Sweet Oliver Huxley. My best friend, and now maybe the father of my child.

"I wonder if it worked?" I say softly.

"It wasn't for the want of trying."

"No." I smile.

He rolls onto his side and props his head on a hand. Then he trails a finger down between my breasts as I lower my feet, and he rests a hand on my tummy.

"Wouldn't that be something?" he murmurs.

"I suppose it's different from last time for you. I mean, when you made a baby, you weren't exactly trying."

He strokes my skin with his thumb. "No." He looks out of the window for a moment at the night sky, and I wonder whether he's remembering that time, and how he felt when Brandy told him she was pregnant. I can't imagine he was thrilled. It must have been a difficult time, and I doubt anyone was blissfully happy about it. I know his parents eventually came around and supported him, but Brandy's were extremely hostile, and even now they're maybe the only people in the world who don't seem to like him. I think it's because he didn't marry her, and it doesn't seem to matter that she insists she didn't want to marry him either.

He looks back at me, sees me watching him, and moves a bit closer. Then he kisses me.

I close my eyes and let him, enjoying the way he presses his lips across mine, butterfly light. The sex was great, but he was right; it wasn't just because he hit the buttons in the right order. He said, *It's the person you have it with that makes it special… that makes it amazing*, and he was right. It felt great because it was him, and it's been a long time coming, and I wanted him more than any other guy in the world.

If I thought I could come out of this unaffected, I was very, very dumb. I've opened the cage to my heart, and it's sitting there, soft, squidgy, and unprotected. And now we've had sex, and all that remains is to see where the tide carries us.

Chapter Eleven

Huxley

"Don't get sleepy," I scold as Elizabeth's eyelids droop. "We've got a long way to go yet."

She smiles. "It doesn't matter how many times you have sex, as long as you do it at the right time."

"Nevertheless. I intend to fill you to the brim."

"Mr. Romantic."

I laugh, roll over, and get up. I search for boxers and pull them on, then tug on my trousers.

"Going somewhere?" she asks.

"I'm going to order us some drinks and a snack. I've got to keep my strength up. Want anything in particular?"

"Mmm... something sweet."

"Okay." I walk around to her side of the bed, lean over her, and kiss her. "We're getting in the hot tub," I tell her as I walk out the room. "Naked, before you start going all coy on me and getting your cozzie on."

I walk through to the living room, flick on one of the lamps. Then I go over to the phone, pick it up, and dial for room service. I put in my order, then go out onto the deck to take the cover off the hot tub and start it up.

"I'm not sure about the naked part," Elizabeth says, coming out in one of the white bathrobes left for guests.

"We're right at the end," I tell her, "nobody's going to walk past, and the neighbors can't see."

"Even so..."

I slip an arm around her, pull her close to me, and nuzzle her ear. "Don't you like the idea of getting all wet and slippery with me?"

"Mm. I'm beginning to see the attraction. You don't think… um… I should avoid it if I'm trying to get pregnant? It won't wash everything away?"

I kiss her nose and release her as there's a knock at the door. "Honey, nothing's getting up there that you don't want up there, believe me. I think I'm going to have bruises."

She pokes her tongue out at me, and I laugh and walk through to answer the door. The guy comes in with a tray and leaves it on the kitchen countertop, and I slip him a note and close the door behind him.

I retrieve a couple of heavy-bottomed glasses from the cupboard, add some ice cubes to each from the freezer, then bring the tray out onto the deck and place it on the table next to the hot tub.

She grins as she sees the Bowmore. "You bought the rest of the bottle?"

"Seems a shame to waste it."

"I kinda like dating a rich guy."

I smile, my gaze lingering on her as I unscrew the top of the bottle. Dating. It's the first time she's intimated that what's happening here might continue when we leave the island. Then again, it might just have been a throwaway word. I asked for one night, and it's possible she might hold me to that.

Well, I'm not going to worry about it now. I know I have to earn her trust. I'm going to make the most of the time I have with her, and hope she enjoys it so much that she decides to give me a chance.

"You're not exactly penniless," I point out as I pour the whisky over the ice cubes.

"No… true. But I'm not a gajillionaire like you guys."

I chuckle. I honestly don't know how much money I've got exactly, but it's probably over a billion once I take all the investments into account.

"Ooh," she says, looking at the chocolate cake I ordered. "Yum." Then she picks up the small dish next to it. "What are these?"

"Chocolate drops. They're for later."

"For a snack?"

"Maybe." I smirk, take them into the bedroom and leave them on the bedside table, rid myself of my clothes, and come back out.

Her eyebrows rise as she skims her gaze down my naked form. I stand there, arms out with my palms up, and turn around slowly. "Take your time."

"I can't get used to seeing you without clothes," she says. "It's like finding out someone can juggle or play the violin. I didn't realize you had such a hidden talent."

I snort, go over to the tub, and slide in. Oh… that's fantastic. Just above body temperature and bubbling joyfully. "Come on," I say. "Get a move on. We've got four more sessions to fit in before the morning."

She chuckles, glances around as if checking whether there are hundreds of people with binoculars spying on us, obviously decides she's safe, and slips the robe off. Sitting on the side, she swings her legs over and then slips in.

"Ooh, that's hot."

"I know. Good for aching bodies." I hold out a hand, and she takes it and lets me pull her toward me. I turn her so she's facing away, then bring her back between my legs. She nestles against me, and I slide my arms around her waist and nuzzle her neck.

She sighs, relaxing against me, moving her hands through the water. "This is nice."

"Yeah." I reach to the side, retrieve one of the glasses, and pass it to her, then get mine. We tap them together and have a mouthful.

"Aaahhh…" We both exhale and slide down a little more into the water. I lean my head back on the side of the tub and look out at the stars. "I think I'm in heaven."

She links the fingers of her free hand with mine. "You can be incredibly sweet sometimes."

"Not sure if that's what I want your abiding memory of me to be." I put down the glass and pick up the dish with the chocolate cake. Removing my hand from hers, I hold the dish, collect a spoonful of the cake, and offer it to her. She closes her mouth around it, and I remove the spoon slowly.

"Mmm…" she murmurs, licking her lips and swallowing. "That's good." Then she laughs and moves her hips from side to side, rubbing her bottom against my rapidly forming erection. "Chocolate cake turns you on, does it?"

"Watching you eat it does." I blow out a breath and have my own spoonful.

"Cake's not the only thing I've been looking forward to tasting." She looks over her shoulder at me mischievously.

"There won't be any of that," I reprimand her. "We need every drop of my baby batter to end up where it's supposed to."

"Baby batter?"

"Is daddy sauce better? How about erectoplasm?"

She chuckles. "I prefer the band names. Like Pearl Jam."

"Yeah. And 10cc. They say that's apocryphal because 10cc is apparently twice the amount a man ejaculates. I don't agree. I think I could have filled a fifty-gallon whisky barrel by myself ten minutes ago."

That makes her laugh.

"Actually," I add, kissing her neck, "my favorite band name for it is The Lovin' Spoonful."

"I like that."

I offer her some more chocolate cake. She opens her mouth, and I deliberately bump the spoon against her nose before sliding it between her lips.

She flicks me a wry look, removes the chocolate from the bridge of her nose with a finger, and licks it off. Taking my forefinger in her hand, she plunges it into the frosting, then deliberately inserts it into her mouth. Slowly, she washes her tongue over it, spending a good thirty seconds sucking it clean.

"Yeah, all right, that backfired," I say.

She grins, has a mouthful of whisky, then lifts her face for a kiss. My lips curving up, I cover her mouth with mine, and she passes me some of the whisky, warmed by her mouth.

I swallow, put the plate down, and lower my arms into the water. I lift her a little so she's sitting on my lap, her legs either side of mine. Placing my hands on her knees, I slide my hands up her thighs. Her skin is silky smooth and warm. Careful not to touch between her legs or her breasts, I continue to stroke her, enjoying just touching her.

She sips her whisky and leans back on me, looking out at the night sky. "Did you know that Titus is working on a project to use artificial intelligence in the search for exoplanets?"

"No, I didn't. What's an exoplanet?"

"A planet that orbits a star other than our Sun, so one outside our Solar System. It can help study a star's brightness over time which might tell us whether a planet is transiting in front of it."

"He's always been interested in astronomy. It's cool that he's able to contribute to its development." She tips her head to the side to give me better access to her neck as I place kisses on her shoulder.

"By the way," I add, kissing slowly up to her jaw, "I haven't forgotten that you set me up with Titus and Mack. That was very naughty."

"It was in response for throwing me in the pool, if you remember rightly."

"Even so. I almost had a panic attack in the boardroom."

She gives a short laugh.

I move her hair aside so I can kiss her ear. "If we hadn't done this tonight, would you have asked either of them to be a donor for you?"

"I thought about it," she says softly. "I... I don't know. I mean, there's nothing sexual about it. And I wouldn't expect the guy to be involved at all. But it's a bit... odd. Isn't it? Do you think it's odd? I didn't really consider that when I asked you. With you it just seemed like the right thing to do because... well, it's you. But it would be different with them. I don't know why. I'm not explaining myself very well."

I run a strand of her hair through my fingers. "Have you ever had feelings for either of them?"

She laughs. "No, never. Mack is far too intense for me. And Titus can be quite moody. I like my men to be meek and mild." She chuckles.

"Again, not sure about that description. Can't you use words like impressive or manly?"

"Horny?" she suggests.

"That's probably nearer to the mark, but I'd prefer something a bit more romantic." I'm genuinely a bit aggrieved. Is that the best she can come up with?

She's quiet for a moment. Then she says, "Generous, loyal, kind, gentle, sexy, genial, affable, wicked, gorgeous... How's that?"

"Okay, that's better," I say, mollified.

"You, Mack, and Titus are similar in many ways, larger than life, like planets or stars. Mack's like the Sun, with all this intense energy, as if he'd burn you to a crisp if you get too close to him. Titus is like Mars, the God of War, defender and protector."

"You're going to make a joke about Uranus now, aren't you?"

She laughs and lifts a hand to stroke my cheek. "You're Jupiter, King of the Gods. How could you be anything but?"

"And you're Venus," I murmur, stroking up her ribs and across her belly. "Made for loving."

She has another mouthful of whisky and shares it with me. I dip my tongue into her mouth, and she giggles as the whisky runs down her chin.

"This is wonderful," she says, leaning back against me again. "I'm having such a great time."

"I'm glad." I stroke down her arms, then back up underneath them.

She looks out at the stars again, her eyes distant. "Can I ask you something?"

"Of course."

"What happened with your brother?"

My hands stop moving. I've never discussed it with her—with anyone, in fact. Not even Mack knows the whole story.

"Sorry," she says, obviously sensing my reluctance. "You don't have to talk about it."

I don't want to tell her everything now. But it doesn't feel right to refuse to talk about it when we're sharing such an intimate moment. "No, it's okay." I start stroking her again, the water swirling around us. "Guy's two years older than me. He was trouble all the way through childhood—he was the sort of kid who fell out of trees, got caught shoplifting, bunked school. I don't know why. All my sisters were impeccably behaved, and although I wasn't an angel, I worked hard. I was head boy, for Christ's sake."

"Were you?" She laughs. "I didn't know that. It doesn't surprise me."

"I don't know why Guy fell so far from the tree, but he was nothing but trouble, and gave my parents permanent headaches. It continued into his teens—he left school after year eleven and stumbled through several jobs. Fell in with a bad crowd. Took harder drugs, lots of alcohol, got into trouble with the police. Mum and Dad did everything they could, but he was out of control. It was always going to end badly."

"What happened?"

"He got caught doing an electronics shop over. Mum was very upset, and Dad—as you can imagine—was furious. He paid for a top lawyer and got him off, but gave him an ultimatum—turn your life around, or he was out of the family. You can guess which Guy chose."

She's quiet for a moment. I stroke up and down her arms and the outside of her thighs.

"Where is he now?" she asks.

"Mum and Dad think he went to Australia, but he came back a year ago. He's in Dunedin."

"You're still in contact with him?"

"Yeah. I send him money from time to time. I haven't told Dad because he wouldn't understand. He believes in tough love, but it doesn't work for everyone. Guy doesn't step up, pull himself up by his bootstraps, or take responsibility. He crumbles. He's weak, and he needs help."

She has a sip of whisky, passing her spare hand through the water. "I'm so sorry. I didn't know."

"Of course you didn't. I haven't told anyone."

"Not Victoria? Or Mack?"

"No."

"Does Brandy know?"

"Why do you ask that?"

She shrugs. "I wonder sometimes about your relationship with her. She had your baby. You look after her. And you're connected by Joanna. I wonder how close you are sometimes." She swirls her hand in a circle, creating a whirlpool. "Do you love her?" Then she splashes, irritated with herself. "No, don't answer that. I'm sorry. It's none of my business."

I kiss the top of her head. "Elizabeth, we've just had sex. It's a reasonable question. The answer is that I love her like one of my sisters. She's had it tough—her parents were very strict, and they were extremely harsh on her when she got pregnant. I mean, really harsh, practically medieval. They wanted to send her away to have the baby so their church wouldn't find out."

"Fucking hell."

"Yeah. It's the only time I put my foot down and said no, she wasn't going."

"I've wondered sometimes… you're so honorable and, well, chivalrous, for want of a better word. Why didn't you ask her to marry you?"

"Because I wanted you."

She turns and looks up at me. I kiss her nose.

"Seriously?" she says.

"Yeah. I didn't love Brandy, not in the way you should love someone when you marry them. I wanted to do the right thing, but equally I'm not going to sign my life away because of a one-night stand when a condom broke. And I didn't want to lose the girl I was crazy about." I sigh. "But I lost her anyway."

Her eyes shine. "You should have told me."

"Forget about it. It's done now. All that matters is what happens next." I turn her away from me again and run my fingers up the inside of her thighs. The refractory period has passed, and I'm ready for round two. "Let's play a game. Intimate questions. You can ask me whatever you like." I suck her earlobe.

She sucks her bottom lip. "Okay. Um… Have you ever fired a real longbow?"

My eyebrows rise and I stifle a laugh. "Okay, I wasn't expecting that."

"What's wrong with it?"

"I just thought… never mind. Anyway, you don't fire a bow. There's no gunpowder involved. You release an arrow or you loose it." I draw circles on her inner thighs. "And yes, I have used a medieval longbow. It had the same draw weight as the ones they found on Henry VIII's warship, the Mary Rose. It had a one hundred- and eighty-five-pound draw weight and a thirty-inch draw—the arrows were thirty inches long. It was fucking hard to use. The guys must have had shoulders like the Hulk."

"That's so hot," she says.

I chuckle. "Longbows turn you on?"

"The thought of you using one does." She wrinkles her nose. "Go on then, your turn."

"What's your favorite sexual position?"

Her jaw drops. "Oh… I get the game now."

"It's okay, I'm more than happy to talk about longbows." She blushes and elbows me, and I grin. "Your answer?"

She pouts and huffs. Then she says, "From behind, I guess."

I give a short laugh.

"What's so funny?" she asks indignantly.

I shake my head. "It's a perfectly reasonable answer."

She frowns. She genuinely doesn't understand why I find her frank reply amusing.

I'm just beginning to get why she's so puzzled about sex. I don't think she's had a single romantic moment in her life. All the men she's been with have been Neanderthals. And she mixes mainly with men, so she's used to the frank kind of dialogue that guys have. All the time I've known her, I would have teased her if she'd said anything remotely romantic or soppy. I don't do it with women normally, but I do it with my friends. So no wonder she was confused when I teased her about sex. Nobody else has ever done it.

She's glaring at me. "Okay," she says. "What's your favorite position?"

I think about it. "I like the woman on top, because it means she's in control. She can touch herself, and I can watch. It turns me on, and I can learn what she likes too. Pressure, speed. Everyone's different."

Her eyes widen.

"Come on then," I say softly. "Tell me why you like it from behind. Do you prefer lying down? Or on all fours?"

"Um… lying down."

"Why?"

She shrugs. "I don't know."

"Is it because the guy has to take charge? Do you like giving up control for once?"

She studies her glass. "Maybe."

I continue stroking her, all the way up from her knees to her ribs and back. "It doesn't surprise me. Women are encouraged not to show weakness nowadays. To be strong and powerful. And that's great out of the bedroom—we're all equal. But there's something earthy and carnal about sex that reduces everything to a base level. In the bedroom, most men naturally want to dominate, and women like to be dominated. And there's nothing wrong with exploring that." I kiss from her shoulder up to her neck and touch my tongue where her pulse is beating.

She sighs. "I also like the physical differences between men and women," she says, hesitantly at first. "Your height, weight, the width of your shoulders. Being heavy on top of me. Is that weird?"

"Of course not. It's why men like breasts and the curve of a woman's waist, and the softness of her mouth. This might sound strange to you because I know I tease you about it, but I love that you're small."

"Really?"

"Yeah. It makes me feel protective. Manly." I kiss her jaw. "You're very beautiful."

"Don't give me false flattery. I know I'm not beautiful."

"You are. You're stunning. Those big dark eyes and that Cupid's bow." I turn her face so I can kiss it. "Your gorgeous hair, swinging forward like a curtain. And you have magnificent breasts."

That makes her laugh. "Yeah okay. My boobs are pretty good."

"They're perfect." I kiss her again, brushing my tongue across her bottom lip. "I want to kiss you all over," I say huskily. "From your ears to your toes. Especially your toes."

"I forgot you have a foot fetish."

"I like *your* feet. They're dainty and sexy, and your toenails are always perfectly painted. I'm going to kiss them when we get out. But first, I'm going to make you come with my fingers."

Her lips part and her eyes flare. "Hux!"

"What?" I stroke up her thighs again, and this time I continue between her legs. She shivers and sighs as I slide my fingers down into her folds. She's still a little swollen. I circle over her clit, making her sigh.

"She was right," she whispers.

"Who?"

"Rachel. You were able to find my clitoris without a map."

I chuckle and tease the little bean with the tip of my finger. "It's not hard to find."

"Mmm. And, apparently, you didn't need a map to find my G-spot either."

"Again, it's not rocket science."

"Honestly? I didn't think they existed."

"Oh… they exist."

"Well I know that now. Trust you to find it."

I move my middle finger down through her folds and carefully slide it about an inch inside her. She's deliciously tight. "Here, you mean?" I press up until I find the area and then massage it firmly.

"Ooh! Wow. Oh."

"You like that?"

"Mmm… it's an unusual… oh… feeling… Mmm… don't stop…"

"I won't. I'm going to touch you here." I rub my thumb over her clit at the same time. "And here." I cup her breast. "And here." I lower my mouth to hers and slide my tongue into her mouth.

She moans and arches her spine, pushing her breast into my hand, and I tug one and then the other nipple gently. They've softened from the warmth of the hot tub, but as I tease them, they tighten in my fingers.

"I'm going to make you come," I tell her, murmuring in her ear. "Then I'm going to take you into the bedroom and arouse you again until you're begging me to take you. And then I'm going to turn you on your front and take you from behind the way you like it, until I come inside you, and fill you with as much of a loving spoonful as I can manage." I kiss her ear. "How does that sound?"

Chapter Twelve

Elizabeth

It sounds like heaven. I think I actually did die at some point, and this is all part of a blissful afterlife where I can make love with Huxley like this until the end of time.

My hips move of their own accord against his fingers, and I rest my hand on top of his, enjoying the sensation of matching his movements inside me.

My head is still spinning his answer to my question: *Why didn't you ask her to marry you?* His reply, *Because I wanted you*, makes me feel thrilled and humble and guilty and ashamed at the same time. I said no to him because he'd broken my heart and I was trying to protect myself. But I never considered his heart. His feelings.

All along, I've thought of him as a tomcat, a man with a short attention span who takes what he wants, albeit wrapped up in a kind, gentle package. Have I been wrong all this time? Is the reason that he's never settled down really because he's in love with me?

I don't want to think about it now. My brain's not working properly. His fingers are teasing me toward the edge again, surprisingly quickly, maybe because of the unusual sensation of the spot he's teasing inside me. It feels… hmm… like a strange internal pressure, a little different from normal… Oh jeez, so much for my jokes about foreplay—he's only been touching me for a few minutes, and I think I'm going to come.

But then the foreplay didn't start a few minutes ago, did it? It began when we got in the tub, with him stroking me all over, arousing all the erogenous zones I didn't even know I had.

"You're going to come for me now," he says, a little smugly, and part of me wants to say no, I won't, just to prove he's not in control, but of course that's not going to happen because I'm already losing it, and his fingers move quicker, stroking me, tugging my nipple, and his mouth is hot on mine, and that's it, the tsunami of pleasure rears up inside me, then crashes over me in five or six huge waves that make me gasp against his lips.

As I drift back down to earth, he moves his arms around me and places soft kisses on my neck.

"How do you know my body better than I do?" I say breathlessly, relaxing back against him.

He chuckles and moves his hips, rocking his erection against my bottom. "Time to get out."

"Just give me a few minutes. I need time to recover."

"Nope." He pushes me up. "I don't want you to recover." He rises behind me and gets out, then holds out a towel for me. Grumbling, I swing my legs over the edge of the tub and let him wrap me in the towel. He rubs me all over, smiling as I look up at him.

"In you go," he murmurs. "On the bed."

I open the door to the bedroom, surprised to find it warm, and realize he must have switched on the heat pump. I finish drying myself, then discard the towel, peel back the duvet, and climb onto the mattress. Less than a minute later he does the same, bringing our drinks in and leaving them on the bedside table.

"Lie down," he instructs.

Unsure what he's up to, I lie back on the pillows. But he gestures for me to scoot down, so I'm lying flat.

He picks up the small dish of chocolate drops and climbs onto the mattress, sitting next to me, cross-legged.

"Where are you going to put those?" I ask suspiciously. "Are you trying to give me a yeast infection?"

He gives a short laugh. "I promise not to insert them anywhere except your mouth." He rubs one along my bottom lip, and when I open my mouth, he slides it in.

"Chocolate melts at body temperature," he states, "and your body is extra warm at the moment. So this should be fun. Lift your arms." I raise them, and he moves them above my head so I'm stretched out. "Now, you're not to move," he instructs.

"Or what?"

He glares at me. "Every time you move, I'll make you wait longer before I let you come."

"Oh. Um… Okay."

He shows me one of the chocolate drops. Then he puts it in the palm of one of my hands.

Slowly, he continues down my body, placing a drop every few inches. Both palms. The inside of my wrists. Halfway down my arm. The inside of my elbows. My upper arm. Even under my arms, which makes me frown. He puts one on the end of my nose and laughs when I glare at him. "Close your mouth," he says, and places one on my top lip and one on the bottom, then one on each cheekbone. He continues down: the hollow at the base of my throat. Several on each nipple. One underneath each breast. One over my solar plexus. Another he rests on my belly button.

He shifts on the bed toward my feet, lies on his side, and parts my legs. Then he places a couple between my toes. Jeez. Him and toes. He carries on up, putting them on my ankle, my knee, one on each thigh, one on the crease of my thighs.

Lastly, he slides one down over my mound and nestles it on top of my clit. I groan, my lips parting, and the drop falls off my bottom lip onto my chin.

"One penalty," he says. "I'm keeping count." He turns and stretches out to lie beside me. "We'll just give them a few seconds to melt."

I scowl at him. "Is it my turn after this?"

He just smiles. Lifting a hand, he trails a finger over my body, avoiding the drops, passing between my breasts, over my tummy, and up my sides. I twitch.

"Two times," he says.

"That's not fair."

"I don't make the rules. Well, I do. What I mean is, you know the rules. You break them, you have to pay the penalty."

I pout, trying not to move the drop on my upper lip. He continues to touch me, his gaze warm on mine. Feeling my face warm, I let my gaze slide down him, taking in his muscular torso, his narrow waist, and his ohhh-so-impressive erection.

"This turn you on, does it?" I comment.

"My favorite girl at my mercy and chocolate. What's not to like?"

His favorite girl. How does this guy know how to melt not only the chocolate drops on my body but also my heart?

He trails his finger all the way up, then touches it to the drop on my upper lip. "Mmm," he says, and he moves it from side to side, smearing chocolate across my lip.

Then he lowers his head and kisses me.

I sigh as he brushes his tongue over my lips several times, feeling an answering clench deep inside me. Oh dear… I'm in serious trouble.

Slowly, sensually, Huxley begins to remove each chocolate drop with his mouth.

He starts with my hands, then progresses to my wrists, arms, and the inside of my elbows. Each time, he moves the drop with his tongue so it smears chocolate across my skin, and then he proceeds to lick it away. The sensation of his tongue moving slowly over me is tantalizing and agonizing, especially because he does it so deliberately, taking his time.

I ascend into a kind of hazy dream state, as if I'm having an out-of-body experience. I feel as if he's heating me over a gentle flame, and I'm like caramel, softening in his hands.

He spends quite a bit of time licking the ones under my arms, which makes me squirm and earns me a third penalty. Then he shifts on the bed and starts moving down my body. He takes a lot longer than I'm sure is necessary on my breasts, sucking my nipples clean. It's quite warm in the room now, and I can tell by how quickly the chocolate is melting that I must be perspiring.

"You're gross," I tell him as he runs his tongue beneath my breasts.

"You taste amazing."

I watch him move on to my tummy, methodically licking up every drop. "You're going to be sick of chocolate by the end of this."

"I'm probably giving myself diabetes," he says, and we both laugh. "It'll be worth it," he adds, moving down the bed to my feet. Closing his mouth over a toe, he sucks the chocolate off it.

I giggle and twitch, and he says, "Four times."

I groan as he moves from one toe to the next. "That's not fair. It tickles."

"You know the rules." He removes all the drops from my feet, then proceeds up my legs. I close my eyes, unable to stop a low moan leaving my lips when he runs his tongue up the crease of my thighs.

"God, you smell so good," he mutters, and then, before I have the chance to catch my breath, he buries his tongue in my folds.

"Aaahhh…"

He licks all the way up, then spends ages removing the chocolate, until I'm aching inside, and my chest is rising and falling rapidly with my ragged breaths. Only then does he rise and move up the bed.

He leans over me, studies my face, then bends and carefully removes the chocolate from my nose and cheekbones. Finally, he returns to my lips, and he gives me a deep kiss, plunging his tongue into my mouth.

When he eventually lifts up, I can only gaze at him longingly.

"Not yet," he says. "Turn over."

My jaw drops. What?

He lifts his eyebrows and rotates his forefinger. Grumbling, I shift onto my front, resting my cheek on my arms.

"Lie still," he murmurs in my ear, and then he places a few more drops on my skin. Slightly less than before—I think this is backfiring, and he's more than ready to slide inside me, but he obviously has a couple of places he wants to pay attention to before then.

He sweeps my hair to the side and puts one drop on the nape of my neck. One between my shoulder blades. One on my spine, and one on my tailbone.

He puts one on the sole of each foot, the back of my knees, on each thigh, on each side of my bottom. And then he picks up one final one.

"I daren't ask where you're putting that," I whisper.

He doesn't reply, but I feel his hands parting my cheeks, and he leaves the drop there, right at the top.

"We'll just let that melt," he says, and I can tell he's smiling.

He moves up, and then I feel his lips at the nape of my neck. Mmm… that makes me shiver. I'm already so turned on that every place he kisses me now only heightens my arousal. He moves down my back, then switches to my feet and kisses up my legs. He takes his time over the cheeks of my bottom, licking and sucking the plump muscles there. And then finally, he places a hand on both sides and parts them.

Resting my forehead on my hands, I hold my breath, then exhale, which turns into a groan as he brushes his tongue right up. He mutters his approval, then does it again, teasing the tight muscle there with his tongue.

"Oh fuck," I whisper, feeling the first tremors of an orgasm.

He lifts up and moves over me. "Not yet," he scolds. Pushing up one of my knees, he directs his erection beneath me. Leaning on both hands, he moves his hips, sliding the tip of his erection through my swollen folds.

We both groan, and he rests his forehead on my shoulder. I lift a hand and clutch it in his hair, and he shudders. He's losing control. Fuck, that's sexy. I like out-of-control Huxley. Come on, grizzly bear. I want to hear you roar.

He grabs a pillow and pulls it down, then taps my hip so I lift up enough for him to slide the pillow beneath me. When he's satisfied, he moves his erection down and presses the tip against my entrance.

Then, so slowly it's agonizing, he slides inside me.

It feels so amazing, I can't stop the long moan that escapes my lips.

"Jesus," he says, "you're so wet."

"Huxley!"

"What?" He lowers down on top of me and nuzzles my neck. "It wasn't a complaint."

I tip my head to the side, my lips parting as he sucks the sensitive skin where my neck meets my shoulder. "Argh… don't give me a hickey."

He laces his tongue over my skin. "I want to. I want to mark you. Tell all those other guys to fuck off because you're mine." He sucks a little harder.

I squeal, and he laughs and slides an arm under me to stroke my breast. "How's this?" he murmurs in my ear as he begins to move inside me. "Is this what you wanted?"

I don't reply, having lost the power of speech with the feel of him heavy on top of me. I feel completely under his control, encased in his strong arms, with his hips thrusting purposefully.

He places hot kisses up my neck. "Tell me, Elizabeth. You like me taking charge?"

"No."

He chuckles and nips my earlobe.

"Ow!"

"Then don't lie to me." He traces his tongue around the shell of my ear, all the while moving inside me. His hand moves down over my tummy, and his finger circles over my clit, firm but gentle. "I think you do like giving up control. Being dominated. Maybe I should tie you down."

I shiver. "Oh God."

"I could take hours to tease you to the edge of orgasm, and there would be nothing you could do about it."

I pull a pillow down and bury my face in it. He laughs and kisses my neck. "I could keep you handcuffed to the bed in my apartment," he murmurs. "Make you my sex slave. What do you think about that?"

I shake my head, but I can't reply.

"All day, you'd be lying there, waiting for me to come home." His hips are speeding up—he's turning himself on. "And at night I'd do whatever I wanted to you, and you wouldn't be able to stop me."

Ohhh… this guy knows exactly what I need. I can feel him holding back, and the thought of the generous, loving Huxley waiting for me makes me want to weep.

"Oh God," I whisper, as the first ripples spread through me.

Carefully, he withdraws, and my eyes fly open in surprise.

"Four times," he says silkily.

I groan. "You're kidding me."

"I warned you." He kisses my neck, waiting about ten seconds before he slides inside me again.

Then begins a slow torture session, with him thrusting me each time to the edge of an orgasm before withdrawing and letting the ripples of pleasure die away. Four times he does it, and by the end I'm drawing deep ragged breaths, aching for release.

"Hux…" I beg. "Please."

He tilts my face up and kisses me. "All right," he says softly. "Hang on, this is going to be a big one."

He starts moving with purpose, and I clutch at the pillow as pleasure immediately spirals within me. "Oh God," I say, "oh—oh—oh," crying out with each thrust, and he lifts up and leans one hand on the headboard behind me as he moves faster, plunging into me, and that's it, I can't hold on any longer. I come hard, and he's right, it's a big one, the orgasm powerful enough to make me squeal as I'm overcome with six or seven incredibly powerful pulses that take my breath away.

"Fuck," Huxley says, and then he groans and comes, his hips pushing forward so he's so deep inside me, hot and hard as he fills me up.

It feels as if we're locked forever in the warm darkness, and his hand finds mine on the pillow and he links our fingers, as if we're drifting together on the sea at night, miles from land, with just each other for company.

It's only when our climaxes finally release us that he flexes his fingers in mine and exhales in a rush.

"Holy shit," he says. "I feel as if someone's used a defibrillator to shock me back to life."

I can feel his heart racing against my back as he lowers down on top of me. Ooohhh... he's heavy and his skin's all hot and sweaty, sticking to mine. I love it.

He moves his hips slowly, still hard inside me. "Just making sure I've filled all your nooks and crannies," he says.

That makes me laugh, and he joins in. "Ouch," he says, withdrawing and shifting a little to the side, so he's not lying right on me.

"Serves you right for torturing me," I murmur, too tired to move.

"Mmm." He nuzzles my neck. "Tell me you didn't enjoy it."

"I didn't enjoy it."

"Liar."

I sigh and hug his arm as he slides it around me. I feel exhausted, in a nice way, limp and loose as if I've run on the treadmill for an hour.

He scoops my hair off my neck and runs a finger down it.

"Tell me you didn't give me a hickey," I say, alarmed.

"Er..."

I lift my head and look over my shoulder at him. "You did not!"

He pulls an eek face. "It's very faint."

"Hux!"

He kisses me. "I told you I was going to mark you," he teases. "Spoil you for other men."

You've already done that. I don't say the words, but I think he might see them in my eyes because his brows draw together, and then he settles down behind me, pulling me back against him.

"I'm sorry," he whispers, kissing my neck. "I shouldn't have said that."

"It's okay."

"It's not. I know we're not dating yet. I was riled up."

"I noticed."

"It's your fault," he insists. "Lying there naked and inviting."

"And covered in chocolate."

"And covered in chocolate," he echoes.

"Well, you've had me now," I say. "Twice. Do you think it's abated your hunger?"

"Maybe for about half an hour. But we're only two-fifths of the way there."

I groan and slap his arm. "I'm knackered. And I don't believe you can have sperm left."

"I do think I've probably ejaculated enough to fill two whisky barrels now."

I laugh weakly. "I think that's probably enough to do the job."

"We'll see. I have all night with you lying next to me."

"Naked and inviting."

"Yeah. Naked and inviting. I'll never make it till daybreak."

I close my eyes. "Well, you know where I am."

"Mmm."

I turn my head and kiss his shoulder, and inhale.

"Did you just sniff me?" he asks.

"You smell nice." I yawn. "I like your aftershave. I haven't smelled it before."

"I bought it for you," he says.

I kiss his arm, warmed through by his words.

I'd like to tell him how great I feel. But I'm too tired.

In less than a minute, I fall asleep.

Chapter Thirteen

Huxley

I'm feeling drowsy. I promised Elizabeth I'd make love to her four or five times, but the after-sex hormones are roaming through my system, and my body is telling me, *You're not as young as you used to be, Hux.*

I kiss her ear and nuzzle her neck. She smells warm and chocolatey, and I smile as I think of all the places I've licked the drops from.

Then something about her deep, even breathing makes me lift my head and look at her.

She's asleep.

I guess we were more energetic than I realized. Plus of course the good food and the alcohol have played a part, too. I think about waking her, but she works hard, and it's rare for her to take time off to have fun. Regarding the baby making, I know that it doesn't really matter how many times we have sex, providing we did it when she was ovulating. I should let her sleep.

Settling down, I wonder whether I should give her some space, but as I go to lift my arm she pulls it tighter to her.

Smiling, I close my eyes, and in a few minutes I doze off, too.

*

I rouse sometime later and look around in the semi-darkness, puzzled. The room is filled with starlight. Then I remember: I'm on Waiheke Island, with Elizabeth.

I tap my watch—it says 2:47 a.m. I'm lying on my side, and she's curled up in my arms, facing me. Our legs are entwined, and our arms are wrapped around each other. We couldn't get any closer if we tried.

SERENITY WOODS

Well, possibly a little closer. I smile and kiss the top of her head. Maybe I'll wake her in a while and see if she's up for a nighttime lovin' spoonful.

But right now, I just want to enjoy having her in my arms.

She's small and slender, almost fragile, although she's stronger than she looks. She's taken tai chi and jiu jitsu classes in the past, and she's embarrassed me by putting me in an arm lock I can't get out of. Despite her height, she's pretty good at tennis, and she can also beat me around an eighteen-hole golf course. She likes dancing and can moonwalk almost as well as Michael Jackson himself. She's fucking smart, and she knows a hundred chemistry mnemonics that she spent a good portion of her last year at university reciting. She taught me the rhyme to remember the first twenty elements of the periodic table, something about 'Here He Lies Beneath Bed Clothes', Hydrogen, Helium, Lithium… I've already forgotten, but she can recite it all.

Of course, she's not perfect. She can't hold a tune. She's impatient, and she's not afraid to speak her mind, which often leads to her and Mack having arguments with lots of yelling. I've learned it's better to walk out and leave them to it than to try and calm them down. She doesn't suffer fools gladly. She's not great at relaxing, and doesn't have any hobbies that I know of, but then neither do I apart from the archery—both of us work all hours under the sun, and when we have any spare time, we either prod ourselves into going to the gym or crash in front of a movie.

But she's whole-hearted, feisty, and fearless, and is never cowed by any man, which I love. I adored her when I first met her, and I adore her now.

And I might have made her pregnant. I stroke her back, thinking about my sperm swimming up inside her to get to the egg. Come on, little fellas. I want to do this for her. I imagine the baby—my baby—forming inside her, growing slowly. It makes my stomach flip. I'd hate anyone else to do this for her. I honestly think I'd kill them with my bare hands.

Her skin is so soft, and silky smooth. I trail my fingers down her spine to her tailbone, and circle them in the little dimple there.

"If you're thinking of heading any further south, please give me some warning," she murmurs.

I chuckle. "I thought you were asleep."

"And decided to cop a sneaky feel?"

"*Carpe noctem.*"

She laughs and lifts her head, and I give her a long, lingering kiss.

"What time is it?" she asks eventually.

"Nearly three a.m."

"Mmm. I'd better let out some of that whisky." She goes to get up.

I tighten my arms around her. "Not yet," I tell her, nuzzling her ear.

"Why?"

"Orgasms are better with a full bladder."

"What? You're kidding. I'll pee all over you."

"Are you trying to turn me on?"

"Hux!" She looks genuinely shocked. "That... gross."

I chuckle and pull her butt toward me so she can feel my hard-on. "You have surprised me. I thought you'd be into all kinds of weird stuff."

"Really?"

"Yeah."

"I haven't had the chance." She sounds wistful.

"I'd be happy to initiate you."

"I bet you would, you kinky bastard."

That makes me laugh.

"What... um... sort of things do you like?" she murmurs, her voice husky.

I kiss her. "Let's just say that I can't think of anything you could suggest that would turn me off."

"Chickens?"

"Okay, maybe one thing."

She giggles. Then she traces a circle on my chest. "You like bondage?"

"Not hardcore stuff. I don't like pain. But pretty scarves and furry handcuffs? Yeah, bring it on."

"I should have known. And you've already mentioned putting tab a) into slots b), c), and d), so I think I can guess what else you're into."

I smirk and nibble her earlobe. "Your body is all soft and inviting. Why wouldn't I want to make the most of it?"

"Yeah. I bet you like giving a girl a pearl necklace too."

I trace a finger across her neck. "Now you really are trying to get me hot and bothered."

"It seems to be working." She slides a hand down my front and closes it around my erection. "Can I?"

"Help yourself."

She strokes me slowly, from the root right up to the tip, which she explores with her thumb. I watch her, my eyelids lowering sleepily, and swell in her hand.

"You like that?" she whispers, doing it again.

"Mm."

She slides her hand beneath her for a moment, and then when she strokes me again, her fingers glide easily up and down.

"Natural lube," she whispers, kissing me.

I let her think she's in charge for a bit, enjoying her touch, but eventually I move her hand away.

"Aw," she says, "I was enjoying myself."

"If you carry on like that, I'll be depositing my lovin' spoonful somewhere other than where I want it to be," I tell her. She laughs as I kiss her, and I slide my hand down her tummy and into her folds. I sigh as I find her swollen and moist. "Already?"

"It's all the talk of bondage and pearl necklaces." She fans her fingers out on my chest. "And touching you. You're not a small man, Hux. It turns a girl on."

"I'm glad to hear it."

She shifts up a little and directs my erection beneath her. "All my talk of foreplay goes out the window with you," she says huskily. "Two seconds of touching your magnificent body and I'm more aroused than I've ever been with any other guy."

It's a flattering thing to say, but I can't reply because I lose the power of speech as she impales herself on me.

"Aaahhh…" She exhales, her breath whispering across my lips. "Oh my God, that feels so good."

Our bodies are touching from the chest all the way to our thighs, and she slides her arms around me, and I wrap mine around her, so we're as close as we can possibly be. It's magical, lying there in the semi-darkness beneath the covers, warm and cozy, my senses filled with the sight, smell, sound, and taste of her, and the feel of her beneath my fingers.

We stay that way for ages, moving slowly under the duvet, kissing, touching, just enjoying being close, being together. It's like an erotic dream, one I never want to wake up from.

Unfortunately, of course, it can't last forever, and as I start to feel the tension begin, Elizabeth hooks her leg over me, her hips moving faster. I slide a hand onto her bottom to hold her there, our bodies heating under the covers, skin sliding, mouths slanting, tongues darting, and she's rocking her hips, grinding against me, and then she shudders and cries out, clamping around me. God, she's going to kill me with her orgasms, I fucking love it. I pause my thrusts and hold her tightly as she climaxes, and wait until her body releases her before I start moving again. It doesn't take long before heat rushes up inside me. I'm consumed by several strong pulses as I come inside her, and I tangle my hand in her hair and yank her head back so I can crush my lips to hers.

When we're finally done, we lie in a tangle of arms and legs, breathing heavily as we calm.

"Oh my God, you're so good at this," she says, resting her forehead on my chest.

"A man's only as good as the woman he's with." I move gently inside her, enjoying the after-ripples of my climax, until finally, sighing, I withdraw.

"Knees up," I instruct.

Lying on her back, she draws her knees to her chest. I lie facing her, head propped on a hand, and meet her eyes as she rolls her head to look at me.

There's so much I want to say to her, and I don't know where to start. I want to ask her if I can see her again when we're back in the city. If she'll start dating me properly. And, connected to that, I want to ask her what will happen if she does find out she's pregnant. Would she want me to be a part of the baby's life? She was so reluctant to give me the one night. But how else can I convince her that I'm serious about her?

I'm just about to say something when she clears her throat. "I really need to pee now!" She rolls over, gets up, and heads for the bathroom.

She's gone a little while, and when she comes back, she's shivering, and pulls the duvet up over her shoulders.

"You okay?" I ask.

"I'm fine."

"Not too sore?"

"A bit tender. I haven't had any action for a while, and then I get three times in one night, so…" She smiles. I lift my arm, and she nestles up close to me again. "This is one of the nicest parts," she murmurs. "You smell so good."

"I am sorry if I was a bit rough."

"No, you were perfect. Huxley?"

"Yeah?"

She sighs and tucks her head under my chin. "Thank you."

I kiss the top of her head. "You're welcome." I look over her head, out at the night sky. It was nice of her to thank me, but for some reason I feel a ripple of uncertainty, deep inside. Her words have a ring of finality to them, as if now she's got what she wanted, and she's going to be heading on her merry way. She can't be saying we're over? She can't turn her back on sex as good as this, surely?

Stroking down her back, I say, "Elizabeth?"

But she's fallen asleep again.

I try to relax into the pillows and close my eyes. But they soon drift open, and I lie like that, Elizabeth small and soft in my arms, for a long time before sleep claims me.

*

Elizabeth

When I wake again, the room is filled with light. Huxley is asleep, lying on his back, head turned away from me.

I can't believe we've had sex three times. The man does have stamina, as Rachel announced in the bar. It might not have been the five times he promised, but he more than made up for it with the quality of his lovemaking.

I pick up my phone from the bedside table. It's still early, not quite seven a.m. We've got time for a leisurely breakfast before we have to check out at ten. I smirk as I think about nuzzling up to Huxley now, while he's all warm and sleepy. I bet he has morning glory. I'm sure I can help him with that, if he's up to it. I'm a little tender still, but I'm willing to overlook that for one more time with him.

Because it might enhance the possibility of making a baby. Not for any other reason.

Oh, who am I kidding? The sex was amazing, and I'd kill to make this last as long as I possibly could.

Out of habit, I open my phone, and my eyebrows rise to see three missed calls and five unread texts. They're all from Titus, from last night.

Are you around?

Elizabeth?

Answer your fucking phone!

Jesus. Where are you?

The last one is longer. *Just spoken to Victoria. She said you've gone away for the night with Huxley. I really need to speak to you. Something's come up with Acheron. Can you come and see me when you get back? Mack's coming over at nine a.m.*

The fact that he hasn't commented on me going away with Huxley tells me that it's something serious. Shit. I text him, *Sorry, I forgot to check my messages. Yeah, I'll come over as soon as I'm back in the city, probably around nine.*

He messages me right back. *Cool, see you then.*

Me: *Is there a problem?*

Titus: *I'd rather not discuss it over text.*

Me: *Bad news?*

Titus: *Not necessarily.*

I blow out a breath. He obviously doesn't want to share on the phone, for whatever reason.

My phone buzzes again.

Titus: *Sorry if I disturbed anything.* He adds a winky face.

I wince. Damn Victoria for telling him. Now Mack will know too, if Huxley hadn't already told him. Oh well, I guess it was always going to come out. The five of us are quite tight, and two of us sleeping together was always going to be big news.

I know Hux will be disappointed that I have to get back. I'm sure he was hoping for a lazy morning and a couple more lovemaking sessions before we left.

Leaving my phone on the bedside table, I roll onto my side and study him. He's still facing away, but I can see the five o'clock shadow on his cheek and jaw. It's unusual to see it because he's always clean-shaven. I lower my lips to his skin and inhale. I just love the way he smells—the gorgeous scent of warm male.

This guy jumped off a building for me. I still don't know whether he did it just to get in my knickers. If so, his thirst should be quenched, and he'll quickly lose interest. But what do I do if he says he wants to continue seeing me?

I've had such a great time, and he's amazing in bed. It's also been wonderful to share myself with my best friend, the one guy I've dreamed about having sex with since I was nineteen. But is it possible there could be anything more between us? Will he want anything more?

As always, whenever I think about it my throat tightens and panic rises inside me. If I don't get involved with anyone, I won't get hurt again. I know that's a coward's way out, and I'm not proud of it. But if anyone has the potential to break my heart to the point of it being unmendable, it's the guy lying beside me.

He stirs at that point, and I watch him open his eyes, then roll his head to look at me.

"Morning, Rip Van Hux," I say.

He stretches and yawns. "What time is it?"

"Just after seven." I reach out a hand and cup his face. "You look younger when you're asleep."

In answer, he slides a hand to the back of my head and pulls me toward him for a long, leisurely kiss. I love the way he does that, lazy and possessive.

"I think we've still got time to cram in two more sessions," he murmurs, guiding my hand down to his morning erection.

Unable to resist, I give him a stroke—ooh, he's so hard, like an iron bar, wonderful—then lean back with a sigh. "I can't. I need to get back."

His eyes widen. "Seriously?"

"Yeah, I'm sorry. I've had several urgent messages from Titus. He wants to see me at nine, something to do with the offer from the English company."

"You can't meet him this afternoon? Or have a Zoom call?"

"He wants Mack there too. I think it's important," I say gently.

He meets my eyes for a long moment. Is he also wondering if this is it? Or is he thinking about where we go from here?

But he just says, "No worries, I know how it is. Come on, then. We might as well shower and get going."

We go into the bathroom and clean our teeth while the shower heats up. Our eyes meet in the mirror, but he doesn't smile. Conscious that I'm naked, I feel suddenly shy. Even though he's my best friend, and we've shared such intimate moments over the past few hours, he still feels like a stranger in this setting. The Huxley I know is jovial, laid back, and always laughing; I don't know this guy who looks at me with such serious, intense eyes.

We get into the shower together, and he turns me so I'm under the water, wets my hair, then pours some shampoo onto his hand. He massages it into my hair, his hands gentle, and the feel of his fingers grazing over my scalp sends me tingling all over.

I look down. He has an erection.

"You're insatiable," I scold, pouring some shower gel into my hand, then smoothing it over his chest and down to his groin.

"You're naked, wet, and slippery," he says with some exasperation as I raise an eyebrow. "What did you expect?"

"It wasn't a complaint." I close my hand around him and stroke him several times. God, he's as hard as a rock, long and thick. Even though I only had him hours ago, I feel a twinge deep inside, and I can't help but raise up onto my tiptoes and kiss him.

He sighs, then pours shower gel over my shoulders, and spreads it over my skin. "I didn't mean for this to happen," he mumbles as he strokes my breasts.

"You thought we could get naked and shower together and not get turned on?"

"I overestimated my power to resist you." His lips twist.

He tucks a finger under my chin and holds me there as his eyes search mine. He looks wistful, and I guess he's thinking about our trip coming to an end, but he doesn't say anything. Instead, he presses me up against the tiles and kisses me.

His mouth sears across mine, and his hands glide over my skin, slippery from the shower gel, making me shiver. After a while, he slips a hand down my front to between my legs, and he arouses me there until I'm aching with need.

"Put your arms around me," he instructs, his voice husky with desire. I lift them around his neck, and hold tightly as he lifts me and pins me against the tiles. I wrap my legs around his waist, and he lets me slide down until I'm impaled on him.

Between fiery hot kisses, he fixes his gaze on mine as he thrusts into me, and I find myself unable to look away from his gray eyes. It's like he's branding himself onto my brain, and I know that from now on, when we're apart, I'm not going to be able to forget the image of him driving us both toward the edge.

"Open them," he demands when I close my eyes as I feel my orgasm approaching, and I'm powerless to do anything but look hazily up at him while I come, pulsing around him. He stops moving to enjoy the moment, and it's only when I'm done that he begins to thrust again. His climax claims him shortly afterward, and I tighten my thighs and clench inside, making him groan and rest his forehead against mine.

"Four times," I whisper, sinking my hands into his wet hair. "You're a fucking marvel, Oliver Huxley."

"I'm a shadow of my former self. A dry husk." He withdraws and lowers my legs to the floor. "You've milked me dry."

"And enjoyed every minute of it." I pull him down for a kiss, and we stand there for a long time, under the hot water, while the steam swirls around us, enclosing us in our own private world.

*

We leave as soon as we're dressed, deciding to skip breakfast. We're both quiet as Huxley flies us back. I pretend to be captivated by the view, but the truth is that I feel emotional and confused, and I'm not sure what to say to him. It's the same guy who flew us to the island, and yet I look at him in a very different way now. When I glance down at his hand where he grips the cyclic, I can see that same hand gliding over my body, brown against the paleness of the skin I rarely reveal to the sun. The smell of his aftershave makes me think of when I kissed down his neck to his chest, and the muscles that lie beneath his shirt. Everything about him makes me think of sex.

He lands at Mechanics Bay, and we walk over to his obsidian Merc and get in. He buckles himself in and turns the engine on, then hesitates and looks across at me.

"How long before you know?" he asks.

I frown, not sure what he means.

"Whether you're pregnant," he clarifies.

My lips part. I'd completely forgotten that's the reason why we slept together.

Except, of course, it isn't, not really. Not if I'm honest with myself.

"Two weeks," I whisper.

He nods. He looks at the steering wheel and scrubs at an imagined mark on it. Then he says, "Would you like to go out for a drink tonight?"

"A date?" I murmur.

He looks back at me. "We should talk." He's not smiling. Serious Huxley. My heart skips a beat, and I nod.

He starts the engine and heads us back into the city. We don't say much as he drives through the gathering traffic.

He pulls up outside my apartment block. "Meet you at the Crescent at eight?" he asks.

"Okay." I pause before I get out. "Thank you," I say softly.

He meets my eyes, and all I can think about is that moment in the shower where he demanded, "Open them," and made me watch him as he came inside me.

I lean forward and kiss his cheek. Then I quickly get out of the car, retrieve my bag, and run up to my apartment.

Chapter Fourteen

Elizabeth

Within fifteen minutes, I'm heading out to my car to meet Titus and Mack.

Usually we meet at Huxley's, but today Titus asked us to come to his office. His company is based in Parnell, not far from Mack's offices, in a smart glass-and-chrome building overlooking Hobson Bay and with views of Rangitoto Island.

I pull up in a Visitors' spot in the car park out the front, sign in at Reception, get my visitor's sticker, and then take the elevator up to the top floor.

"Morning, Ms. Tremblay," Elaine, his PA, greets me as I exit the elevator. "Please go straight in. They're waiting for you."

"Thank you." I push open the glass door and go inside.

They're sitting in the cream chairs that circle a coffee table at one end of his office, and they both raise a hand as I approach and take one of the chairs next to them.

Titus—as his nickname suggests—is a big guy, an inch or two taller than Huxley and Mack, and with shoulders that reflect the fact that he played Lock for his university rugby team. He was even considered for the Blues—Auckland's Rugby Union team—but decided to focus on his work rather than take up the chance to become a sportsman, although he still plays at a casual level.

He has dark-brown hair, cut like the other guys' in a modern short fade, longer on top, and he has attractive green eyes. We've been friends for a long time, and we work well together, maybe because neither of us has ever shown any sexual interest in the other. His girlfriends are always tall, leggy blondes, and although I'm happy to admit he's good looking, he's more brooding than the genial Huxley, and quieter than the sometimes explosive Mack. He's a little too brooding and quiet for me, but I like that he's interested in healthcare, and that he's always open to new ideas and willing to listen to others. Not every guy in his position is like that.

At university, Titus, Mack, and I all decided we wanted to run our own companies, but we were keen to work together as often as we could because we'd built up a strong friendship and trust. As a chemist, I enjoyed the development of and research into drugs, and it was clear to me from the start that was the area I wanted to work in. I was lucky enough to get an internship at a major New Zealand pharmaceutical firm, and in my first year my work on developing a new drug that boosted the immune response against melanoma cells won me a lot of interest in the scientific community, and led to some major funding for further research.

I've always been more interested in the bigger picture than the smaller elements of projects—I like to see how things are implemented and how the project I'm working on will benefit others. I prefer working with the patient in the forefront of my mind, and I liked the idea of shaping the culture of a company, rather than having to fit in with an established one. And so I started up my own firm, initially with a low headcount and a small research and development team. But it proved to be so successful that over the past three years we've tripled our number of employees, and we're starting to be a major player in drug development in New Zealand.

Mack was always going to be a genius computer engineer, and his construction of the fastest supercomputer in New Zealand has been both amazing and useful in the development of Titus' and my businesses.

Titus is also a computer engineer, but from the start his fascination was with artificial intelligence. It has so many uses, many of which he has an interest in: robotics, astronomy, and climate change to name three, but his greatest passion is healthcare. He heads a company that works with Mack's supercomputer, Marise, to find ways to use AI to deliver better healthcare faster and at a lower cost, to discover links between genetic codes, to maximize hospital efficiency, and to power surgical robots, amongst many other things.

When I approached him and Mack with the idea of a joint project involving using AI to improve IVF, both of them said yes immediately. We've all been working closely on it over the past six months, and once we realized its potential, we immediately began looking for extra funding. All three of us are excited because an English company called Acheron Pharmaceuticals approached Titus a couple of weeks ago offering a huge investment in the project. The owner of the company is a Kiwi who moved to England, but he's keen to maintain a close connection with his homeland, and he's excited about this new research from up-and-coming Kiwi companies. I'd rather have kept it in New Zealand, but it's too generous to pass up on, and the research is too important for me to pick and choose.

"Coffee?" Titus asks as Elaine pops her head in, and when I nod, he says, "Yes, please," and she goes out to make it.

"So what's so important?" I ask, settling back and crossing my legs.

"To the point as always," Mack says, amused.

"Time is money, my friend."

"True."

"I've been talking to Alan Woodridge," Titus says.

I nod. Alan is the owner of Acheron Pharmaceuticals. "They're still interested in investing?" I ask.

"Yeah…" Titus exchanges a glance with Mack. "But he has come up with a condition."

"Oh?"

"He wants the project to be headed by Acheron, based in Exeter, in Devon."

My eyebrows lift. We all study each other for a moment. The door opens, and Elaine comes in with our drinks and leaves them on the table with a plate of cookies before withdrawing. I pick up my mug and sip the steaming coffee, my brain whirring.

Acheron's investment is a significant amount of money—five hundred million dollars. It can cost billions to develop and approve a new drug, but they will almost certainly increase their investment when they see the first successful results and realize its potential.

"It's a fair enough request," I say slowly.

They both nod. "That's what I said," Titus replies.

"Did they have someone in mind to run the project?"

"A senior member of our team is all he said. Basically, he means one of us three."

We all give a rueful smile.

"What do you think?" Mack asks. "It's your project. We're just the machinery behind it."

"Ah, now you're being modest."

"I'm summarizing," he says. "Come on, it's your baby—almost literally. You're the driving force behind it."

"Are they looking for a permanent move?" I ask.

"No," Titus says. "He's requested two years—enough time to get the project up and running."

Two years. It's a significant amount of time to be away from home. Oh God, Huxley.

My heart's pounding, and my mouth has gone dry. "Are either of you interested in heading it?"

"I can't," Mack says immediately. "I need to be near Marise." His supercomputer needs constant attention, and I'm not surprised he's not interested. "And I'm right in the middle of developing a new microprocessor, too. Plus Sidnie won't want to move to England, especially while her father is still sick." Her dad has bowel cancer, and is still undergoing treatment.

"Fair enough." I look at Titus. "How about you?"

"Well… I'm single," he says slowly, "so I don't have that pressure. If you say absolutely not, I'll give it some serious thought. If I'm honest, though, I think they're hoping it will be you. Like Mack says, it's your baby—you're the chemist, and it is a pharmaceutical company. It's going to be… not impossible, but difficult for you to run it from here if they want the research to be carried out there."

"Yeah." I tip my head back and staring up at the ceiling. "Shit. Why couldn't this have happened years ago?"

"You're at your peak, Elizabeth," Titus says. "Young, beautiful, incredibly smart. You know this is a huge opportunity. You'll be inundated with funding after this project concludes. You'll be able to do anything you want."

I close my eyes. The other two are quiet for a moment.

Then Mack asks, "Is this about Huxley?"

I open my eyes. He's not smiling.

"It's nothing to do with us," Titus says quickly, glancing at him. Clearly, they've been talking about us.

"It is when it impinges on our businesses," Mack says. His gaze is direct. He's annoyed. I know him well enough to suspect it's nothing to do with business. He's worried about Huxley's feelings. Well, I'm not going to discuss that in front of Titus. He doesn't need to know the ins and outs of my love life.

"When do they need to know by?" I ask briskly.

"There's no rush," Titus says, "I think we can take a few weeks to work it out. But obviously the sooner the better."

"Yeah." I clear my throat. "I'll have to give it some thought, if that's okay."

"Of course." Titus pulls a folder toward him. "Alan gave me a few figures to go through. Shall we take a look at them?"

I nod, and he proceeds to read out the notes, and we take half an hour to discuss them.

"I'd better get going," I tell them when we're done. "I've got a bit of work to catch up on."

"Yeah, me too," Mack says.

Fuck. That means he wants to talk to me.

"I'll call you," I tell Titus, and Mack and I head out to the elevator. We wait for the doors to open, go inside, press the button for the ground floor, and the doors close.

Mack leans against the wall of the carriage, hands in his pockets.

"Don't glare at me," I say impatiently. "It's not my fault."

"Are you thinking of going?" he asks.

"Of course I'm thinking of going. It's five hundred million dollars, Mack. That's a significant amount of money, and this cause is very important to me."

"Is it possible you're pregnant?"

The elevator walls are made of mirrors, so I'm able to see my face turn completely scarlet.

"That's none of your business," I snap. How dare he ask me that?

Unrepentant, he says, "What would you do if you are?"

"They do have babies in England." My voice drips with sarcasm.

"Yes, I know," he bites back. "Don't be snarky. You know what I'm asking. You'd really think about going after the two of you finally get together?"

"We're not together. I asked him if he'd donate his sperm for me. He said no, he'd only do it the old-fashioned way. It was his choice."

The elevator stops, the doors slide open, and I march out. Walking at lightspeed, as usual, he moves in front of me, and I have to stop.

"So you had no intention of seeing him again?" he demands.

"He asked for one night, and that's what I gave him."

"Don't be so naïve. You know he wants more. I assumed you were using it as a way to kickstart a relationship, and so did he."

"That's not my fault."

"Elizabeth!" he yells.

"He's a grown man," I yell back. "Perfectly capable of forming his own sentences. He doesn't need you to speak for him."

"Yes, he does, because he would never say what I'm about to say. He's too nice. I'm not. You're being exceedingly cruel."

"Cruel?!"

"He jumped off the Sky Tower for you."

My irritation flares into outright anger. "He jumped off the fucking Sky Tower because I'm the one girl who'd never opened her legs to him. Well, now I have, so he can finally leave me in peace and go about his merry way."

Mack stares at me. "You're kidding me."

"What?"

"You know this isn't about that."

"Do I? He asked for one night with me. And he made the most of it, Mack. Do I need to say more?"

He winces. "No."

I'm so angry and upset now that I'm not watching my words. "What, now you're squeamish? I thought you wanted to know all the intimate details about my love life? Well, Huxley fucked me four ways till Friday because he knew one night was all he was getting. I made myself quite clear. He's a fucking smooth bastard, and he always gets what he wants. You know that. Well, he got me, and now he's had me. And yes, I might be pregnant. That's what I wanted. And if I am, I'm going to have the baby in England and bring it up there. Why shouldn't I? I don't owe him anything."

Mack stares at me. He looks genuinely shocked. "He's asked you out every month since you were twenty."

"Mack, that was a joke! You know what he's like! Name one girl he's dated for more than four or five months."

"Because he's been waiting for you!"

"Bollocks!" I'm nearly tearful. "Stop talking about this as if it's the love of a lifetime. The thing is, England is the opportunity of a lifetime. The chance to work with top scientists. To make a difference, Mack. You of all people should understand how I feel about that."

"I do. Of course I do. But I thought you wanted Huxley. If I didn't think that, I wouldn't have convinced him to go through with the jump. And now you have him in the palm of your hand, and you're just throwing that away? That's what I meant by cruel. Is this about revenge? You want to hurt him like he hurt you?"

Silence falls between us.

"Shit," Mack says. "It is." He runs a hand through his hair. He looks genuinely upset.

His words have shocked me, because I want to protest, and I can't. It wasn't a calculated plan. But deep down, I know he's right. Consciously, it makes no sense. Huxley did the honorable thing, acknowledged his mistake, and decided to stand by the girl he'd knocked up and wait until his baby was born before he dated another woman. Subconsciously, though, it comes down to one fact: he chose Brandy over me.

I know it's ridiculous. The guy was nineteen. It was an ice age ago. And it makes me a vengeful, hateful person.

I like to think maybe it also says something about my feelings for him. I love him with all of my broken heart. It wouldn't hurt half so much if I didn't.

"Ask him to tell you," Mack says, hands on his hips, "about…" His voice trails off, and he looks away.

"About what?"

He purses his lips. Then he looks back at me. He's breathing heavily.

"Nothing," he says eventually.

"Ask him to tell me about what, Mack?"

But he just shakes his head. "Forget it." He turns and walks away.

I run after him and catch his arm. "No, come on, what were you going to say?"

He detaches my hand. "It's not my story to tell. And you're right. This is none of my business. Do what you want. You usually do—both of you." He walks away again, and this time, I don't follow him.

*

I need to think about England objectively, but I'm not going to be able to do that today. I go to my office for a while, hoping to lose myself in work, but I'm distracted and irritable, and my staff are heartily sick of me by the time I decide to head home at five p.m. It's early for me, but I'm tired and emotional, and I don't like working when my mind's not on the job.

My brother, Arthur, is a dog breeder, and he looks after Nymph whenever I'm busy. I stop off at his kennels and pick her up, drive home, then take her out for a walk for half an hour around Albert Park.

My brain feels as if it's overstuffed with too many thoughts. I feel a bit feverish, like I'm coming down with something. I argue with Mack all the time, and I'm used to him yelling at me, but for some reason his words today really upset me. Maybe it's because what he said hit me so close to home. He and Huxley are like brothers, and I know Mack's worried about him. He genuinely wants him to be happy.

My muscles are warming up now, and I breathe deeply, enjoying the exercise. I need to think about this properly, break it down into parts. Two years isn't twenty. There's no reason Huxley and I couldn't have a long-distance relationship for a while.

But there are so many other factors, the main one being that he's surrounded by other women at the club. Would he really be able to resist them? I know Mack would say I'm being unfair, but I don't have that high an opinion of myself to assume any man would choose being faithful to me over the attraction of short-term sex with a variety of other women.

And I'm not even considering bringing a baby into the equation. I really didn't think it through. I'm such a fucking idiot. If I am pregnant, what am I going to do? Huxley is going to want to be a part of the baby's life. Of course he is. He gave up everything for a woman he'd had a one-night stand with because she fell pregnant; what's he going to want to do for one of his best friends? So would I tell Titus that I'd pass on the move to England and risk losing five hundred million dollars—oh my fucking God—stay here, and make a go of it with Huxley?

Me, him, and the baby—one big happy family? Of course it's not going to happen. Real life doesn't work out like that. This isn't a fucking romance novel. Now Mack's with Sidnie, he wants everyone to be as happy as he is, but what's happened with him is an aberration, not the norm.

Deep down, in the secret parts of my heart that nobody else sees, I'm envious of Mack and Sidnie. He's so fucking happy, it makes me want to throw up.

Oh, I'm thrilled for him, don't get me wrong. I'm absolutely stoked that he's found someone who understands him, and who adores him.

He deserves it, because he's such a nice guy, a true philanthropist, and he works so incredibly hard.

But I'm still green as the Hulk, because I know how unusual true love is, and I wish it could have happened for me and Huxley. I wish we'd gotten together when we were young, and we'd dated for a year or two, and then we could have married, and I might even have had a baby by now the proper way, in a settled, committed relationship.

The thought makes my eyes sting. I don't want to think about it anymore.

Luckily, my phone buzzes in the back pocket of my jeans, and I take it out. It's a text from Penelope—my sister.

Have you got time for a coffee? she asks.

Sure, I reply. *I've got until eight. I'm on my way back from walking Nymph. I'll be there around six.*

See you then x

Glad of the distraction, I pick up the pace with Nymph and head home. By the time I get in, it's five to six, so I switch the coffee machine on and start brewing two lattes.

It's a beautiful evening, and the apartment is filled with late summer sunshine. It's not a huge place—I'm not quite as rich as the boys—but it's still spectacular. It's all open plan—one big living room, dining room, and kitchen—with a view of Auckland Harbour Bridge through the huge windows. The furniture is mostly Tasmanian blackwood and cream, and I bought a couple of Helene Huxley's paintings for the walls, which give the place a splash of color. I love it, and I feel very at home here, but tonight it brings me no pleasure. All I can think about is that I'm meeting Huxley at eight this evening, and I'm going to have to tell him about England. Oh God. What's he going to say?

Chapter Fifteen

Elizabeth

Pen texts me to say she's on her way up. While the espresso fills one of the cups, I go over to the front door and open it to see her walking up the corridor. I smile. "Hey, you!"

Nymph runs past me and dashes up to her, and she stops briefly to fuss her before following her up to the apartment. We exchange a kiss, and she comes in.

She's six years older and a couple of inches taller than me, but other than that we're relatively alike, with the same light-brown hair, although hers is longer and wavier, and she often wears it up in a bun, like today.

"The coffee's nearly ready," I tell her, going over to steam the milk. "How are you doing?"

She dumps her purse on the breakfast bar and sits on one of the barstools. "Honestly?"

I glance over at her. "Oh, what's up?"

She gives me a sad smile, and her bottom lip trembles. Only then do I see how pale she is, and the dark patches under her eyes, before she puts her face in her hands and bursts into tears.

"Oh, no…" I run around the counter and put my arms around her. "You've had a miscarriage?"

She wipes her face, but it's pointless, and more tears stream down her cheeks. "I'm sorry. I was determined not to get upset, but…"

"No, girl, you let it out, don't worry." I pull a barstool toward me and perch on it so I can hold her while she cries.

Pen and her husband, Paul, have been trying for a baby since she was twenty-eight. After two unsuccessful years, they finally decided it was time to get help. Tests revealed nothing apparently wrong with either her eggs or his sperm. First they tried ovulation induction, and when that was unsuccessful, they had four cycles of IUI. Finally, when that didn't work, they moved onto IVF. The first two cycles resulted in miscarriages, but she told me a week ago that she felt different with this cycle—more positive and hopeful, and I thought maybe it was a good sign. My heart breaks to think her dreams have been dashed once again. And for some reason it's even worse that nobody seems to have any idea why it's happening. It's just one of those unexplained mysteries.

"I'm so sorry." I kiss the top of her head and rub her back. Her sobs are already dying down. I'm guessing she's all cried out.

"Every time we've tried something, I've done my best to rein in my hopes," she whispers. "We've both tried to be practical. But this time... I really thought it was going to work. I was absolutely convinced, third time lucky. And then a couple of days ago I began spotting, and yesterday I started bleeding heavily, and Paul took me to the clinic, and they confirmed I'd miscarried."

She was only seven weeks' pregnant, but I know there's no point in saying it was only the size of a blueberry and wouldn't have looked much like a baby. She knows all that, and it doesn't matter. It's about the destruction of a dream and the loss of hope. And it's incredibly cruel.

I pull the roll of kitchen towel toward me, tear off a sheet, and hand it to her. She wipes her face and blows her nose.

"Go and sit on the sofa," I tell her. "I'll get the coffees and join you."

Pen nods and goes through to the living room, Nymph following her as if she can feel her pain and wants to help. I quickly pour the hot milk onto the espresso, then bring the cups through, sitting beside her.

"How are you feeling?" I ask. "Are you in pain?"

"A bit achy. A few cramps. Not too bad." She blows out a long breath, then picks up her coffee cup and takes a sip. "Ah, that's good."

I have a mouthful of my latte. "How's Paul?"

"Tired. Upset. Angry."

"Yeah."

"Thanks for asking, though. People tend to forget about the guy. It's a physical and emotional strain on both of us."

"Yeah, well, it's his dream too, right?"

She doesn't reply, and meets my eyes for a moment. "It was," she says slowly. "But last night he said he didn't want to go through it again."

My lips part, but words desert me. "Fuck," I say in the end.

Her lips twist. "Yeah. The thing is, I get it. It's been such a strain on our relationship."

"Aw, but he loves you so much."

She wipes under her eyes again and leans her head on her hand tiredly. "Yes, he does. But everyone has their limits. It's so hard to describe how this dominates your life. It's the first thing we talk about in the morning, and the last thing we discuss at night."

I feel a big twist inside. I'd be lying if I said Pen's experiences haven't influenced my decision to try for a baby. I know I'll only be twenty-nine in May, and that's not old at all to start a family in this day and age. But a small part of me wonders whether the reason she can't get pregnant could be hereditary. It's probably not; it could be a problem with Paul's sperm that they haven't found, or maybe she's got an autoimmune disorder, or literally any one of a hundred other factors. But there's a chance it's an issue that I have too. And I don't want to wait until I'm thirty-five to start trying, then discover I have years of IVF ahead of me with my fertility rate dropping like a stone.

"Paul's reaction was probably knee-jerk," I say. "As you said, he's upset and angry, and at the moment the thought of going through it all again is just horrendous. But give him some time to calm down, and I'm sure he'll feel better about it all."

She blows her nose again. "Maybe. But there's also a small part of me that wonders whether it would be better to accept it's not going to happen."

I feel as if someone's punched me in the stomach. "Aw, Pen… You've still got lots of other treatments to try. What about donor options? Or surrogacy?"

"After the first couple of years, we began to understand that pregnancy was going to be a bit harder for us than for a lot of people. We realized it was rarely the idyllic experience it's portrayed as in the media, and that there might be miscarriages, nausea, the stress of being tested, issues with the pregnancy or the baby, pre-eclampsia, all those things. We felt like it was a trial we were being put through, as if we were being tested to see how serious we were. You only get given what you can cope with, right? We were convinced we'd get there in the end."

"And you will, I know you will."

But she shakes her head. "It's not just about having a baby. It's about having that connection with your partner. Don't get me wrong, I do want a baby, but what I really wanted, more than anything, was a little piece of Paul that will always be mine, you know? I wanted to share myself with him in that way. To have a baby that was part of us both. And I don't know if I want a baby enough to use a donor egg or sperm."

She swallows hard. "The thing is, it's not just about having a baby anymore. It's about our marriage, too. We're struggling. Mainly because our sex life isn't great and hasn't been for some time." Her eyes water again. It's a tough subject to discuss, but we've always been close and talked about everything.

"I'm so sorry," I murmur.

"I don't enjoy it anymore," she says honestly. "And I know he's just going through the motions, too. He's still relatively young, and he has a high sex drive; he should be with someone who wants it five times a week, who can't wait to get him into bed. I love him so much, but when we're making love all I can think about is if it's going to make a baby. And so… if he suggests anything else, you know… I just think what a waste…" She stops, fighting tears again.

"I understand."

"I feel as if I'm at a point where I need to choose between my marriage and having a baby," she says.

We study each other for a moment. She looks surprised at having finally said what's obviously been on her mind, and maybe even a little bit relieved.

"Perhaps what you need right now is a break," I say slowly. "Maybe a holiday. It seems perfectly natural to me that it's put an incredible strain on your relationship. What you need is to rediscover why you're together. Concentrate on yourselves. Give yourselves the opportunity to fall back in love again."

She nods and brightens. "I think you're right."

"You don't need to make any big, final decisions right now. It's not all or nothing. There are still options available to you. Maybe pre-implantation genetic testing is what you need, to increase the chances of having a healthy embryo before it's even implanted."

"Maybe. How is the research going on that, by the way?"

"It's good. Actually, I have something to tell you. I didn't want to say before because I didn't want to get your hopes up, but we've been working on something that might end up being useful to you."

"Oh?"

"You know Titus Oates?" His real name is Lawrence, but everyone calls him Titus because it was the nickname of the Antarctic explorer of the same name who died on Scott's expedition to the South Pole when he walked from his tent into a blizzard.

"Yeah, I met him at a party here once. Big guy, dark hair, gorgeous, and brooding?"

"That sums him up."

"Isn't his father from Norway or something? I seem to remember some impressive tats on his arms."

"Yeah. I call him the Striking Viking. Anyway, his company, NZAI, has been working with MediTech on some new research involving using Artificial Intelligence with IVF."

"In what way?"

"We're exploring its use in identifying early markers of quality in gametes and embryos. We know that things like follicle size in the female gametes and morphology and motility in sperm directly correlate with IVF success, but selection depends on the operator making the right decisions. AI removes subjectivity and objectively ranks gametes based on quality." I know I'm slipping into science speak, so I stop there. "It's complicated, but there are really good signs it could predict blastocyst formation and even live birth prior to fertilization."

"It sounds amazing. But I'm guessing that's years away."

"Not at all. We're well into the development and we'll hopefully be running trials soon. The best news is that a big English medical research company wants to invest in the final stages of the project."

She smiles. "That's great news." She knows how hard I've worked over the past few years, and how hard it is to come by funding.

"There is one drawback," I say softly.

"Oh?"

"They want someone from here to go over there to head the project. It's a condition of their investment."

She stares at me. "Go over where?"

"England."

"You're thinking of moving there?"

I tip my head from side to side. "Not permanently. They want a two-year commitment."

"But it doesn't have to be you."

"I'm the head of the company. They're asking for me."

"What about Titus?"

"We've talked about him going, but to be honest, I'm quite excited about the challenge. It'd be an opportunity to make a huge advancement in fertility treatment, Pen. It would change so many lives." *Including yours.* I don't say it, but she'll know that's what I'm thinking.

Her brows draw together. "Well, obviously, I can't say I wouldn't miss you, but I know how much you love your work. We can always keep in touch on FaceTime I suppose."

We both know, though, that it's not the same as being able to call in for coffee.

"What about Huxley?" Pen asks. "Have you told him?"

I suck my bottom lip. "No. And it's a bit more complicated now."

"Oh shit, of course, you went away didn't you?" Her eyes sparkle. "How did it go?"

I hesitate, meet her eyes, and then we both start to laugh. "It was amazing," I admit. "But I came back to the news about England, and now I don't know what to do."

"So… you could be pregnant?"

I bite my lip and nod. Telling her about my plans to get pregnant was a difficult conversation, because even though we're close, her infertility makes it a delicate issue. But when I told her, she hugged me and said she understood. She's been nothing but supportive, and now her face breaks into a big smile.

"Are you going to tell him about England?" she asks.

"I have to." I know Mack or Titus will tell him even if I don't.

"What will you do if you're pregnant?"

"I don't know. It's turned out to be a terrible mess, and it's all my fault." Whatever I said to Mack, I know I'm to blame for the state of affairs. I should have said no when Huxley said he wanted one night with me. I'm not stupid. I wanted him, and I wasn't strong enough to say no.

We sit quietly for a while. I've opened the window that overlooks the harbor, and the late summer breeze drifts through, bringing with it the faint scent of the ocean.

"How serious do you think he is about you?" she asks eventually.

"He jumped off the Sky Tower for me. I guess that's pretty serious. I'm still not sure whether he just did it because he wanted to have sex with me. Mack says it's more than that, but I'm not sure. I think I'm a distant moon he hasn't yet discovered, you know?"

"I bet he really enjoyed planting his flag, though."

That makes me laugh. Then my smile fades. "I knew the sex was going to be great. But I don't know what happens now. I guess the first thing I need to do is wait and see if I get pregnant."

Her brow furrows. "Even if you don't, the fact that you knowingly slept together to make a baby changes something between you. It's intimate and wondrous and magical. It connects you, and it binds you together in a way that can't be undone."

I look at my latte, feeling a complex mix of emotions. "I wish he'd agreed to be a donor. That's all I wanted. I didn't want this. And now… There are bigger things at stake. This is hugely important research, and there's a lot of money involved. I feel like I have a responsibility to see it through. And I want to. It's important to me."

"Elizabeth," she says softly, "you know you don't have to do it for me, don't you?" I just look at her, and she reaches out and cups my face. "You're so sweet," she murmurs. "But you mustn't sacrifice your own happiness for me."

"I know what you're saying, and I do want to do this for you. But it's not just about me and you. I want to make a difference, Pen. It's my chance to do something big, you know? It could change so many lives. Every woman should be able to bear a child if she wants one. I have this opportunity to help all those women who've struggled with infertility. And if I turn my back on that, what kind of person does it make me?"

She gives me a pained look. "But you can't put it before your own happiness."

I don't say anything, because that's exactly what I'm planning to do. "I'm seeing Huxley at eight," I say. "I guess we'll talk about it then, and maybe things will become clearer."

"All right. Will you call or text and let me know how it goes?"

"Yeah, of course."

She changes the subject then, talking about Mum's birthday and asking what present she thinks we should get, and then shortly after that she says she'd better get going. Nymph and I see her to the door, where we have a hug, and then she heads off, promising to let me know what Paul thinks about the idea of going on vacation for a while.

I close the door behind her, and go and sit on the sofa. Nymph jumps up beside me, and I bury my hand in her fur.

What's Huxley going to say? Will he understand my predicament? Or will he think I'm being deliberately obstructive? I remember his reply when I asked him why he didn't marry Brandy all those years ago: *Because I wanted you.* How much truth is in that statement? Was he just saying what he thought I wanted to hear? I can't believe that somehow, because one thing he's not is insincere.

But in the end, it doesn't matter what our feelings are for each other. I have this wonderful opportunity to help people. How can I face myself in the mirror if I choose my own happiness over that?

Chapter Sixteen

Huxley

The Crescent is a bar halfway between the club and Elizabeth's apartment, and we all occasionally meet there for a drink. This is the first time Elizabeth and I have met on our own, though, and I head out, conscious that my pulse is racing faster than normal.

The days are still humid and warm, but as we head toward autumn, the nights are cooling down, and I'm glad of my jacket. The sun has almost set, and the streets are flooded with a deep orange light and lengthening shadows.

I'm looking forward to seeing her, but I feel anxious too. I'm not sure why. Maybe because we haven't yet talked properly about what comes next. I'm hopeful, but she hasn't texted me today, even though I've messaged her a couple of times, and I have an odd feeling that this isn't going to end well.

I arrive at The Crescent and go inside. She's not here yet, so I go up to the bar and order two whiskies, choosing the Ardbeg Islay malt I know she'll like. She'll be walking because the bar's not that far away.

The bar is, unsurprisingly, crescent-shaped, and the room is divided into individual nooks that provide places to chat. The decor is all dark wood and dim lighting, making it seem private and intimate. It's about half full, not bad for a Wednesday night. The music playing is Ella Fitzgerald's *Dream a Little Dream of Me*.

"Hey."

I look around to see Elizabeth standing there, and my stomach flips. She's changed from her outfit this morning, and now she's wearing black wide-leg pants, a white shirt, and a fawn blazer, with gold bangles and gold hoops hanging from her ears. She looks elegant and sophisticated, and I've never wanted her more than I do at that moment.

I wish we were dating, and I could greet her with a kiss and a hug. But despite how great the sex was last night, we're not officially a couple, and even though I often kiss her on the cheek, suddenly I feel unsure about approaching her.

"I got you a whisky," I say instead, picking up both glasses. "Shall we sit over there?"

She nods and leads the way to one of the nooks, and we slide onto the benches on opposite sides of the table. Her hair is sleek and shiny, like a sheet of milk chocolate. She's taken time over her makeup. She's dressed up for me.

I'm still wearing the suit I changed into for work—navy today, with a light-blue shirt. It's warm in the bar, and I take off my jacket, remove my cufflinks, and turn up the cuffs of my shirt, more to give myself something to do than anything else. She watches me, her gaze brushing over me like a feather, making a shiver run down my back.

"You look nice tonight," I say, leaning back again and sipping the whisky.

"So do you," she replies. "But then you always do. You know how to wear a suit."

"Thank you." We're being very polite. You'd never know we had amazing sex last night. Four times.

She meets my gaze for a moment, then drops hers to her glass and studies the amber liquid. The suspense is killing me.

"Go on then," I say eventually. "Out with it."

Her eyebrows rise. "What do you mean?"

"You obviously have something to tell me, and I'm guessing it's not good news."

She still doesn't say anything.

I lean on the table. "Spit it out, for Christ's sake. You're making me nervous."

She inhales deeply, then exhales slowly before beginning. "You know the project I'm working on with Titus?"

"The IVF one?"

"Yeah. I think I told you that we've had an incredible offer from a leading pharmaceutical company wanting to invest in the research."

"That's great."

"It is. It's a significant amount of money—five hundred million dollars."

"Shit."

"Obviously, it's a drop in the ocean where drug research is concerned, but we're hopeful they'll stump up some more cash once the first results come through. Titus is thrilled—he's worked really hard to get them interested."

I nod. I can't yet see where this is going.

She clears her throat. "The thing is… they want a senior member of our team to head the project."

"Okay…"

She meets my eyes. "Over there."

My heart gives a heavy thud. "In England?"

"Yes, in Devon."

We stare at each other for a long moment.

"Does it have to be you?" I ask. I feel nauseous. It's not even as if she's said Australia—it's the other side of the world.

"Titus said they're expecting it to be me. It would be a fantastic experience. I've never worked in England, and the opportunity to learn from their scientists is something I didn't think I'd get, to this extent anyway."

My heart's racing. Her expression is hopeful and cautious. She wants me to be pleased for her. But she's expecting me to be angry.

"Is it a permanent move?" I ask.

"They've requested a two-year commitment."

Two years. I give a short, humorless laugh, lean back, and look away, out through the window. It's dark now, and the round lights in each alcove make me feel as if we're on life rafts floating on the ocean, each nook its own small world.

"Say something," she pleads.

I turn my gaze back to her. "What do you want? My blessing?" My voice is sharp, but I don't care.

She winces. "I understand why you're angry."

"I'm not angry. I'm incredibly hurt."

Her brows draw together, and she bites her lip.

"Last night," I continue, "I'm pretty sure I remember us having sex."

"I know."

"Four times."

Her eyes glimmer with a touch of humor. "I know."

"Tell me it wasn't amazing."

She gives me a look that says *You know I can't.*

"You're just going to walk away from that?" I ask.

"It was just sex," she says. Her eyes are a touch cool.

That hits me like a blow to the stomach. I'm not stupid—I know women can have sex without emotion the same as men. But is that really what happened here? I don't believe it.

"Tell me you don't feel anything for me," I snap.

"Of course I feel something for you," she says gently. "You're my best friend, and I don't want to lose that relationship. But I had no intentions of it becoming anything more than that. I asked you if you'd donate sperm for me because I want a baby and I think you'd make a great father. But I don't want a relationship. It was you who demanded one night with me, who made the grand gesture of jumping off the building. How could I say no after that? Mack practically put me in an arm lock to make sure I went through with it. And... I'm attracted to you. Of course I am. I was curious. And the sex was amazing. But it was never going to be more than that. I thought you understood."

I'm so shocked, I can't speak. She's right. At no point has she intimated that she's interested in a relationship. I'm the one who's pushed it all along.

Her eyes meet mine, and she drops her gaze again. And it's only then that I realize just how much I hurt her all those years ago. Part of me thought she was concentrating on her career, and it was only a matter of time before she came around. I was convinced we'd get together eventually. But she was obviously determined all along to keep her distance.

I have a large mouthful of whisky and welcome the sear of the firewater down to my stomach. I watch her sip from her glass, and then something occurs to me. "What happens if you get pregnant?"

She looks into her glass for a moment, then lifts her gaze to mine. "They do have babies in England."

There's a long pause. I feel as if she's slid a dagger between my ribs and twisted it.

"Right," I say eventually.

"Two years isn't that long. You never know, when I get back..." She bites her lip.

For the first time, anger rears up inside me. How can she feed me little pieces of hope like that?

"You might meet someone else over there," I say, knowing it's very possible. "Or I might meet someone else here. What then?"

There's another long pause.

"I don't want you to meet someone else," she says.

"That's not fair," I tell her resentfully.

"I know."

"It's dog in the manger."

"I know."

"You can't just disappear for two years and expect me to wait for you."

"I know, Hux. I'm not saying it's fair. I'm just saying how I feel—the first thing that comes into my mind." She swallows hard. "I'm sorry. I shouldn't have said that." She's gone pale.

"I know your career is important to you," I say. "So's mine to me. But in the end, they're just jobs."

"No," she says. "It's more than that to me." She sighs. "My sister's had a miscarriage."

My breath leaves me in a rush. "Shit. I'm so sorry."

"She's devastated. And Paul's told her he doesn't want to go through it again."

"Ah, that sucks."

"I get it," she says, "of course. The stress that couples—and single people—have to go through is horrific. She said it's taken a terrible toll on their marriage. And Hux, I have the chance to help people like that. To make a difference."

I understand then. She's never going to be able to turn down this opportunity. Beneath her ambition and her drive to achieve are even bigger abstract nouns—responsibility and duty. She has the opportunity to help people, to help her own sister. And I know her well enough to understand that she wouldn't be able to live with herself if she turned her back on that.

But it still doesn't explain one thing. "Can't Titus go, and you oversee things from here?"

She hesitates, then says, "He thinks they're hoping for me." There's a strange emotion flickering behind her eyes, and it's not guilt or disappointment. I think it's resentment.

And then it all becomes clear. The work is important to her, and I can't blame her for being bound by duty and responsibility, because that's a curse I'll always be plagued with. But that's not the whole story. She does have feelings for me. But she's not going to give in to them.

Not just because she doesn't want to be hurt again, although I'm sure that's part of it. But because she wants to punish me for hurting her.

I finish off my whisky and leave the glass on the table. Then I pick up my jacket and walk out of the bar.

Even though it's a Wednesday, the streets are busy-ish, the bars mostly full. I walk fast, not caring if I bump into people, half hoping someone will stop me so I can get into a fight and knock someone's lights out. But people part for me and let me pass, maybe hesitant to engage the guy who looks as if he's lost something precious to him.

Life is so fucking unfair. I did the honorable thing, and it cost me the girl I wanted. If only I could turn back time and have another chance.

Would I do it differently?

I think about Joanna, and my pace slows. She's my daughter, and she's played such a big part in my life. I wouldn't be without her. No, I wouldn't do anything different.

I understand why Elizabeth's hurt. But it was ten years ago. We were nineteen—still kids really. She needs to build a bridge and fucking get over it. I'm done with hanging around waiting for her. If she gets pregnant, I'll just treat it as if I was a donor. She can go to England, meet someone else, and play happy families for all I care. I don't give a fuck.

I ignore the way my heart feels as if someone's grabbed it in their fist and is squeezing it hard. I'm done moping over Elizabeth Tremblay. It's time to move on.

*

Elizabeth

After our conversation in the bar, I do my best to put the events of the past few weeks behind me and concentrate on my career.

I tell Titus and Mack that I'm going to England, and Titus calls Alan and lets him know. Everyone at Acheron Pharmaceuticals is overjoyed, and I have several long phone calls with people talking about practical details like where I'm going to live and what office I'll use.

I don't see much of Huxley. For the first time in years, I don't hear from him for three days—no calls or messages. I don't speak to him at all until I turn up at the club for our usual Friday meeting. When I walk into the boardroom, he greets me with a smile. He's polite and funny, like he always is, bustling around making sure we have coffees and food. But he avoids my eyes, and when the meeting is over, he's out of the door first, saying he has things to do.

I'm sure Mack has picked up on the mood, and I half expect him to wait behind to admonish me. But he doesn't. He gathers up his things too and heads off without a word.

Sad, a little tearful, I pack up my briefcase and head out.

We continue like that for a couple of weeks. I try to keep myself busy, and I'm sure he's doing the same. I work long hours, conscious now that I might not be in the office for much longer, and knowing I need to start preparing for someone else to take over. I have several meetings with my senior management team where we talk about various options, and in the end we decide the team will continue to run things together, and they'll just refer to me if they can't decide on an issue.

I don't like leaving behind the company I've worked so hard to build, but it's never been easier to run a business online, and anyway, it's not forever.

In the evenings, I take Nymph for long walks through the park, and it's only then that I let myself dwell on my personal life. I know I've made the right decision, but whenever I think about Huxley, my eyes prick with tears, and I have to fight not to let them fall. I can't remember a time in the past when he's been angry with me, or when more than a few hours have gone by without us contacting one another. I miss him, so much it physically hurts. But it was my decision, and so I can't complain.

The days tick by, faster than I would have thought possible, and it's not long before my period's due. I have a short cycle of only twenty-five days, and I'm hardly ever late. So it's with some nervousness that I rise on day twenty-six.

It's almost impossible to concentrate during the day. The achiness I feel and the tenderness in my breasts could easily be down to PMS, and I don't want to get excited.

And anyway, my feelings are very mixed. In many ways, it would be better if I'm not pregnant. That way I can sever the connection between myself and Huxley, because it will really complicate matters if he were to be the father of my child. And it would also, if I'm really honest with myself, be easier to deal with moving to England if I'm not. I know women have babies over there, but I wouldn't have my family and friends around me, and that would be a shame.

I tell myself this all day. I'm therefore completely shocked when I go to the bathroom around five p.m. and discover that my period has started.

I sit on the toilet seat, my face in my hands, and fight against a wave of emotion, surprised at how devastated I feel. I really thought it had worked. I thought he'd made me pregnant. I thought I was going to give birth to his child. The feeling of loss completely overwhelms me, and it's the first time I really understand how much of an impact Pen's infertility must have had on her.

"It's for the best," I repeat like a mantra, but the physical ache in my belly matches a deep ache in my heart. I feel so incredibly sad, which is ridiculous because it's not like I've had a miscarriage. There was never anything there. But of course, that's not the point. Just like Pen didn't really lose a baby, it's about the loss of a dream.

Oh, Huxley. Yet again, it feels as if we held an opportunity in our hands, and yet again it's been ripped away. It feels as if Fate is trying to tell me we're not meant to be together.

The ridiculous thing is that now, out of all my friends, he's the one I want to talk to. And anyway, I need to tell him he's off the hook. He deserves to know.

Will he be disappointed? Or relieved to get me out of his hair?

I take out my phone, intending to text him, then pause and put it away again.

Leaving the bathroom, I tell my PA I'm going out for a while. Then I get in my car and drive the short distance to the club.

I go up in the elevator and come out in reception. "Hey," I say to Gail when she smiles at me. "Is Huxley around?" It suddenly occurs to me that he might be in a meeting, or even out somewhere—I should have checked.

But she says, "Yes, he's in his office. Hold on." She lifts up her phone and buzzes him. "Ms. Tremblay is here to see you," she says. She listens, and I imagine him closing his eyes for a moment, maybe massaging his forehead. Will he refuse to see me? But then she says, "Of course," and she puts the phone down. "Please," she says, "go in."

"Thank you." I head down the corridor, knock on the door, and go inside, closing the door behind me.

He has a large office, not unlike Titus's, with a great view over the city. Two of his mother's abstract paintings hang on the walls, bringing a blaze of color to the room. His desk sits in front of the large windows, and it's currently covered with paperwork. It looks as if he's working on his accounts. He's alone, though, standing behind his desk, in the process of putting on his suit jacket. He does that when he's being formal, meeting clients or going into a meeting, donning it like a suit of armor.

"Hey," he says. He smiles, but it doesn't reach his eyes.

"Hey." I walk forward and stand in front of his desk hesitantly. "I'm sorry to bother you."

"It's okay, I'm just going through some figures." He drops his gaze to the desk and squares some papers. "What can I do for you?"

"I wanted to let you know…" I swallow hard. Why is this so hard to say? Out with it, Elizabeth. I take a deep breath. "You're off the hook. I'm not pregnant."

His gaze snaps up to mine. "Oh," he says softly.

We stare at each other for a long time. He doesn't say anything, but his beautiful gray eyes are filled with a mixture of emotions.

"It's a good thing," I say brightly.

"Yeah."

"It's for the best."

"Yeah."

"I should never have asked you," I say huskily. "I've ruined our friendship, and that was the last thing I wanted. I'm absolutely gutted to have lost you, and… I'm so sorry."

He tips his head to the side. His eyes lose the frosty look they've carried since our conversation in The Crescent, and survey me gently. "You haven't lost me. Time heals most wounds. I'll always be here for you."

His unexpected words are my undoing. I press my hand to my mouth and burst into tears.

I'm horrified, because I rarely cry, and I'm sure it's the last thing he wants. I don't want him to think I'm trying to manipulate him. I half expect him to just watch me, to snap at me, or even to ask me to leave.

But he just says, "Aw," and he walks around the table and pulls me into his arms for a hug.

"I'm sorry," I squeak.

"It's okay."

"I really thought it had worked."

He sighs. "Yeah. Me too."

I bury my face in his shirt. He smells familiar, warm and masculine, and his arms are tight around me. I've missed him so much.

"I know it's for the best," I whisper. "But I feel so incredibly sad."

He blows out a long breath. "Me too."

We stand there like that for a long time. To anyone else, it might look romantic, or at the least like two good friends comforting each other. But I'm sure he feels the same as me—that it's an ending, like the last glimmer of a firework, the final chance we had to make it work before it faded away to nothing.

Chapter Seventeen

Huxley

The next two weeks pass swiftly. I'm busy at work, and I throw myself into the rest of the refurbishments, getting under Victoria's feet until she yells at me to go home for Christ's sake and give her some space. At the weekends, I have Joanna, and that passes a few pleasant hours. I take her to the zoo and the aquarium, and we also have a movie night, and watch TV while we're in our pajamas, eating popcorn.

When I do get some spare time, I do what I can to help Mack and Sidnie plan for their wedding. They want to keep it relatively simple, and Cameron Brown, who owns the yacht they're hiring, is happy to organize the food and entertainment. But there are other bits and pieces that need arranging, and I call on some of my contacts to help Mack get what he wants, as it's at relatively short notice.

The invitations go out, and they state they want the wedding to be smart casual, so I'm not going to have to worry about wearing a tux. Instead, Mack and I choose a cream linen suit for the big day, with a light-blue shirt for a touch of color, and decide to omit a tie.

Sidnie will be wearing a white dress, but she's decided not to have bridesmaids, as they both want to keep the affair very relaxed and more like a summer party. Her father has just finished his last round of treatment and appears to be doing well, so all she wants is for him to be able to give her away.

I'm looking forward to seeing my best mate marry the girl of his dreams. Mack's been a different man since he met Sidnie, and he's worked so hard over the last few years and deserves some personal happiness.

Of course, Elizabeth will be on the yacht, which means we'll be in relatively close contact for a couple of days. That's going to be hard. Even though I insisted she hadn't ruined our friendship, there's no doubt that things between us have changed. I don't blame her. I blame myself. I'm the one who blackmailed her into giving me one night after I jumped off the Sky Tower. She made it quite clear she didn't want a relationship, and it's my fault that I ignored that.

I know I've been cool toward her, and that it's upset her, but I can't help it. I'm shocked and embarrassed that I wildly overestimated my powers of seduction. I honestly believed that once we slept together, she wouldn't be able to walk away. Somehow, I thought it was just a matter of time before we got together. And I'm stunned that even though we had fantastic sex, she's chosen to go to England over being with me.

I was also secretly taken aback that I didn't get her pregnant. I know the experts say there's only a thirty percent chance of it happening during sex, but I'm a relatively young, fertile, red-blooded male. I've only got to look at a girl and I'll knock her up, right? That's what your parents and the school warn you when you're young, anyway. I also felt that my enthusiasm in the bedroom would be a factor in encouraging my little swimmers to reach their destination.

I know it's not a tragic failure. For God's sake, some people, like Elizabeth's sister Penelope, try for years without falling, and have to resort to scientific help. But I was so sure it would happen. I've always felt that if I worked hard enough, and if I switched on the charm, I'd get what I want, but this is the first time I've had to accept that I have no control.

I hate that I let her down. But there's nothing I can do about it if she's decided it's over between us.

Things have been a little easier since she came to my office, but I'm not sure we'll ever be the same. I'm very rarely moody, but I know I've not been myself since it happened. I've been off my food and feeling low, which is very unusual for me. Mack told me I'm lovesick, and even though I told him to fuck off, privately I conceded he was right. I miss her, and I'm angry and frustrated—not with her necessarily, but with the world, with Fate, and with myself.

I have great belief in my ability to talk other people into doing what I want. It's a talent I developed at a young age, and it's very rare that I fail. So I feel as if the rug has been whipped out from under my feet. It's shaken me, and even though my feelings toward her haven't changed, I find it difficult to be around her. I want to try and convince her to stay with me, to force her to listen, to browbeat her into submission. But I can't do that. I've got to let her go, and it's turning out to be the hardest thing I've ever had to do.

In a way it's a good thing that I haven't seen much of her at all over the past few weeks. She's been busy working on the IVF project with Titus and Mack, and the only time I've seen her is at our usual Friday meetings, when she's been the last to arrive and the first to leave. But at the wedding we're going to be in close proximity, and that's going to be a challenge.

The guests have been requested to arrive by one p.m. with the hope of being ready to sail at two. I catch an Uber and get there at twelve, hoping I can help Mack with any last-minute organization. He's already there when I arrive, and tells me that Sidnie is picking up her folks and will be there shortly.

"Come and look around the yacht," he says. "It's fucking amazing."

I have to admit, it's a great location to tie the knot, and maybe the most sumptuous place I've ever stayed. It has twenty-eight passenger cabins, all of which will be filled tomorrow night when we pick up his family in the Bay of Islands, and over a hundred crew. It has a helipad on the bow, a swimming pool, spacious viewing decks, a dining saloon, a licensed bar, and an observation lounge. The free-flowing layout encourages indoor-outdoor living, with curved sofas and chairs both inside and on the deck, lots of cushions, glass tables, and plenty of lamps for when the sun sets. The whole place is decorated in creams, light blues, oak, and mother of pearl.

"Snazzy, isn't it?" Mack comments as we make our way back.

"It's fantastic."

We lean on the railing on the upper deck and look down at the gangway, where the crew are carrying supplies onto the yacht.

"It's a shame Joanna couldn't come," Mack says. "There are going to be other kids here. She'd have loved it."

"Yeah, she's sorry she's missing it, but Brandy's parents insisted she be present for their big do." It's Brandy's parents' fortieth wedding anniversary, and they're having a huge party where they live in Wellington. "I could have argued with them, but I wanted to be able to concentrate on my best man duties."

Mack grins. "Fair enough."

"Brandy's taking Billy down to meet them," I tell him.

His eyebrows rise. "Oh, that's a big step for her. Do you think they'll like him?"

"I think they'll adore him."

"What do you think of him?"

"He's solid and dependable, just what she needs. I'm pleased for her. And he gets on well with Joanna."

Mack glances across at me. "You okay with that?"

"Of course," I say, surprised. "Why wouldn't I be?"

Mack studies me for a moment. He hesitates. Then he says, "You should tell her, you know."

"Tell who what?"

"Elizabeth."

"What about her?"

"You should tell her the truth," he says. "About Brandy."

I look at his odd, planetary eyes. "I don't know what you mean."

"I think you do."

There's a long pause. My heart's racing. He's never spoken to me about this before.

"You fucking idiot," he says, with some affection. "What am I going to do with you?"

My throat tightening, I look down at the dock and watch a group of people getting out of a taxi. "Your blushing bride's here," I say. "We'd better go down."

"Yeah, come on." He claps me on the back, and we descend the steps to where Sidnie and her family are walking up the gangway.

The beautiful autumn day feels more like late summer, and the breeze that blows across us is warm and pleasant. Sidnie looks absolutely stunning today, full of joy and excitement at her upcoming wedding. Her blonde hair hangs around her head in crazy curls that bob in the breeze, and her eyes are bright and sparkling. She throws her arms around Mack, and they exchange a long kiss before breaking apart so he can greet her family.

"Welcome," I say when they're all done. "Come with me and I'll show you to your cabins, and then you can explore."

Mack's put me in charge of cabin allocation. It took a surprising amount of time to organize. Couples are easy, but there are a lot of single people coming, and not everyone's keen on sharing a cabin. I'm sharing with Titus, and Victoria's sharing with my sister, Evie, as they're good friends, but I've given Elizabeth her own cabin. I figured it's the least I can do.

The next hour is busy as everyone arrives. Even if Mack hadn't asked me to be his best man, I'd still have wanted to help make the day run smoothly, but now I'm determined that nothing is going to go wrong for him.

First, I introduce myself to the Chief Steward, and ask if he would mind finding me rather than Mack if there are any issues, and promising to help wherever I can.

Then I go through the cabins introducing myself to everyone, checking to make sure they're settled and comfortable, and sorting out any problems. I show Sidnie's parents to the large cabin I allocated them at the end where it's nice and quiet, and make her mother promise to let me know if they need anything at all. I pass on to the chef that Mack's colleague, Eoin, is a diabetic, and that Sidnie's friend, Caro, is gluten-free, as both of them forgot to let anyone know about their dietary requirements. Mack's brother, Jamie, and his girlfriend Emma are pregnant, and I source some extra pillows for her as she's having some issues sleeping.

I make sure everyone has a drink as they come into the main saloon and out onto the viewing decks, move umbrellas around to make sure people are in the shade, source sun lotion and shawls for those who hadn't realized it would be both sunny and breezy, and quietly tick names off on my list so we know when everyone's aboard.

"You were born to play best man, weren't you?"

The amused voice comes from behind me, and I turn to see Elizabeth watching me with a smile. I hadn't seen her come aboard, and the sight of her makes me catch my breath. She's wearing a navy-and-white-striped top and a navy blazer with white cropped trousers and deck shoes, and a pair of gold-rimmed sunglasses shaped like hearts.

"You look like you were born on a yacht," I tell her.

"So do you," she says with a smile.

I look down at myself—I'm wearing a casual light-blue shirt over the top of cream chinos and my usual Ray Ban aviators. "I'll change into shorts later," I say. "Have you seen the pool?"

"Not yet. I had to drop Nymph off with Arthur so I'm a bit late."

"Come with me," I say, gesturing inside with my head. "I'll show you to your cabin."

"Thank you." She follows me inside, and we walk slowly through the saloon, smiling at Sidnie's sister and her husband, who are sitting up at the bar, sipping their first cocktail.

"What a gorgeous place to get married," Elizabeth says.

"Yeah. Perfect if you want to keep it relatively small." I indicate for her to precede me through the doorway, and we go down the stairs to the lower deck where the cabins are based. "I put you down here," I tell her, showing her to the cabin in the middle and opening the door. It's a twin, but she's the only occupant. "It should be quieter here with fewer people passing to go up the stairs."

One of the stewards has already brought her bag here, and she lifts it onto the bed, then looks around. "It's lovely. Are you sure I don't need to share with someone? I don't mind."

I lift my sunglasses onto the top of my head and lean on the door jamb, sliding my hands into my pockets. "Not so far. It'll get busier tomorrow when we pick up Mack's family in the Bay, but I've worked it all out and you should be okay."

"Thank you." She sends me a smile. "So you're sharing with Titus?"

"Yeah, we've got a twin."

"He knows you snore, right?"

I give her a wry look. She chuckles. "I'm teasing. You didn't snore. I probably did though."

"No, you were as quiet as a rather elegant, beautiful mouse."

She meets my eyes, and for a moment our gazes lock, as I think about that night—that one, wondrous night—when she curled up close to me, and I held her in my arms as we slept.

Then she clears her throat and looks away. "I'd better unpack."

"Yeah. I think everyone's here, so we'll be casting off soon."

"Cool, okay."

I give her one last look, my gaze lingering on her chocolate-brown-silk hair as it swings forward to hide her face, and then I go out and close the door behind me.

There's no time for me to dwell on our exchange because it's just past two p.m. Cameron Brown greets everyone on deck and makes sure we all have a drink, and he gives a brief safety talk, then a longer welcome speech, and ends by saying he hopes we have a fantastic two days. Then party time begins as they cast off the ropes and the yacht slowly heads out through the harbor to the deeper blue waters of the Pacific Ocean.

It proves to be a fun and relaxing afternoon as everyone gradually settles in. Champagne flows freely, and the stewards regularly bring out trays of canapés for the guests to soak up the alcohol. Most of us change into swim gear, and we're in and out of the pool for several hours, interspersing a swim with having a drink or a snooze on one of the sun loungers as the coastline of the North Island slowly sails by.

I try to avoid Elizabeth without looking like I'm avoiding her. When we're near each other, I either want to kiss her or get on my knees and beg her to stay with me, and neither of those seems like an option she'd be pleased with. So I figure it's better if I try to keep my distance and, if possible, not even tempt myself by looking at her.

It's not easy, especially when she changes into the smallest bikini I've ever laid eyes on, with two miniscule turquoise triangles that barely cover her breasts. She's lost weight over the past couple of weeks, and she's on the slim side, but she's still hot enough that I have to stop my tongue rolling on the floor like a cartoon character. Mack glances at me and nudges Sidnie, who giggles, and Victoria rolls her eyes and whispers something to Evie, who looks at me with much amusement.

"Glad I can provide some comedic entertainment," I tell them, disgruntled, and walk off to the bar to drown my sorrows.

Titus joins me there and tries not to laugh when I glare at him.

"Don't start," I say.

"Wouldn't dream of it." He leans on the bar, gestures out at the pool, and says quietly, "Are they an item?"

I follow his gaze to where Victoria and Evie are lying on the loungers together, whispering together and laughing. "I think it's heading that way."

"I didn't realize." He smiles. "It's about time."

He's referring to Victoria. She's very private about her love life, and because of that I'm not sure how many partners she's had over the years since her transition, but I don't think it's many. Evie's been out since she was sixteen though, and she's not afraid to speak up when she's attracted to someone.

"What about you?" I ask him, and have a swig from the bottle of Speights I just ordered. "I thought you might have brought a date to the wedding."

"Nah, I'm on a hiatus from dating," he says. "I'm working fourteen-hour days at the moment and there's just no time, and anyway I don't want the complication. Sex is great. It's everything else that comes with it that I find frustrating. You know what I mean?"

"Yep."

"I feel bad saying that. It's not that I'm not prepared to make an effort. But I just find the constant communication exhausting."

"Well, you did insist on dating the fastest talking girl on planet Earth," I point out. "Most people speak at around one hundred and forty words a minute. Maisey spoke at least double that."

"True." He swigs his beer and gives me a mischievous look. "She even talked during sex."

"I'm guessing you don't mean in a dirty sense."

"Oh no. I mean literally discussing what she needed at the supermarket while we were at it."

That makes me laugh. "Seriously?"

"I've never met a girl like it. She was sweet and sexy, but it was like she had no filter at all. Most off-putting when you're, you know, trying to concentrate."

I chuckle. "I'm not sure there's anyone coming on board who you'll find interesting either."

"Nah, that's cool. I'm going to drink myself into a coma and sleep for forty-eight hours."

"Sounds like a plan." I have another drink, then tell him, "I heard from Heidi a few days ago, by the way."

His lips curve up. "Oh? How is she?"

"She's okay. She's had a bit of a nasty breakup with her boyfriend."

"Oh no, really? What was he like?"

"I never met him, but he sounds like a cunt. God knows why she hooked up with him. She said he was very controlling and jealous. Made her life a misery by the sounds of it. I was tempted to fly over there and sort him out."

"Well if you do form a posse, count me in."

"Will do. Anyway, she's coming back during the summer holidays for six weeks." Heidi is a primary school teacher in Exeter, in England. Our mother is English, and after she finished her teaching degree, Heidi went over there to visit our grandparents during her big Overseas Experience, and loved it so much that she decided to stay and teach there.

"Cool," he says, "it'll be great to catch up." I hold his gaze as I sip my beer, and he gives me a wry look. "Stop it," he says. "That was a long time ago."

"She was sixteen," I say. "I had to stop Dad from getting his shotgun."

"It was one kiss," he scolds. "She might have been only sixteen, but she was wearing this bikini that was…" He trails off as I raise my eyebrows. "Anyway, it was her fault. I said no, but she was all young and… tempting," he finishes, somewhat lamely.

"Actually, I believe you," I tell him. "She's always been a minx." I tap my bottle to his. "Come on. Let's see whether Mack's managed to dunk Sidnie yet."

It turns out that he has, and now the two of them are dancing in the middle of the pool, kissing occasionally, bathed in the warm April sun. Usually, when Mack's away from his laptop he gets a twitch in one eye and a thousand-mile stare, but today he looks deliriously happy, as if work couldn't be further from his mind. I never thought he'd be like that with a woman. I feel a deep and uncharacteristic stab of envy that he managed to get his girl.

I stop at the edge of the pool and look over at Elizabeth, letting my gaze linger for a while, as she's not looking at me. She's lying on a sun lounger, reading a book, dressed only in her skimpy bikini. Jesus. It shouldn't be allowed. I wish I was her boyfriend, and I could go over to her, kneel by her side, and offer to rub sun lotion into her soft skin. I wish I could kiss her, and dance with her in the pool, and have people compliment us on how happy we look.

But it's not meant to be, and so I turn away and begin going around seeing if anyone wants a drink, and try to put her to the back of my mind.

Chapter Eighteen

Elizabeth

The first day on board the yacht passes smoothly. Around six, we gravitate indoors to the saloon for dinner, and I'm awed by the amazing buffet the crew have put on—platters filled with freshly caught fish and seafood, cured meats, and a variety of gorgeous salads, as both Mack and Sidnie are vegetarians.

Afterward, we move back out onto the deck for more swimming, conversation, champagne drinking, and dancing, as the music is turned up, and the sun begins to sink behind the land to the west.

Huxley's avoiding me. It's quite obvious to me, although I don't know if anyone else has picked up on it. He's not cold, exactly, and he includes me in the conversation, and is quick to get me another drink or anything else I might need. But our usual teasing camaraderie is gone, and he spends most of the time on the other side of the pool, or off mingling with the guests.

I should have expected it, but it makes me sad. I can't rant and rail at him though, because it's all my fault. I suspected this would happen if we slept together. Two people can't turn off their passion for one another like a tap and not expect consequences. I've hurt him badly, and I've made things ten times more difficult for myself. And in the end, it was all for nothing. Now I'm tortured with memories of that one night, and I don't even have a baby to show for my misery.

But it's done, and there's no point in crying about it. I just have to get through the next couple of days as best as I can, and then I can bury myself in work and keep any contact between the two of us to a minimum.

It would be easier if I just stayed in my cabin, but this is Mack's wedding, and I don't want to be a stick-in-the-mud. So I pin a smile on my face, join in the conversation, and do my best not to look as if

I'm missing my left arm every time Huxley sees me and turns the other way.

It doesn't make it easier that he looks so gorgeous. He's lost a little weight over the past few weeks, which concerns me, especially when I see the faint shadows under his eyes, but he's still easily the most gorgeous guy on the yacht. He spends most of the afternoon bare-chested in his swim shorts, and honestly the guy has such a fantastic physique that it makes me feel a little faint. Those muscular arms and amazing biceps a girl could sink her teeth into… And those legs… all tanned and muscled. And his flat stomach with that happy trail of hair disappearing into his shorts… And the way he walks around as if he owns the place, with those sunglasses and his sexy smile. Does he know how good he looks? Of course he fucking does. He's doing it on purpose to show me what I'm missing, I'm sure of it.

But we keep our distance, and I pass the evening talking to Caro and Hana, and Victoria and Evie, as we all gradually get drunk on champagne while we watch Mack and Sidnie dancing together on the deck.

"I'm so jealous," I announce when I've had far too much to drink. "They're far too happy. It shouldn't be allowed. Happiness should be doled out proportionately."

"Aw," Hana says, "we need to get you a date."

"You might stand more of a chance if you don't sit talking to four lesbians all night," Evie points out, causing us all to dissolve into giggles.

"The pickings are a bit slim this weekend," Victoria states. "Not many single guys."

"What about Titus?" Caro asks. "He seems nice. And he's gorgeous."

"Too moody," I reply. "He's like the Dark Knight without the cape."

"Or Huxley?" Hana suggests. "He's single, isn't he?"

I just sigh.

"Oh yeah," Evie says, "I keep meaning to ask. How did the trip go?"

I roll my head to look over at him. He's sitting talking to Mack's colleagues, Cherry, Eoin, and Kai and his wife. He's changed into a blue-and-white-quartered polo shirt and cream chinos. As I watch, he picks up a navy-blue sweater and pulls it on, briefly revealing a strip of tanned skin on his stomach as he lifts his arms before he tugs the sweater down.

"Amazing," I say, and sigh again.

"What's this?" Caro and Hana ask together.

"Elizabeth wants a baby," Victoria states. "They went away for the night and Hux tried to knock her up, but it didn't work."

"That's the most depressing one-sentence summary of my life I can imagine," I tell her, and they all laugh.

"But the sex was good?" Hana asks.

"Oh yeah. The sex was fucking amazing."

"So… I don't see the problem?"

"I'm moving to England for two years."

"Ah."

"Do you have to go?" Caro asks.

"No, but it's such a great opportunity, and anyway, all relationships sour eventually." I wince as they exchange a look. "I meant all my relationships. And I don't want that to happen to us."

Even as the words leave my mouth, though, I feel a pang of regret. Things have already soured between Hux and me. Damn, I'm such a fool.

A steward comes over with a platter of nibbles, and the conversation moves on. It's dark now, getting late, and it's going to be a big day tomorrow. I'm tired, I've drunk more than I should, and I feel suddenly weary.

"I think I'll call it a day," I tell the others. They protest politely, but I smile and say goodnight, then head inside.

Part of me wonders whether Huxley will catch up with me and try to stop me leaving. But he doesn't. I walk down the steps to my cabin, go in, and lock the door. Then I sit on the edge of one of the beds and flop back.

I feel weighed down by sadness and regret. I shouldn't have slept with Huxley. I've spoiled everything. I want things to go back to the way they were, but that's physically impossible. I've made my bed, and I have to lie in it, I know that.

It doesn't mean I have to be happy about it, though.

I get ready for bed, then slide beneath the covers and lie there looking out at the stars, feeling the yacht rocking beneath me, and imagining Huxley curled up behind me, his breath warm on my neck as we both fall asleep.

*

I sleep well in the end, and wake up naturally just after six. I have a quick shower and dress, then head up to the saloon for breakfast around seven.

We moored overnight at Urupukapuka, the largest island in the Bay of Islands, and we've not yet set sail for Paihia, where we're picking up Mack's family. Outside, the rich green bush that covers most of the island contrasts with the deep blue of the ocean and the cornflower-blue sky. It's a beautiful morning, already hot and sunny, and the forecast is the same all day.

I'm guessing a few people are nursing hangovers as most of the tables are empty. Mack and Sidnie are there. They aren't bothering with the tradition of not seeing each other before the wedding and are happily tucking into a cooked breakfast at a table with Huxley and Victoria.

I ask the chef for scrambled eggs to go with my bacon and toast, and take the plate over to join them, as it seems rude to sit at another table on my own.

"Morning," they all say as I take the remaining chair.

"Hey." I smile at the steward as he comes up to offer me coffee. "Yes, please." I wait until he's poured the cup and retreated before I continue. "How are you two doing today?"

"We're good," Mack says. "All ready for the big day."

"Get plenty of sleep?" I ask innocently.

Mack opens his mouth to reply, then catches my eye and grins. "Some."

"Yeah," Huxley says, "don't think we didn't notice the boat rocking when the two of you went to bed."

Sidnie blushes, and I scold, "Hux, honestly."

"You started it," he says.

"It's a beautiful day for getting married," I say, sending him a mock glare before changing the subject. "How excited are you on a scale of one to ten, Sid?"

"Fifty-two," she says, and giggles. "I am sorry. We must be very annoying at the moment."

"Of course not," Victoria says, "if you can't be excited on your wedding day, when can you?"

"True. I just can't wait to show you my dress," she says to Mack. "It's so beautiful."

"You're beautiful," he says, and pulls her toward him for a kiss.

Huxley rolls his eyes, but smiles at me. "Sleep well?" he asks.

I nod. "The bed was lovely and comfortable. You?"

"Titus snores."

"Oh, I thought there was something wrong with the engine."

He chuckles, and I grin. His eyes meet mine then, smiling and warm, and my heart lifts. Oh, it would be so nice if we could return to the way we were. I miss him so much.

I'm not going to get much of a chance to talk to him this morning, though. As soon as he finishes breakfast, he's off helping the staff to get organized for the day. By nine we've cast off and we're heading for Paihia, and once there it takes an hour to ferry Mack's family onto the yacht. Huxley's kept busy showing the guests to their cabins and making sure everyone has everything they need.

I'm happy to help, but it seems as if everything is well organized, so I keep out of the way on the deck and just sit and read while everyone comes on board. It's only when I spot Huxley and Mack deep in conversation to one side, looking concerned, that I put my book down and go over.

"Everything all right?" I ask.

"Yeah," Mack says, "we've just had one more person turn up than we anticipated. My grandfather's brother, Wiremu, told us he wasn't coming, but he changed his mind at the last minute, which isn't very helpful."

Huxley has spread out his list of guests and what cabins he's allocated them to on the table. I join him in looking at them, and quickly spot the problem. "My cabin's the only one with a single occupant."

"It's okay," Huxley says, "I'm working on it."

"Put him in with me," I say. "I don't mind."

He gives me a direct look. "That's very kind, but I'm not putting a strange older man in your cabin."

Mack runs his hand through his hair. "I'll tell Wiremu we don't have the space. He did say he wasn't coming. He'll have to go back, that's all there is to it."

"Of course not," I say swiftly, not wanting anything to upset Mack on his big day. "Look, Hux, put him in with Titus, and you'll have to share with me."

Huxley raises an eyebrow. "Seriously?"

I hesitate. "If you'd rather not, then you share with Wiremu and put Titus in with me. It's only one night. I'm planning to party into the early hours anyway." I smile at Mack.

"Are you sure?" he says, relieved.

"Of course. Go and tell him he's fine to stay."

Mack nods and goes off.

Huxley looks at his piece of paper and hovers his pencil over his cabin. Then he looks up at me. "Who would you prefer to share with?" His eyes are gentle. "I don't mind if you choose Titus."

"I'd rather share with you, silly. But I understand if you'd rather not."

We study each other for a moment. Then he drops his gaze to the paper, crosses his name out, and adds Wiremu's name to the cabin. He writes his own name above mine.

"Thanks," he says. "Mack was freaking out at having to send him away."

"Oh we couldn't have that. We'll be fine. We can be grown-ups about it, can't we?"

"Of course," he says.

But my heart's racing, and from the look in his eyes, I'm sure his heart is too.

It doesn't mean anything. Like I said, we'll be up until the early hours, and then we'll probably crash out without a second thought. The last thing we should do is sleep together again. I'm already miserable; I don't want to make things worse.

But there's magic in the air today. Mack and Sidnie's happiness is like glitter floating on the air through the yacht, and I can't help but get some of it on me.

*

The yacht sets sail from Paihia, and begins its tour of the Bay of Islands, following which it will pass the Cavalli Islands and sail up to Doubtless Bay before looping back once again.

The yacht is a lot busier now everyone's on board. Sidnie is already locked away with her mother, sister, and best friends getting ready for her big moment. Huxley and Mack spend a couple of hours introducing people and playing hosts while stewards go around with drinks and canapés, and then around midday everyone starts disappearing for a short rest before they get ready for the wedding.

As Sidnie's getting ready in their cabin, Mack joins Huxley in his old cabin to change, leaving me alone in mine, at least for now. They wanted a relaxed wedding, and I thought I'd go for trousers as I didn't want to spend the whole day trying to stop the sea breeze blowing up my skirt. I was going to pick something cream or maybe light blue to go with the ocean theme, but then my gaze fell on the outfit I ended up with, and I was lost. It's cherry-red, with a boned bodice, shoestring straps, and wide-leg pants. It's perfect for a summer wedding, and I rarely wear red, so it's also a little different.

I leave my hair down but add a clip with a small red flower behind one ear, and touch up my makeup, adding a red gloss to my lips that again I rarely wear.

When I'm done, and it's around 1:30 p.m., I take a deep breath and head up the stairs to the saloon.

I see Huxley immediately, standing with Mack in the wide doorway leading onto the deck, talking to Cameron. They're both wearing cream linen suits and light-blue shirts, and they're both heartbreakingly handsome.

Huxley glances around and spots me, and I have the pleasure of watching his eyes widen as he sees my outfit. He doesn't smile as I walk toward them, and when I stop before him, he just lets his gaze slip down me, then slowly brushes it back up.

"Hey, Elizabeth," Mack says. "Wow, you look gorgeous. Doesn't she, Hux?"

"Mm," he says noncommittally.

"Don't worry about him," Mack says, "he's lost the power of speech, that's all."

Huxley shoots him a wry look, then turns away to talk to Cameron as he asks him something about the guest list.

"Look at you," I say to Mack, not sure whether Huxley likes my outfit or not. "You scrub up well."

"Even brushed my teeth," he says, holding up an arm so I can hug him.

"She's a lucky girl," I tell him, kissing him on the cheek.

"I'm the lucky one. I still can't believe she said yes." He walks me away a few feet, then lets me go. "How are you doing?" he asks.

"You just worry about yourself on your wedding day, Mack Hart."

"I'm sorry I shouted at you at Titus's office," he says. "You know it's only because I'm worried about the two of you."

"I know. But you shouldn't be. It's all over."

"Yeah," he says, "right." He glances at Huxley, then back at me. "He's not doing great."

I follow his gaze, and watch Huxley laughing with Cameron. "He looks okay to me."

"It's a cover. He's lost a load of weight." He runs his gaze down me. "So have you."

"I've been busy."

"I know it's none of my business, but you're both killing me." He looks genuinely pained.

My throat tightens. "Don't. It's hard enough as it is. I'm hanging on by my fingernails."

"He loves you, you know."

My eyes water. "Mack! You'll ruin my makeup."

He sighs, then smiles as Huxley walks up to us. I sniff and study my shoes.

"Everything all right?" Huxley asks.

"Yep," Mack says. "What's going on?"

"I wondered if you felt like getting married, bro?"

Mack grins. "Yeah. Let's do it."

"Come on then. Cameron says it's time to get organized." Huxley glances at me and frowns, but I give him a small smile, and he steers Mack out onto the deck.

"You okay?" It's Victoria, who comes up and slips an arm around my shoulders. "Those guys making your life a misery?"

"Nah. *I'm* making my life a misery." I sigh and then smile at her. She's wearing a smart navy pantsuit with a petal-pink blouse, and she's twisted her hair up in an elegant chignon. "Wow, you look stunning," I tell her.

She flushes. "Thank you. So do you. I love that outfit. No wonder Huxley's jaw was scraping the deck."

I'm saved from a reply as her gaze is drawn to Evie. Hux's sister isn't as tall as Victoria, but she looks striking today in a long silvery-gray dress, with her dark-blonde hair that she normally wears in a tight bun when she's working as a police officer now tumbling around her shoulders in bountiful curls.

"Ah," I say. "So that's why you're all glowy."

Victoria laughs, but she's lit up like a streetlamp, and she doesn't deny it.

"I'm so happy for you," I tell her. "You deserve it."

She tears her gaze away and brings it back to me. "So do you," she says. "You act like you don't think you deserve love and affection, but you do. You've been unlucky in love, and that's going to make you wary, but you mustn't close your heart off forever."

I look away, out at the coast drifting past us, the emerald-green forests in the distance, and the golden sands leading to the rich blue water.

"Sweetie," she continues, "it's none of my business, and I understand why you've made the decisions you have. And I know Huxley's been a bit of a tomcat at times. But he's the best man I know. Mack comes a close second, and Titus a moody third, and Hux isn't perfect by any means, but he's not far from it."

"You've been friends a long time," I say softly. "You've never had feelings for him?"

"Of course I have, darling. I've been half in love with him for donkeys' years. He's an easy man to love. But we know each other too well. Nobody wants to know how the sausages are made, you know?"

That makes me laugh. "Nicely put."

She looks out at where he's on the deck directing guests to their seats. "Elizabeth, about what happened all those years ago... I know he hurt you, but give him a break. I can't say any more, but it's not what you think."

I frown, because it's so similar to what Mack said at Titus's office. "What do you mean?"

She hesitates, but she's stopped from saying more by Evie walking up. "Hey you," Evie says, reaching up to kiss her cheek. "Time to find a seat."

"Yeah. Come on, Elizabeth. Let's go and watch Mack get hitched."

I follow them out onto the deck, puzzled by her words. What are she and Mack implying? And why won't they tell me instead of hinting at the fucking thing?

But there's no time to ponder, because people are taking their seats among the rows of folding chairs that the crew have placed in lines on the deck. They've erected a canopy to protect us all from the sun, and at the front is a simple white altar where Mack is standing talking to Cameron.

Huxley is directing people to chairs, making sure there aren't any gaps and that Sidnie's family and Mack's grandparents are at the front, ensuring Jamie's Emma is comfortable with a cushion, and bending to chat quietly to Mack's young cousins, explaining that if they sit quietly for the duration of the ceremony, he'll let them dunk him in the pool later, which makes me smile.

I sit at the end of the second row near the railing, with the ocean on my right, and a perfect view of the ceremony. Seagulls cry overhead, mingling with the song that one of Mack's cousins has just started playing on his guitar. Mack had told me that Sidnie had left the choice of entrance music to him, and I smile as Stevie Wonder's *Isn't She Lovely* fills the autumn air.

With everyone seated, Huxley joins Mack at the front, and we all turn as Sidnie and her father appear in the saloon. The crew are standing in a line either side of the path through to the deck, all dressed in smart white uniforms, and they toss handfuls of rose petals in front of them as they walk through.

Tears prick my eyes as I get my first glimpse of Sidnie. The floor-length skirt of her gown consists of layers of white tulle, and the bodice has a layer of lace that flows down to her wrists. It's backless, with a simple tie at the nape of her neck that dangles down her back with a single pearl. Her blonde hair hangs past her shoulders in a riot of curls, with the sides rolled back and pinned over the circlet that holds her veil. The breeze has come up a bit, but it just makes her look as if she's floating, as her hair and veil and skirt flutter.

I look at Mack, and I can see he's genuinely taken aback at her beauty. This has all happened fast for him, and I have to admit I wondered whether he was getting married too quickly, but right now I can see that it doesn't matter how long they've known each other. He's deliriously happy, and he just wants to put his ring on her finger and promise to love her in front of all his friends and family.

I look at Huxley, and my heart jumps. He's not looking at Sidnie; he's looking at me. He holds my gaze for a long moment, and I can't look away, captivated by how handsome he is, and unable to miss how he takes my breath away.

I thought it was all over. *Yeah, right*, Mack said when I told him that. And he was right. It's not over. I'm not sure it'll ever be over. God, I'm such a fool.

Chapter Nineteen

Huxley

It's the first time I've been a best man. I've spent the past twenty-four hours making sure people are comfortable and happy, and it's just felt like an extension of my day job, which comes so easily to me I'm convinced anyone could do it.

But as I stand with Mack, and I watch him tremble as his bride-to-be approaches down the aisle, I suddenly feel the real reason I'm here. I'm the equivalent to Sidnie's father for the groom. I'm a symbol of Mack's past, and I'm giving him away to her, helping him pass from bachelorhood to the respectable role of husband and, God willing, father, in time.

For so long we've all—me, Mack, Victoria, Titus, Elizabeth—lived without a thought for the future. Selfishly devoting our lives to work and fun, convinced we'd be young forever, and certain that we didn't want the tie of a relationship, not wanting the complication, as Titus said. I wonder if he's feeling what I am right now—that sudden shock like a bee sting inside me, as I watch Mack waiting for his bride, and realize I'm experiencing not smugness at being the single one, but envy, bone-deep, at the thought that he's making that transition onto the train into manhood that I've somehow not managed to board.

He inhales deeply and blows out a long breath, and I rest a hand on his shoulder and squeeze. "She looks like a princess," I murmur.

"I don't deserve her," he whispers. "I don't know why she picked me."

"Because you're soul mates."

"I didn't think you believed in that."

"I didn't, until now."

He glances at me and smiles. "I'm glad you're here."

"Me, too," I say, my voice husky. "Good luck, bro."

I let him go, and he moves forward to stand next to Sidnie as she reaches the altar, turns to face him, and lifts her veil back.

Cameron begins to speak, reciting a Māori karakia or prayer, to invoke the spiritual goodwill of the gathering, and increase the likelihood of a good outcome. After this, he greets everyone, first in Māori, then in English, and the ceremony proceeds, blessed by the autumn sun. I feel a strange sense of surrealism as I listen to them say their vows and promise to love each other for the rest of their lives. I've been to weddings before, of course, but the words they're saying to each other seem to hold more meaning today.

When it's time for them to exchange rings, I fumble at the box with uncharacteristic inelegance, oddly emotional as I hand them over. But maybe it's not odd. I know why I'm feeling like this.

I look across at Elizabeth, and I'm not surprised to find her watching me. Her eyes are wet, and as I watch she smiles and brushes at her cheeks.

Do I believe in soul mates?

If so, then does that mean I have one, too?

I can buy a girl chocolate and flowers the same as any man, but I've never thought of myself as a romantic person, and I've tended to mock anyone who talks hearts and flowers. But what if there is such a thing as my soul mate? If there is one woman who's meant for me?

Looking into Elizabeth's eyes, my stomach flips.

Have I lost her, just before I even realized who she is?

But there's no time to ruminate on it, because the short, simple ceremony is coming to an end.

"I now pronounce you man and wife," Cameron says, smiling. "You may kiss the bride!"

"That's the easy part," Mack says, pulling her toward him, and she laughs and throws her arms around his neck as they exchange a long, heartfelt kiss.

After that, they sign the official documents with me and Sidnie's sister as witnesses, and then it's time for photos, which always takes longer than you think. Then it's cocktail hour, while a couple of Mack's cousins play guitars and one of his aunts sings.

When Cameron comes over to me and says it's time, I nod to Koro, Mack's grandfather, and he gets to his feet and starts organizing Mack's family into two lines for the celebration that we've secretly planned. Mack's eyes widen, but I just grin and get everyone else, including many of the crew, who are eager to watch, to stand in a semi-circle facing them, and direct Mack and Sidnie to the center of the deck. I catch Sidnie's eye, and she winks at me. Mack has no idea we've practiced this.

I can see Elizabeth standing to one side with Victoria and the others, and I feel a frisson of nerves for a second at the thought that she's going to be watching me perform, but it's too late now.

As everyone falls quiet, I take my place in the front line, down from Titus and Jamie, who've been practicing with me, and Mack's cousin starts playing his guitar. First, we sing a Māori song, *Pōkarekare Ana*, and as it's a traditional song, many of the guests also join in.

When the song comes to an end, Koro begins walking behind the line as he begins the call and response to start the *haka*—the Māori ceremonial war dance. The rest of us respond with the aggressive calls and warlike gestures that provide the challenge to Mack and his wife to step up to their new role.

Most New Zealanders know the *Ka Mate haka* that the All Blacks rugby team performs, but this is a special *haka*, called *Tika Tonu*— 'What is right is always right'—written at the beginning of the twentieth century by a Māori chief whose son had gone to college and was having trouble there. Mack already knows it off by heart, but I know he'll be touched that we're all performing it for him. I'm conscious that he lost his father some time ago, and Koro agreed that this *haka* was the perfect way to show him that the rest of his family and friends will always be there for him.

We go through the whole thing once as he and Sidnie watch. This *haka* is often taught to young people as a lesson when they're making difficult transitions in their lives, and the words are surprisingly powerful.

Tika tonu atu ki a koe, e tama
Hiki nei koe aku whakaaro, pakia!
He hiki aha to hiki?
He hiki roa to hiki?
I a ha hā!
E tama, te uaua ana
E tama, te mārō
Roa ina hoki ra
Te tohe o te uaua na

E tāu nei.
Āna! Āna! Āna! Aue... Hī!

It means:
Be true to yourself, my son!
You have raised my concerns, so listen up!
What is this problem you are carrying?
How long have you been carrying it for?
Have you got that? Right, let's go on.
So son, Although it may be difficult for you
and son, Although it seems to be unyielding
No matter how long you reflect on it
the answer to the problem
is here inside you.
Indeed! Indeed! Indeed! Yes, indeed!

The Māori words are performed with vigorous gestures and facial expressions, and the sound of stomping feet, hands slapping chests, the deep bellows of the men, and the ringing voices of the women, reverberate through the whole yacht.

I can see Mack getting emotional as he watches us all perform, and feel a touch of pity for him as he doesn't know what's coming. Sure enough, as Koro calls to repeat the *haka*, "Tika tonu! Tika tonu!" and Sidnie adopts the wide eyes and trembling hand gestures of the women and calls back, "U-e!" Indeed! and begins performing the dance, Mack's emotion spills over, and he has to stare hard at the ground, fighting for control. Emotional herself, Sidnie doesn't stop but touches his arm, encouraging him, and after a few seconds he finally joins in too, copying our movements as he says the words. He locks eyes with me—he knows I set this up—and for a moment time slips away, and we could be any two guys in Māori history, doing their war dance. It's a powerful performance, especially with everyone in their wedding finery, a celebration of their new life together, and I don't think there's a dry eye on the yacht by the time we're done.

The other guests cheer and give a huge round of applause, and everyone breaks up to hug and congratulate us on the performance. Mack comes over to thank all his family, hugging them all in turn starting with his grandfather. When he's done, he stands before me, and we smile at each other.

"Your idea, I'm guessing," he says.

I glance at Sidnie, who's chatting to some of his family.

"Actually it was hers," I say. "She wanted to learn it for you."

He glances at her, with her curly hair lifting in the autumn breeze, slender and gorgeous in her wedding dress.

"She's one in a million," I say, my voice husky with emotion. "*Ko te mea nui ko te aroha.*" The greatest thing is love.

"Yeah," he says, and brings his gaze back to me, smiling. "Thanks. For everything."

"Least I could do."

He gives me a bearhug, and we stand there like that for a moment before Sidnie finally comes up and says, "Are you two trying to make me cry?" following which we break apart with a laugh.

Everyone forms two lines between which Mack and Sidnie walk while we toss rose-petal confetti over them and cheer. Gradually the guests filter in and find their places around the long tables in the saloon.

I'm sitting on Sidnie's left, and it's only when I take my seat, I see with surprise that the placeholder on my left bears Elizabeth's name.

"You can thank me later," Sidnie says.

I glare at her. "Stop meddling."

"I like meddling," she says cheerfully. "Anyway, it was Mack's idea. He's determined to get the two of you together as much as we can until you sort things out."

"It is sorted," I reply.

Mack leans forward to speak around her. "No, it's not. So for Christ's sake work things out tonight, now you just happen to be sharing a cabin." He gives me a look that says *Fooled you there.*

My jaw drops. "You engineered that?"

"I did. You're welcome."

"For fuck's sake."

"Serves you right for springing the *haka* on me."

"That was your wife's fault," I point out.

His lips curve up. "My wife," he says. "Oh-ho, I like that." He pulls her against him and nuzzles her ear. "I'll inspect your ring later on."

She giggles, and I roll my eyes. "Jesus."

"You're only jealous," he says.

I open my mouth to reply, then shut it again as Elizabeth appears beside me. "Was this your idea?" she asks Mack suspiciously.

"Yes," he says, "and it's my special day, so the two of you need to sit down and stop arguing."

She pokes her tongue out at him as she takes her seat.

"I mean it," he says. "Things have been weird lately, and I don't like it. I want you two to sort yourselves out."

"He engineered us into sharing a cabin," I tell Elizabeth.

Her eyes widen and she glares at him. "You did not."

"I did," Mack says. "Now the two of you need to drink some champagne, get drunk, and have really dirty sex, because you're both doing my head in."

That makes me laugh, while Elizabeth closes her eyes and mutters, "Oh my God."

"Just ignore him," I tell her. "He's going to be unbearable for the next few weeks."

"Damn straight," Mack says, leaning back as the waiters bring around the starters.

I grin and nudge Elizabeth with my elbow. "I mean it. Don't listen to him, he's only teasing."

"No, he's not," Mack says. "And I'll be checking."

"Checking what?"

"Whether you've had sex."

"May I ask how?" Elizabeth asks.

"I'll be able to tell," Mack states. "So be warned."

She blows a raspberry and picks up her fork. He gives me a look that says, *I'm not joking.*

"How many glasses of champagne have you had?" I ask him suspiciously.

"I haven't touched a drop."

"He's had four," Sidnie replies. "He was very nervous, bless him."

"I might need a snooze after dinner," Mack says.

"We'll have a little lie down together." She whispers something in his ear, and he laughs.

"You are too fucking happy," Elizabeth complains. "It shouldn't be allowed."

I chuckle and tuck into my starter. The vegetarian option is mushroom bites stuffed with walnuts, spinach, and sun-dried tomatoes, a creamy butternut squash linguine with fried sage for a main, and vegan cheesecakes for dessert, but there are seasonal fish and meat alternatives for each course too, like grilled chicken and salmon with lemon.

Elizabeth and I make polite conversation during the meal, chatting about the yacht, the food, and the guests, but I can sense she feels as awkward as I do. It's as if we have so much to say to each other that we can't get the words out, so in the end we talk about stupid things, like how tasty the chicken is, and don't Victoria and Evie seem happy? In the end I give up and accept that whatever Mack's wishes, things aren't going to magically right themselves over dinner. Maybe later, when we get some time alone, we'll be able to talk.

Ultimately, though, what am I expecting she'll say? I know she's still planning on going to England. So there's really nothing to discuss. Mack has good intentions, but it doesn't matter how much he pushes me to alter the situation. Elizabeth is the one who's making the rules, and unless she changes her mind, things are going to stay the way they are whether he likes it or not.

*

Elizabeth

I can't believe Mack put me next to Huxley for dinner. I'll have words with him about that later. I'm annoyed that he's trying to force the issue. What good will pushing us together do now? It's only going to make us more miserable.

Huxley is his usual polite, charming self, but things aren't going to go back to the way they were. We've slept together. He's been inside me, for fuck's sake. Without a condom. You can't forget something like that. I can't, anyway, and judging by the way he's quieter than usual, neither can he.

Eventually, I feel I have to say something, so I murmur, "You're quiet today."

"I'm thinking about my speech," he says.

"Oh, I'd forgotten about that. Have you written it down?"

"Nah. I'll make it up as I go." He smiles. His light-gray eyes rest on me, and it feels as if they're curtains hiding all the things he wants to say. I so want things to go back to normal. I open my mouth to ask him if he's forgiven me, but at that moment Cameron calls for quiet and announces that it's time for the speeches, and Huxley gets to his feet. He'd previously taken off his jacket, but now he slips it on and does the top button up.

"Welcome, everyone," he begins, "to the wedding of one of my very best friends, Mack Hart, to his beautiful new wife, Sidnie. I'm Oliver Huxley, and I've known Mack since our first year at high school. We've been rivals for as long as I can remember, so it's kind of nice to have it confirmed that I am, in fact, the best man."

Mack groans as there's a ripple of laughter. "Is this what we can expect from your speech?"

"Oh, there's plenty more where that came from," Huxley says enthusiastically. "But I should add that I've been instructed to keep the speech smut free, so if I come across any innuendo, I'll whip it out immediately."

Sidnie dissolves into giggles, which makes the rest of us laugh.

"Don't encourage him," Mack says wryly.

Huxley grins. "I looked up some etiquette on being a best man, and apparently I should start with some embarrassing tales about the groom. My problem is there are so many to choose from!"

I chuckle, because there's something about the way he speaks that draws you into the conversation and makes you feel as if he's talking just to you. I've always liked listening to him speak in public. It's a rare gift, and although I've done it on several occasions, I'm nowhere near as natural as Hux.

"Let's go right back to the beginning with a sporting story," he says. "We were fourteen and in the same class at high school. We were both in the year ten cricket team, and we got to the final against one of the local grammar schools. Being the superior batsman," and he glances at Mack, who tips his head from side to side, "I was in to bat first. I had a great innings, and I made it to ninety-nine runs before the other batsman was caught out. So, out strolls fourteen-year-old Mack onto the field, walking so fast they have to announce a warning in case the grass catches fire."

We all laugh, and Mack grins, because his walking speed is legendary.

"He's determined to impress the spectators," Huxley continues, "especially the group of girls who happen to be there cheering our team on. So he takes forever to get to his position in front of the wicket, strutting around and showing off. The bowler sends him the ball. He hits it to short leg. I yell to wait. He ignores me and sprints up the pitch—which I have to point out, in case you're not aware, is just short of lightspeed, because two years later he would go on to win first place in the hundred meters in the New Zealand Athletics Championships. And so he promptly runs me out. On the first ball."

"I did do that," Mack says as everyone chuckles. "Sorry."

"I missed my century by one run," Huxley adds. "Not that I'm bitter or anything. Anyway that story's just a warm up. Let's turn to something much more embarrassing. Picture this: we're fifteen years old, and it's my older sister's twenty-first birthday party."

"Oh no," Mack says.

"Oh yes. You had to know this was coming, bro." He gives me a mischievous glance before addressing the room. "So, the party's at my parents' house, and my mother tells me I can invite one friend as long as we both behave. Well, that was my first mistake, inviting Mack. I should have known better. He's always egged me on. I had every intention of behaving. It was his idea to steal a pack of six bottles of Steinlager from the fridge. And it was also his idea, after we'd downed four of said six bottles, to go to the pool where my sister was hanging out with her friends. The thing is, we were both tall and, being all of fifteen, incredibly sophisticated, as you can imagine, and we were convinced we could pass for twenty-one. So we decided to make our way around the pool toward the hot girls sitting sunbathing in their bikinis and chat them up."

Sidnie grins at Mack. "I can picture it now," she says, and he winces.

"Moose, our Labrador, was asleep on the side of the pool," Huxley continues. "I was in front, and I stepped over him. Unfortunately, Mack had donned a pair of dark sunglasses in an attempt to look cool." He glances at Mack, who's trying not to laugh. "He didn't see the dog, tripped over him and fell forward, reached out a hand to steady himself, grabbed the back of my swim shorts, and in full view of all the hot twenty-one-year-old girls, pulled my shorts down, exposing them to the last turkey in the shop."

He stops as we all erupt into laughter. "The poor girls are probably still in therapy," he adds when he can get a word in. "And I haven't finished. As he overbalanced, he crashed into me, and the two of us fell in the pool, me with my shorts still around my knees. Needless to say, we did not pull any of the hot girls that night. And even now, Abigail's friends still laugh when they see me."

He glances at me and smiles. It's such a Huxley story—on the face of it, it's about mocking Mack, but underneath it all he's being self-deprecating and mocking himself.

Could I want him any more at this moment? I honestly don't think it's possible.

"So," he continues, "let's move on to our university years. When we were nineteen, we all went to play paintball…"

He carries on in that vein, telling a few more stories involving the two of them getting up to madcap things and making a fool of themselves that have everyone in stitches.

"I just want you to know what you're letting yourself in for," he says to Sidnie eventually.

"*Now* you tell me," she replies, "when the deed's done and it's too late to back out."

Huxley grins and waits for the laughter to die down. "All joking aside," he says, "I was thrilled to be here today to watch Mack declare his love for his beautiful bride. The two of you are perfect for each other. *Kia hora te marino, kia whakapapa pounamu te moana, kia tere te Kārohirohi i mua i tōu huarahi.* May the calm be widespread, may the surface of the ocean glisten like the greenstone, and may the shimmer of summer dance across your path forever."

Sidnie presses her fingers to her lips, and Mack bends his head and kisses her shoulder.

"Everyone, please join me in toasting the bride and groom," Huxley says. "To Mack and Sidnie."

We all raise our glasses. "To Mack and Sidnie," I whisper before taking a sip of the champagne.

Everyone cheers and claps then, and Huxley sits down.

"It was a fantastic speech," I tell him honestly.

He taps his glass to mine, and looks as if he's about to say something, but in the end he just smiles and finishes off his champagne.

My gaze lingers on him, though. I'm sure I'm not the only woman here today who's more than a little in love with him. His performance of the *haka* with Mack—my two favorite guys in the whole world—had tears rolling down my face. I feel torn in two between my head and my heart. Victoria's words have continued to rumble away in my mind like thunder rolling around the hills: *You act like you don't think you deserve love and affection, but you do. You've been unlucky in love, and that's going to make you wary, but you mustn't close your heart off forever.*

I've been trying to protect myself. But it's not working. I'm miserable and lonely, and all I've done is lose my best friend. Is it too late to put everything right?

Chapter Twenty

Elizabeth

When the meal is finally over, the music starts, and the guests filter out of the saloon. It's dark now, but the deck is lit with fairy lights, and it's just the start of the party.

True to his word, Huxley changes into his swim shorts and lets the kids dunk him in the pool. I sit with Victoria and the others on the poolside, sipping champagne and laughing as they pile on top of him and try to drown him.

"I think I drank half the pool," he says when he's finally able to extricate himself and climb out.

The others laugh, but I can only stare at him, as he dries his back with a towel, his chest shining with water droplets. He walks off to get changed, and I give a private sigh before looking around and realizing Mack is watching me.

"I'll be able to tell," he mouths.

I give him the finger, and he chuckles and returns to his conversation.

Huxley returns five minutes later in his blue shirt and linen suit, and he then spends a while circulating amongst the guests, checking that everyone has a drink before he finally starts asking the women to dance. He's always done this—he hates people being alone, and he'll ask anyone—grandmas, teenage girls, and single mums—to dance with him so they don't feel left out.

I pull on a thick sweater, slide down in my chair, and drink my champagne as I watch him dancing with an older Māori woman and making her laugh, wondering what it would be like to be married to someone like him. I've honestly not thought about it much before. I never talked about marriage with any of my exes, and they certainly never broached the subject. It always seemed like a bit of an outdated institution. Why commit yourself for life to someone and have to go through a divorce when it's over when you can just move in with them and see how it goes?

But being here today, watching Mack and Sidnie saying their vows, has given me a new perspective on things. Maybe marriage isn't about owning the other person. Perhaps it's not a bear trap you catch them in. Is it possible it really is as magical as today has made it seem? Or am I just very drunk?

What was the saying that Huxley ended with today? *May the calm be widespread, may the surface of the ocean glisten like the greenstone, and may the shimmer of summer dance across your path forever.* I wonder what he thinks about it all.

He's not doing great, Mack told me. *He loves you, you know.* Okay, he'd had four glasses of champagne when he said it, but even so.

Give him a break. It's not what you think. Once again, Victoria's words haunt me. I wish someone would tell me what's going on.

There's mainly been dance music playing, but now a slow song begins, and I realize with a bang of my heart that it's one of my favorites oldies—The Beatles' *Don't Let Me Down*. Couples start gravitating toward each other—Jamie and his pregnant girlfriend, Kai and his wife, Victoria and Evie, Mack and Sidnie, Caro and Hana, even Sidnie's parents—and they all begin to circle slowly to the music.

A shadow falls over me, and I look up to see Huxley standing there, hand outstretched. "Dance with me," he says.

I poke my tongue out at him. "Working your way through the spinsters on board, are we?"

He flicks his fingers up. "Don't be grouchy. I know you like this song. Dance with me."

"I'm too drunk, Hux. Find another old maid to bother."

"Old maid… You're not even thirty yet. One of Mack's maiden aunts has a mustache. You're the sexiest girl on board by a long shot."

That makes me laugh. He flicks his fingers again. "Come on, I'll hold you up. Don't make me put you in a firefighter's lift."

Grumbling, slightly mollified by his compliment, I ignore the sniggers of those around me and let him pull me to my feet. I'm wearing deck shoes rather than heels today, so I'm a lot shorter than him. He moves me to the edge of the dance floor and turns me into his arms.

As we settle into a rhythm, he sings softly, causing goose bumps to rise on my skin. I study the triangle of skin visible at his neckline where he's left the top two buttons undone as we move to the music. "Can I ask you something?" I say.

"Sure."

"Is there something you haven't told me about what happened when we were nineteen?"

His left hand curls around my right, and his other hand splays at the base of my spine. "No," he says.

I brush my thumb over the seam of his shirt where it runs around his shoulder, feeling his muscles beneath. He didn't say, *What do you mean?* And he didn't look surprised. He knows what I'm talking about. But he's not going to tell me.

"Please?" I whisper.

He looks down at me then. His pupils are large in the semi-darkness. "There's nothing to say."

I don't reply, and in the end he just pulls me toward him a little more, and we dance quietly.

He doesn't trust me enough to tell me his secret. We're not married, and we're not partners, and I'm not even sure we're close friends anymore. He's shutting me out, and I only have myself to blame.

He continues to sing, telling me he's in love for the first time, and that it's going to last forever, but they're just words, and I know it's not the truth. It's like torture, his hand in mine, his lips close to my temple, his hot breath whispering across my skin. I can smell his aftershave, and I can't stop my thumb from stroking his shoulder. Part of me hopes he'll throw caution to the wind, slide a hand beneath my chin, and lift my face to kiss me, or that he'll catch my hand in his, drag me back to our cabin, throw me onto the bed, and make mad passionate love to me, refusing to take no for an answer.

But he's not going to do that. I know he won't. In his world, no means no, and even though I wish with all my heart that at this moment he could let go of his lofty principles for just one second, that would never happen. I made my bed, and I have to lie in it, even though it's lumpy and uncomfortable, and I know I'm not going to get any sleep at all.

When the song ends, we thank each other politely, and I go back to my seat and return to my champagne.

I feel like I'm drinking lemonade, though. It's not doing the job quickly enough. So after a while, sick of watching Mack and Sidnie and the other couples smooching on the dance floor, I go into the saloon, sit up at the bar, and order myself a whisky. I down it probably a little too quickly, but I don't care, and order myself another one.

Outside, the music continues, entwining with the guests' laughter and conversation, and spiraling up into the night sky. I should go back out there with my friends, but suddenly I don't have the energy. Mack and Sidnie's happiness is a brilliant light that has only served to show me how much my life is in shadow. And I'm angry with myself, because it's my choice, and I have this wonderful opportunity to go to England, and I should be celebrating, but instead I just feel miserable and low. Not wanting to tarnish Mack's beautiful day, I know the only answer is to keep to myself.

Quietly, I finish my drink, then make my way down to my cabin.

It's empty and dark. It wouldn't surprise me if Huxley doesn't appear tonight. I expect he'll just doze off on one of the sunbeds or something.

Sadly, I take off my makeup, change into a T-shirt nightie, and slip beneath the covers of the left-hand single bed. I lie on my side, looking at the smooth covers of the other bed, and then let my gaze drift out of the porthole to the stars of Orion's belt, twinkling against the blackness of the sky.

Then I fall asleep, my pillow wet with tears.

*

Sometime later, I jerk awake. It's still dark outside, but a small, dim light emanates from the other bed. Huxley is lying there, the duvet pulled up to his waist, bare-chested, one arm tucked under his head, reading on his Kindle. I hadn't heard him come in. How long has he been there? I can't hear any music, so the party has obviously come to an end.

For a while, I don't move, afraid of breaking the spell. I let my gaze linger on him, on his muscular arms, and his handsome face, lit by the Kindle. An ache begins, deep in my heart. Why does everything have to be so complicated?

He glances over at me then, and sees I'm awake. "Hello," he murmurs.

"Hey." I don't move. "What time is it?"

"Just after three a.m. but the clocks have just gone back, so it's two a.m. again."

My stomach flutters. I know it's ridiculous, but my first thought is that someone's given us an extra hour of time to put things right. It feels like the witching hour, magical and precious.

"How long have you been here?" I whisper.

"About half an hour. You didn't even stir when I came in. Why did you disappear? We missed you."

I don't reply, unable to put my misery into words.

His gaze lingers on me for a while. Then he returns it to his Kindle.

"What are you reading?" I ask.

"*The Life of Pi*," he says, surprising me. "I'm wondering whether there's a tiger like Richard Parker on board here somewhere."

I try to smile, but I feel too sad. I want to ask him if he'll kiss me, if he'll make love to me. But I can't, because that wouldn't be fair, and it would only make things worse. Or would it? I don't think I can feel worse than this. A tear runs down over my nose and drops onto my pillow. I know it's just tiredness and alcohol, but my heart still aches.

He glances at me again briefly. Can he see my tears? It's very dark in here. He doesn't say anything, and returns his gaze to his Kindle. A minute passes. Then, without looking at me, he lifts his arm. "Come over here, and I'll read to you," he says.

My heart bangs against my ribs. Is he serious? He doesn't lower his arm, still reading. I mustn't. I shouldn't.

"*Ka pao te tōrea,*" he says. It's his motto, of a sort, at his business club; it means 'as the tide recedes, the oystercatcher strikes.' We might say 'strike while the iron is hot.'

I pull back the covers, get up, go over to his bed, and slide in next to him. There's not a lot of room as it's a single bed, but I find no reason to complain as I nestle close. He's only wearing his boxers, and his skin is warm. Mmm, he smells good, of his musky evening aftershave and the scent of healthy male. He's so young, strong, and alive.

He tucks the duvet around me, then lowers his arm and pulls me close.

"He's just escaped in the lifeboat," he says, and starts reading, telling me the story of the Indian boy whose ship sinks and who ends up in a boat with a hyena, a zebra, an orangutan, and the tiger, Richard Parker.

He reads for about fifteen minutes, and I rest a hand on his chest, feeling his voice rumble there as he murmurs the words, finding it oddly comforting. We could be any normal couple, resting after a busy day. Tears prick my eyes. This isn't sexual; he's comforting me the only way he knows how. He knows I'm hurting, because I'm pretty sure he's feeling the same way. He's trying to reconnect, and it makes me so incredibly sad.

Eventually, when he gets to the end of the chapter, he stops reading, turns off his Kindle, and puts it on the bedside table. It's dark now, the only light coming from the stars outside.

He puts his arms around me, and I slide my arm around his waist beneath the covers and hug him.

"I miss you," I whisper.

"I miss you, too." He kisses the top of my head.

Tears trickle out of my eyes, and I bite my lip hard.

"Ah," he says, obviously feeling wetness on his skin. "Don't cry."

"I'm sorry," I squeak. "I fucked everything up. I'm so sorry."

"You didn't do anything. It was all me. I shouldn't have pushed you to sleep with me."

"You didn't push me. I wanted to. I've always wanted to."

He sighs then, a long, deep sigh that seems to go on forever. "Elizabeth," he says, just that one word, but he makes it sound precious, as if he's rolling an emerald around on his tongue.

I lift up onto an elbow and look down at him. "Hux…"

He lifts a hand to tuck a strand of my hair behind my ear. "Jesus, you're so fucking beautiful. How are you so beautiful, even without makeup, with your hair all messed up?"

I swallow hard. "Do you want to kiss me?"

He cups my face and gives me a helpless look. "More than I've ever wanted anything in my whole life."

More tears spill down my cheeks. He brushes them away with his thumb. And then he slides his hand to the back of my head and pulls me down to kiss me.

Oh God, at last… I open my mouth and touch my tongue to his bottom lip, and he groans and sweeps his tongue inside. He moves his hand to my thigh and slides it up, groans again as he discovers I'm not wearing any knickers, then slips his fingers further up under my nightie to cup my breast. I arch my back, and he rolls my nipple beneath his thumb, then tugs it in his fingers, and it's like a bolt of electricity shooting through me, exploding somewhere between my thighs.

"I want you," he whispers as he shifts so I'm on my back and he's leaning over me. "I can't bear it any longer. It's all I can think about. I'm obsessed with you."

Fresh tears sting my eyes. "I thought I'd lost you."

"Never," he says, and kisses me hard, delving his tongue into my mouth. Half-crying, filled with relief, I part my legs as he slides his hand down, and I can't help but give a long moan as he slips his fingers into my folds.

"Ahhh…" He lets out a long breath, as if he's coming home, and slides two fingers right down inside me. I can barely see his face, but his eyes glitter in the starlight.

He arouses me gently, moving his fingers while he kisses my breasts and teases my nipples with his tongue, eventually removing the nightie to give himself better access. I don't know if it's the alcohol, or the fact that I'm keyed up and I've been thinking about this almost non-stop ever since we parted, but it feels like only minutes before a deep ache grows in my belly.

"I want you inside me," I tell him softly, moving a hand down to stroke him through his boxers, the silky fabric slipping over his iron-hard length.

He divests himself of the boxers, kisses up my neck to my jaw, right up to my mouth, then pauses, and I look up into his star-filled eyes.

"Do you want me to use a condom?" he asks.

I hesitate. My brain's muddled, and I can't think straight. I'm pretty sure I'm close to ovulating again. Elizabeth… don't complicate things. Take this for what it is—a brief moment of comfort, some quiet, private, nighttime delight. Tell him yes, that he should wear a condom.

But staring into his eyes, I can't bring myself to do it, and I give a small shake of my head.

Half of me thought he might frown, and even say he was making the decision to use one. I'm completely unprepared for his beautiful smile.

He moves on top of me, which isn't easy in the tiny bed, and for the first time we both laugh as he nearly falls off. Impatiently, he pushes the duvet away, then moves up my knees and opens them wide. He slides the tip of his erection down through my folds until he just enters me, then watches as he pushes his hips forward and buries himself inside me.

I arch my back and cry out at the exquisite feeling of being stretched and filled—ohhh… that's amazing.

"Shh," he says, laughing and covering my mouth with his. "You'll wake the rest of the boat."

"Sorry." But it's so hard not to say anything as he moves inside me. Mmm… I welcome his weight as he settles down on top of me, and wrap my legs around his waist. Oh, he feels good. I love the way his muscles bunch and furl beneath my fingertips as he moves. Sliding my fingers up his back, I curve them and draw my nails lightly down either side of his spine, and he shudders.

"Fuck," he says, thrusting harder, and I match each movement of his hips with one of my own. It's sensual and sexy and superlative, and I'm filled with such relief, such wondrous joy, that my eyes prick with tears again.

"Don't cry," he whispers, slowing a little and kissing the tears from the corner of my eyes.

"I can't help it," I say with a sniff.

He touches his tongue to the tears. "Don't be sad."

"I'm not sad. I'm so incredibly happy."

Our gazes lock, and for a moment I can't breathe as he looks into my eyes, moving inside me. I know this is a mistake, I know I'm going to regret it, but right now I'm just so fucking happy, I don't care. I'm so glad he kissed me. Oh my God, I'm so fucking relieved.

"Hux," I whisper, bottom lip trembling, and he says, "I know," and kisses me again. I can feel his body taking over his attempts to go slowly, as he lifts up onto his hands and thrusts harder, and it's so surreal, with the rocking of the boat and the glitter of the starlight on his skin, and oh fuck, I'm going to come, and Huxley crushes his mouth to mine as everything tightens inside so I know I'm crying out, but I can't stop as the beautiful pulses claim me.

"Ah Jesus," he says, his body stiffening, and I wrap my arms around him and hold him tightly as he comes inside me.

When we're done, he opens his eyes, and I wonder whether they're going to show regret. But they don't. All I can see in them is affection.

He kisses me. "Hey, you."

"Hey, you." I brush my fingers over his skin. "Mack will be pleased."

That makes him laugh, and then he winces and withdraws. "Lie still," he instructs. "Knees up."

I pull my knees to my chest and clasp them, rolling my head to look over at him as he stretches out on his side beside me, trying not to fall off the edge of the bed. He pulls the duvet over us, then props his head on a hand, and we lie there quietly, looking at each other.

"This isn't why I got into bed with you," I tell him.

"I know. Seems a shame to waste the lovin' spoonful, though." He smiles.

"I've missed you so much," I whisper.

He lifts a hand, picks up a strand of my hair, and lets it slide through his fingers. "I've missed you too."

"I don't know what I'm doing," I say, tired and muddled.

"Join the club. We've got jackets."

"About England—" I begin, but he shakes his head, and I stop.

"Not now," he says. "You don't have to say anything." I bite my lip, and he brushes his thumb over it, making me release it from my teeth. "We're grownups," he says gently, "sort of, aren't we? And we're best friends. We both know what's going on here. I love you, and I'm pretty sure you love me. But you've been hurt, and you have your career and your need to help other people, but I love that about you. It's complicated, and that's okay, I'm coming to terms with that. Elizabeth... I'll take whatever you can give me. And if it's just today, right here, right now, that's all right."

My eyes brim with tears. "I don't deserve you."

"Yeah, I know." He smiles, then leans forward and kisses me. "Turn over," he says when he moves back, "and I'll give you a hug."

I roll onto my side facing away from him, and he moves up close to me.

"Actually this might backfire on me," he says, pressing his groin against my butt.

"You're incorrigible."

"Thank you." He wraps his arms around me and slides a hand beneath my arm, onto my belly. Then he kisses my shoulder. "I hope it's worked this time."

"It would make things much more complicated," I whisper.

"I know. But in the end, pregnancy would trump everything, wouldn't it? Everything else would pale into insignificance if we made a baby. Wherever you were in the world, I'd know there was a little piece of me with you always. Or until he grew up and went to university, anyway."

"He?" I say, trying to hide my emotion at the thought of having his son.

"A little Huxley running around causing havoc. I quite like that idea." He yawns and nuzzles my neck. "I hope I impregnated you."

"Oh you're so romantic."

"I think it's incredibly romantic. All my little swimmers, racing through your body to fertilize your egg. Fuck Valentine's Day, this is what it's all about." He strokes my belly. "Go, boys, go."

I close my eyes. "It's like Casanova all over again."

"I might have inseminated you tonight. Tell me that's not the most romantic thing you've ever heard."

I smile, and slowly drift off to sleep.

Chapter Twenty-One

Huxley

When we go up to the saloon at seven the next morning, the first people we see are Mack and Sidnie, sitting at a table, eating breakfast.

We put an order in with the chef, then join them at the table. I slide onto the bench next to Mack, and Elizabeth takes the chair next to Sidnie. The steward comes up and pours us a steaming hot coffee. Mack watches us as we sip it, his lips curving up as our eyes meet.

"You put the banana in the fruit salad, then," he says.

Elizabeth blinks. "What?"

"The horizontal tango? Parallel parking? Riding St. George? Opening the Gates of Mordor?"

That makes me laugh, but Elizabeth still looks baffled. "Are you speaking English?"

"Foxtrot Uniform Charlie Kilo?" Mack suggests.

"Mack!" Sidnie looks mortified. "I'm so sorry," she says to Elizabeth. "He's not worked for two days and his ADHD has gone into overdrive."

"I don't need to ask whether you had sex last night," Elizabeth says to him tartly.

"What can I say?" He crunches on some toast. "I'm irresistible."

"Jesus." Sidnie gets up. "I'm getting some more toast."

"I'll join you. Anything to escape this madman." Elizabeth joins her at the food table.

Mack grins at me. "So is it all sorted?"

"Mind your own business."

"Did you put a bun in her oven?"

I give him an exasperated look. He raises his eyebrows.

"I'm working on it," I concede.

He smiles then. "Good lad."

"Don't talk to me like you're my father."

"I'm wise and insightful now I'm married. I'm practically a sage."

"More like parsley if you ask me. The flat-leaf sort, not the curly sort."

He chuckles.

The two of us watch the girls at the breakfast table, chatting and laughing, and we exchange a smile.

"She looks happy," Mack says. "Elizabeth, I mean. Happier than she did yesterday, anyway."

"Yeah. She was pretty low, I think."

"But you cheered her up."

"I did."

"Orgasms tend to put a smile on a girl's face."

I shake my head. "You really are in overdrive this morning, aren't you?"

"I like being married."

"I can tell."

He grins. "Have you talked about what happens next?"

"Nope." I sip my coffee. "I'm going to leave it in the hands of Fate."

"While giving her multiple orgasms."

"As many as I'm physically able."

"That's quite sneaky."

"Whatever ammunition is to hand, you know?"

Sidnie drops a piece of toast butter side down, says, "Fuck," and glares at Mack as he laughs.

"I love that girl," he says.

"She is lovely."

"She's my wife."

"Yeah, I know."

"The old ball and chain."

"I wouldn't say that to her face."

"I called her it this morning. She thought it was adorable."

"I'd bet my apartment that she didn't."

He laughs. "Maybe not."

I watch Elizabeth choosing from the small dishes of jam, and feel a tug deep inside. She's wearing her cut-downs again this morning with a russet-colored sweater, and she's bathed in the golden sunshine that's spilling across the room, as if the goddess of autumn has appeared to visit us. I sigh.

"Man, you've got it bad," Mack says.

"Tell me something I don't know."

"I hope she stays."

"Yeah, me too."

"Have you thought about keeping her chained up in your apartment?"

"Every day, bro."

We both laugh.

"What are you two sniggering at?" Elizabeth says as they come back to the table with their toast.

"Hux's hair," Mack says.

I touch it defensively. "What's wrong with my hair?"

"It's sticking up at the front. It looks as if someone's been running their fingers through it all night."

The four of us laugh, and the conversation continues as the guests filter into the room, and the sun's rays sweep across the floor.

*

We sail back to Paihia and drop off Mack's family, then continue down the coast, taking all morning and most of the afternoon to get back to Auckland. The day passes slowly, those of us who are left sitting together on the deck in the shade, chatting and nibbling on the snacks that the stewards bring out, and watching the beauty of the North Island slip by.

Elizabeth and I chat with our friends, and occasionally we exchange small, private smiles, but mostly we stay apart. I'm content to watch her from afar, and sometimes when I glance over, I catch her watching me, too.

Part of me wishes we could just head past Auckland and sail south, tour New Zealand, head off to Australia, maybe even keep going to the Pacific Islands. But all good things must come to an end, or so they say, and mid-afternoon we head into Auckland Harbour, and eventually it's time to disembark.

Mack and I go around thanking the crew, and then say goodbye to Cameron before we walk down the gangway and join the rest of the guests. Slowly, everyone gets in their cars, or their taxis arrive, and we wait and say goodbye and make sure they've got their transport before we turn to each other with smiles.

"I feel as if the ground's still moving," Sidnie says with a laugh.

Mack chuckles and kisses her cheek. "Come on. The Uber's here." He smiles at me. "Thanks for all your help."

"Oh, we had a great time." We exchange a big hug, and the girls do too, and then Mack and Sidnie head off.

Elizabeth and I turn to each other with a smile.

"You off to the club?" she asks.

I nod. "Just to make sure it's not burned down or anything. You going to the office?"

"I'll pick up Nymph first, then yeah, I might go in for a bit."

"Okay. Well, I'll catch up with you later?"

"Of course." She hesitates, then she comes up and slides her arms around my waist, and we have a big hug.

I kiss her hair. "Take care of yourself."

"You too. See you later."

We part, she gets in her Uber, and it drives away.

I watch her go, then turn and look out across the harbor. A few clouds hover on the horizon, suggesting it might rain later on. I'm glad it held off for the wedding.

In the distance, there's a faint rumble of thunder. I shiver, and walk back to my Uber.

*

The days slip by, faster than I would have thought. The club receives another favorable online review that leads to a flourish of new visitors, and after twelve or fourteen-hour days I'm not good for much except crashing out in front of the TV.

I don't see Elizabeth, who's also busy, but we start messaging each other again, which is nice. Her Snapchats and messages are lighthearted and funny, making me smile when they pop up during the day.

I don't know when, or even if, I'll see her alone again. I know she's still organizing things for England. As far as I know, she's still going in June. That's only a couple of months away. But I try not to think about it, and do what I told Mack and leave it up to Fate. *Que sera, sera,* Huxley. If it's meant to be, it will be.

I'm turning into an old romantic. I never thought I'd see the day.

Normally I work until midnight on Saturdays, but even though the club is busy and I'm there for the lunchtime rush, I'm not in the mood to stay late. I feel tired but oddly buzzy. Victoria tells me she's happy to oversee the evening, so I leave around four and go to the archery club for a while. I shoot a couple dozen arrows, then go to the gym where I run for half an hour then do some weights, but it doesn't dispel the buzzy feeling in my stomach. Maybe I'm hungry. I head home, thinking about what I should order from Uber Eats. Curry? Pizza? I don't feel in the mood for anything in particular.

I think about texting Elizabeth and asking if she'd like to go out to dinner. I type out the text. Delete it. Type it again. Then I delete it crossly and pocket the phone.

I live within walking distance to the club, in a really nice apartment I bought two years ago. I let myself in and toss my keys onto the table by the door. I like space, I hate clutter, and I also hate decorating, so I got a firm in and asked them to kit the whole place out with a minimalist look that matched my favorite pieces of my mother's artwork, most of which feature bright, primary colors. They went for lots of chrome and glass, and a light-gray sofa and chairs to contrast with the bright paintings. A couple of strategically placed mirrors bounce the early evening sunlight around the room and fill it with a golden glow. It's a great place, but tonight it feels too big, as if I'm rattling around in it.

Sighing, I go through to the main bedroom—simply decorated again in dark blues and greens—take off my suit, and have a quick shower. Afterward, I change into an old tee and track pants, and go back through to the living room. Actually I shouldn't have takeout, I should cook myself something healthy. Maybe I'll do some pasta. I go into the kitchen and look moodily in the cupboards. I feel restless and irritable. I should have texted Elizabeth. But then I'd only feel like shit when she said she was busy.

In my back pocket, my phone buzzes.

I take it out. She's sent me a text. *Watcha up to?*

I take a selfie pointing at my tee and track pants holding a beer and a PlayStation controller and send it to her.

She sends one back of herself and Nymph sitting on a brick wall looking sad. I stare at it, and then my lips curve up. I recognize the wall—it runs around the garden behind my apartment.

Me: *Wanna come up?*

Her: *Well, if you're asking…*

Heart fluttering, I buzz her in.

Like a teenager, I run around the place throwing clothes in the laundry bin and making sure it's tidy, then go over to the front door and lean on the post as she comes out of the elevator with Nymph. She lets go of the poodle's lead, and Nymph bounds up to me. I fuss her up, then let her run inside and straighten to look at Elizabeth. She's wearing jeans, a mint-green sweater, and a long black jacket. Her hair's all mussed by the wind. She's so fucking beautiful, it makes my heart ache.

"Hello," I say, sliding my hands into my pockets.

"Hi." She tucks her hair behind her ear. Her gaze skims down me, light as a feather, then returns to mine. "You look nice."

"I look scruffy, but I didn't have time to change during my manic cleanup. You want to come in?"

She gives me a helpless look. "I don't know why I'm here."

I shrug. "Hot sex? Because, you know, that's okay."

Our gazes lock. I smile, and her lips gradually curve up.

"I don't want to use you," she whispers.

"I told you, I'll take whatever you can give me." I hold out a hand.

She smiles shyly and slides her hand into mine, and I lead her inside.

My heart is racing. She's not here by coincidence—it wasn't as if we were in the same place at the same time and she decided she might as well make the most of it. She chose to come here, of her own volition. The thought fills me with joy.

I let the door close behind her, and pull her into my arms.

"I'm glad you're here," I murmur, cupping her face in my hands.

Her huge brown eyes look up at me, and she moistens her lips. "I wasn't sure if you'd want me to come in."

I just laugh and kiss her, slanting my lips across hers so I can delve my tongue into her mouth. I sink my hands into her hair, filling my senses with her—the smell of her perfume, the taste of the mint she'd eaten before she came up, the silky feel of her hair between my fingers, the sound of her sighs that sends a shiver all the way down my spine.

"God, I want you," I murmur, kissing up to her ear, then nibbling the lobe.

"I want you too." She kisses my jaw, then moves back to look at me. "I've thought about you all week. I couldn't stop. I don't know what you've done to me, Oliver Huxley, but you're haunting me like the ghost of Christmas Past, and I can't get you out of my head."

Thrilled, I watch as she goes over to the beanbag I sit in when I play on the PlayStation and steers Nymph onto it, who promptly flops down and stretches out. "We've just been for a long walk and a play in the park," she says. "She'll crash out for a while."

"Do you want anything?" I ask. "Something to eat or drink?"

"Only you." She comes back over to me and throws her arms around me, and I bend and pick her up. Laughing, she wraps her legs around me and kisses me.

"I missed you so much," I say, walking through the living room, still kissing her.

She cups my face and brushes my jaw with her thumbs. "You've got bristles. I hardly ever see you with bristles."

"I promise I'll be careful on your thighs."

She laughs and kisses me again, and it feels like coming home; like my birthday and Christmas and Valentine's Day all rolled into one. I don't think I've ever felt this happy.

I take her through to the bedroom, go over to the bed, and toss the duvet onto the floor. Turning, I sit and lie back, bringing her with me. Astride me, she makes herself comfortable and strokes my hair back off my forehead.

"You're so handsome," she murmurs. "You make my heart ache." She kisses my jaw, brushing her lips against my stubble, to behind my ear. "Your hair's damp. You've had a shower."

"I went to the gym. I tried to run off my lust, but it didn't work."

She laughs and presses her lips around to my mouth. "Can I help with that?"

"I wish you would."

She kisses me, and I smooth my hands down her back over her sweater, enjoying the feel of her small, slim frame, her sexy curves. Holding her butt, I tilt my hips up, and she sighs as I press my erection into her mound.

I can't feel much though because she's wearing jeans, so I push myself up, get to my feet, and let her legs slide down until she's standing. "Clothes off," I instruct, pulling up my tee.

"No," she says, eyes sparking. "Make me."

My heart bangs on my ribs. "With pleasure." I grab the bottom of her sweater and yank it over her head in one easy move, and she squeals, turning to flee. I'm too quick for her though, and I throw an arm around her waist, pick her up, toss her back on the bed, flick open the button of her jeans, and peel them down her legs.

"Oh my God," she says, wriggling as I finish removing them, "that was quick."

"I don't hang around when there's a prize like this waiting." I quickly remove my track pants and boxers, then grab her arm and roll her over, and flick open the catch of her bra. Leaving her on her front, I draw her underwear over her bottom and down her legs, and she sighs, her arms tucked beneath her, as I start kissing up the back of her legs.

She trembles, her flesh quivering, and I kiss over her bottom, then move up to cover her with my frame as I nuzzle her neck. "Are you cold?"

"No." But she trembles again.

I reach over the edge and retrieve the duvet, and bring it over us. Turning her to face me again, I toss her bra away and pull her close against me, skin to skin, so we're nestled beneath the warmth of the covers.

"I'm not cold," she says. "It's just being near you."

I look into her eyes, warming all the way through. She shivers again, and I kiss her nose. "Elizabeth Tremble-ay," I murmur, touched by her words.

"I can't believe I'm here," she whispers. "With you."

We kiss for a long time, just enjoying the feel of each other's skin, stroking, touching. Her body is so soft, her gentle curves like satin cushions beneath my fingers. Her hands travel over the muscles of my shoulders and arms, then slide around me to trace up my spine and over my shoulder blades. I kiss down to her breasts, take each nipple in my mouth in turn, and tease it until she clutches her fingers in my hair.

Now I've got her here, I'd like to spend hours arousing her, and give her multiple orgasms until she's begging me to stop, but she obviously has different ideas. While we're lying on our sides, she hooks a leg over my hip, lifts up, and moves until the tip of my erection parts her folds. I can't help but push up, and in one smooth move I slide inside her.

We both groan, our mouths slanting as our tongues thrust and delve. I clutch the plump muscles of her bottom and encourage her to move, my hips meeting hers. She rocks slowly, moving back until I'm almost out of her, then sliding down my length until I'm buried deep inside.

"I want to make love to you for hours," I tell her, "but you're making it very difficult."

"Later," she whispers, suggesting she's going to stay for a while, which sends tingles through me. "Right now, I'm not going to last that long. You're too hot, too sexy. I want you too much," she whispers, her mouth teasing mine.

"Come for me then," I demand, rolling her onto her back so I can thrust with purpose, making sure I grind against her clit with each push of my hips. "Look at me."

She opens her eyes and looks into mine, and it strikes me then that this is the first time we've made love completely sober. We've not had to use alcohol to encourage us to give up our inhibitions, or to persuade us that we're not making a mistake. This is just us, pure and raw, and the thought fills me with joy.

"Oh God," she whispers. "Hux…"

"Yes…" I thrust harder, and her lips part and her eyes close as she comes. I thrust slowly through her climax, watching it sweep over and loving the thought that I've given her such pleasure, then rise up onto my hands and let my body do what it wants, hips pumping fast, until heat rushes up through me and every muscle in my body tightens. I come inside her, jubilantly, exultantly, and her name filters from my lips as I drift slowly back down to earth.

I nuzzle the place where her neck meets her shoulder for a moment, reveling in the feeling of just being inside her, of being joined to her in the most intimate way I can. Then, as carefully as I can, I withdraw.

"Knees up."

She draws her legs up, and I pull her as close as I can and wrap my arms around her.

For a long while, we just look at each other. I brush her hair back off her face, and trace a finger over her nose, her cheekbones, and across her eyebrows. She eventually lowers her knees and turns toward me, and we exchange a long, leisurely kiss.

"Can I stay?" she whispers. "For a while?"

"As long as you like. Are you hungry?"

"I'm ravenous, actually."

"I'll make us some dinner in a minute."

She nods. "Hux?"

"Yeah?"

"Thank you."

"What for?"

"For not turning me away."

I kiss her nose. "I'll always be here for you."

Her brow furrows, and her eyes glisten.

At the beginning, she told herself I'd lose interest once we slept together, and convinced herself I was a playboy who would break her heart again if she gave it to me. But I think, maybe, she's starting to accept how serious my feelings are for her. And that's why she's conflicted. Because now she's giving up the love of a lifetime for her career, and that is not an easy decision.

Her eyes are filled with pain, still shining with tears. I know I'm forcing her to make a decision, to realize how she feels about me. It's not my way. I don't want anyone to be in pain because of me. But I want her so much, and I don't know what else to do.

Chapter Twenty-Two

Elizabeth

I eventually fall asleep, and when I finally awake, the room is filled with bright sunshine. I roll onto my back and stretch out an arm, and discover Nymph's curly fur rather than the muscular body I'd been hoping to find. Outside, in the kitchen, comes the sounds of someone preparing coffee.

Rising, I dress quickly, then click my fingers at Nymph, and she jumps off the bed.

I go out into the living room and cross to the breakfast bar. He looks over from where he's making the coffee. He's wearing his track pants and a fresh tee, and his hair is all ruffled.

"Morning," he says, and smiles.

"Hey. I'll... um... just take Nymph out."

"Sure. Take the keys with you—they're by the door."

I nod, collect the keys, put my shoes on, and take Nymph down with me to the garden. While she sniffs around and does her business, I sit on the wall where I took the photo last night, my stomach a jumble of emotions. Overriding them all, though, is the undeniable joy I feel at being here, with Huxley. Whatever happens, I'm so glad I came here last night.

I go back upstairs, and let myself into his apartment.

"Toast?" he asks as I go over to the breakfast bar.

"No thanks, coffee's fine."

He crunches into a piece spread with peanut butter and gestures at one of the stools, and I perch on the edge, while he leans on the counter on the other side.

"What are you up to today?" he asks.

"I'm going into work for a few hours," I admit. "What about you?"

"I've got Joanna today. Brandy's dropping her off soon. I'll take her to the cinema later, I think. We haven't been for ages."

I nod. "How's it going with Billy?"

"Good! He took her and Joanna to meet his family up in Kaitaia. That went well, apparently. And her folks are made up that he's an accountant. Very respectable in their eyes."

"I've never understood why they didn't like you," I say softly. "I think they're the only people I've ever met who didn't."

"Ah, I didn't get the chance to charm them. They'd already made up their minds about me before we met." His phone vibrates on the table, and he picks it up and looks at it. "That's them now," he says, finishing off the slice of toast as he goes over to buzz them in.

I blink and stare at him. "What? They're coming here?"

"Yeah. I said, Brandy's dropping Joanna off."

"Oh shit." I get up in a panic. "Hux!"

"What?" he says, laughing.

"It's early morning. They're going to know I was here all night."

"So?"

"But… Joanna…" I flush at the thought that his daughter will know we've been sleeping together.

"She knows how I feel about you," he says, amused. "She'll be pleased."

"I… what?"

But he's going over to the door, and I can only stand there, flustered, as he opens it and smiles to see his daughter run up. "Hey you!"

"Daddy!" She throws her arms around his waist, and he gives her a big squeeze. At that moment, Nymph runs up to them and bounces about, and Joanna squeals and bends to kiss her.

"Nymph!" she says, "what are you doing here?" She looks past him, sees me, and waves. "Hey, Auntie Elizabeth!"

"Hi," I say, blushing.

They come into the apartment, Brandy following, and her eyebrows rise as she sees me.

"Elizabeth!" She beams at me. "I didn't know you'd be here."

"No, I… um… it was a last minute thing… um…" I know it's clear I haven't just turned up as my hair is all ruffled. We look like we've just got out of bed.

But she just comes over and gives me a hug. "It's good to see you."

"Are you staying today?" Joanna says. "We 're going to the cinema."

"No, I've got to work," I tell her, touched when she looks disappointed.

"Want a coffee?" Huxley asks Brandy, and when she nods, he goes through to the kitchen and starts making it.

I listen to Brandy telling us what she's up to today, while Joanna kneels on the carpet to play with Nymph, and watch Huxley move about the kitchen, completely at ease with the strange situation. I know it's been a long time since it happened, but it feels so odd to think that they were once together, and that he made her pregnant. I have to fight not to rest my hand on my stomach. I still have another week before I'll be able to find out whether our time on the yacht has resulted in a baby. I don't know what's going to happen if I discover I'm pregnant. Huxley said he'll wait for me, but will he still be okay with me going to England if I'm pregnant with his baby, or will he expect me to stay?

Most importantly, maybe, what do I want? People always say to follow your gut feeling, but I honestly don't have one. I'm so muddled and confused, and a baby is only going to make that worse.

My musings are interrupted as there's a knock on the door.

Brandy stops talking, her eyebrows rising. "Are you expecting anyone?"

"No," he says. "Nobody ever knocks here." Wiping his hands on a tea towel, he walks across to the door and opens it. "Fuck," he says.

It's enough to make me look around, because he never swears in front of Joanna. A man is standing there. He's a little shorter than Hux, and much thinner, and at first I think he's a lot older because his face is quite lined.

"Wait," Huxley says, but the guy comes into the living room, then stops as he realizes there are people there. Nymph goes to rush past me, barking, but I grab her collar and hold it firmly.

Next to me, Brandy gives an audible gasp, and says, "Guy!"

Guy? Huxley's brother? I stare at him, shocked. No, it's true, now he's closer I can see he must only be a few years older than Hux.

He looks at Brandy, frowns, and then his face clears as he obviously recognizes her. His jaw drops. "Brandy?" he asks slowly.

Huxley walks up to him and pulls his arm. "Out, now," he snaps.

But Guy yanks his arm out of his grip. His gaze passes over me, then snags on Joanna, and he stares at her before looking back at his brother. "What's going on?"

"I told you not to come here," Huxley states. His eyes blaze—he's furious. Once again, he tries to manhandle Guy out, and this time they scuffle before Guy breaks free and walks behind the sofa to get away from him.

Brandy's hand has crept up to her mouth. Her daughter gets up and comes over to her, and Brandy puts a protective arm around her. "Mum?" Joanna asks uncertainly.

A silence falls in the room. I look at the steaming Huxley, then from Guy to Brandy, confused, my heart racing. Clearly there's an unspoken conversation going on.

Guy turns his gaze to Joanna. "How old is she?" he asks.

Brandy doesn't say anything. I can see that she's shaking.

"She's mine?" he asks.

My heart bangs on my ribs. Oh my God. I'm thoroughly confused, and then, at the same time, it's like the sun coming out, and everything becomes clear.

Huxley moves around the sofa. "No, Joanna's my daughter."

But Guy shifts the other way to avoid him, still staring at her. "Jesus." He looks at Huxley. "Why didn't you tell me?"

"Not now," Huxley says, his words clipped as he looks at Joanna.

But Brandy, her arm tight around her daughter, says, "Hux, it's okay." She kisses Joanna's head. "She knows."

Huxley's eyes widen. "What?"

"I told her last year," Brandy says. "I didn't want there to be any secrets between us."

He stares at Joanna, horrified. She looks up at him with big eyes, her bottom lip trembling.

Brandy looks back at Guy. "I found out I was pregnant just a few weeks after you left. I was absolutely terrified—you know what my parents were like. Huxley found me sitting outside your house, crying. I told him I was pregnant, and that I didn't know what to do. I thought my parents were going to kill me. Huxley said you weren't coming back—that you'd gone to the South Island. He said he'd find you and tell you if I wanted him to. Then he gave me an alternative—he said he'd say he was the father of the baby. We talked about it for ages. And in the end, we decided it was the best option, for me and for the baby."

She looks at me then, her face creased with sorrow. "Elizabeth, I'm so sorry. I didn't think about anyone else except myself. I didn't know how that decision would affect you."

I look at Joanna, who's white-faced and silent, then at Huxley. He's standing with his hands on his hips, looking at the floor, but now he lifts his gaze and meets mine. I can see the truth in his eyes. He took on his brother's child because Guy had run off and abandoned her.

Holy fuck.

Guy also looks completely stunned.

"Oliver's name is on Joanna's birth certificate," Brandy says. "For all intents and purposes, he is her father. Do you understand?"

He nods. He looks completely shell-shocked.

Huxley leaps across the sofa, and this time Guy stays puts. "Come with me," Huxley says firmly, tucking a hand under his arm. Guy doesn't resist as Huxley propels him out of the apartment, letting the door close behind him.

*

Huxley

"What the fuck?" I say in a furious whisper as I frog-march Guy down to the corridor. "I told you never to come here. What the hell do you think you're doing?"

"I needed to see you," Guy says miserably.

I bang on the button to call the elevator, still holding onto his arm in case he tries to go back to the apartment. I've never been this angry. I can't believe he just turned up, right when Brandy and Joanna were there.

I also can't believe Brandy told Joanna that I'm not her birth father. I feel hurt and shocked. Why didn't she discuss it with me? She said she did it last year. So Joanna's known for months? She's never said anything to me. Why didn't she talk to me about it?

Fury boils in my veins. I made a huge sacrifice to be her father. I'm not going to have Guy waltz in now and ruin everything.

And Elizabeth... I've worked incredibly hard to keep my secret over the years, for Brandy and Joanna's sake. What is she going to think now?

The elevator doors ping and open. I push Guy into the carriage, go in behind him, press the button for the ground floor, and the doors close.

"What do you want?" I snap.

He hesitates and studies his shoes.

"Money?" I ask, and he nods.

"What happened to the job I got you?"

"I'm still there," he mumbles. "It's not what you think. I've… met someone."

I stare at him. "What?"

"Her name's Claire. We're moving in together. I'm still clean. I have been for three years. I'm doing my best. I work hard. But the room I'm in is too small for two of us. I want to get us a place together, but I need a deposit. And I wondered whether you could loan me the money. I'll pay you back, I swear."

I'm so shocked, and my brain's whizzing around so fast, I can't think what to say.

I've spent ten years trying to get Guy on the straight and narrow. For seven years, he drank and took drugs, gambled and stole, and got himself into all sorts of trouble. It all came to a head when he tried to take his own life. He was found having taken an overdose, and in the hospital he gave them my name. When they called me, I went down to Christchurch to visit him. He was in a pitiful state, very low, and said he'd hit rock bottom. And for the first time, he asked for help.

I got him into a clinic, and he slowly started getting better. When he eventually left the clinic, I got him a job working in a technology store, as he's always been good with computers, and found him a room in a pleasant part of the city.

I've kept a close eye on him, but I can only do so much. Part of me has been waiting to hear that he's moved out, lost his job, and returned to his old ways.

To hear him say he's met someone, and they're moving in together, brings a wave of emotion crashing over me that I never expected.

"I can't believe you did that for me," he says. "Took on a baby that wasn't yours."

"Brandy needed help. She's religious, so she didn't want to terminate the pregnancy, but she was absolutely terrified what would happen when her parents found out. I felt a duty to provide for her."

Guy gives a ghost of a smile. "Duty and responsibility," he murmurs. "That about sums you up, doesn't it?"

"I had to do something. So I said to tell everyone that we'd had a one-night stand and that Joanna was mine. I told her I'd look after her financially, and make sure she didn't want for anything. She hasn't. And Joanna's grown up into a beautiful, spirited girl."

The doors ping and open, and we walk out into the foyer.

"Do Mum and Dad know?" Guy asks.

I shake my head.

"I'm glad," he says. "Dad already thinks I'm a loser. God knows what he would have thought if he'd known I'd knocked a girl up."

I don't say anything, thinking about the lectures I received when I told him I'd gotten a girl pregnant, and his cruel, vocal disappointment. He still occasionally drops sarcastic comments about my lack of discipline, even though I like to think I've proven myself many times over since then.

"Why did you come here?" I ask, my voice husky. "Why not just call me?"

"Claire wanted me to meet her parents—they live on the North Shore. And I wanted to see you, and tell you that I'm doing all right. Because of you, bro. It's all down to you."

I sigh, and we exchange a cautious bearhug.

"I'm sorry," he whispers. "For everything."

I release him, taking deep breaths to contain my emotion. "I'm just thrilled to see you turning things around." I take out my phone, bring up my banking app, and transfer a generous amount of money over to his account. "It's all done. Buy her something nice for your new place."

"I will. Thank you." Guy shoves his hands in his pockets. "Will you tell Brandy I'm sorry? I was a different man back then."

"Of course."

He looks at the elevator, as if he's holding himself back from returning to the apartment. "A daughter," he whispers. "She was pretty."

I fight with the resentment that rises in me at his discussion of my girl. I need to show pity, not anger. He missed her birth, her first steps, her first words, and all the love she's shown me over her nine years of life. He'll never have the relationship with her that I have.

"She's gorgeous," I admit. "And with a beautiful nature to go with it."

"Does she… take after Brandy?"

I know what he's asking—does she have his flaws? "She's the perfect daughter. She works hard at school, she's well behaved, and she does what her mother tells her. She's going to do just fine."

"Thank you," he says.

I nod.

"Are you and Brandy an item?" he wants to know.

I shake my head. "Never have been."

"But you're not married?"

"Not yet."

"Who was the brunette?"

I decide not to tell him that she's the girl I lost because of him. "An old friend."

"She's pretty."

"Yeah."

"She looked pissed off. She didn't know you weren't Joanna's father?"

"I *am* her father."

He meets my eyes for a moment. "Yeah," he says softly. "Sorry."

He gives one last, longing glance at the elevator. Then he nods at me, turns, and heads out of the front door.

I blow out a long, shaky breath, then go back into the elevator and hit the button. The doors close, and the carriage ascends.

When the doors part again, I walk slowly along the corridor toward the apartment. Part of me doesn't want to go in. Joanna hasn't shown any sign of knowing about Guy, but I can't help but wonder if she feels any anger toward me for lying to her for so long.

It's also possible that Brandy will be furious with me for staying in touch with Guy and not telling her.

And what about Elizabeth? What's she going to think? It's possible that all three of the women in my life are going to yell at me when I walk through the door.

I take out my key and insert it, then pause, half tempted to turn and go back down. But I've got to face the music at some point.

Taking a deep breath, I turn the key and go inside.

Chapter Twenty-Three

Elizabeth

The door opens, and Huxley quietly comes in.

Brandy, Joanna, and I are sitting in the living room, but we all stand as he walks toward us. Nymph goes up and nuzzles his hand, and he ruffles her ears before stopping by the sofa, and slides his hands into his pockets.

"Do I need a crash helmet?" he asks.

Brandy promptly bursts into tears.

He sighs, goes up to her, and puts his arms around her.

"I should have told you." She buries her face in his shirt. "I'm so sorry."

"It's all right." He rubs her back. "I'm sorry for being in touch with Guy and not telling you."

"He's your brother," she says with a sniff. "You didn't have to tell me."

"I know, but even so. I didn't want you to get hurt. But he says he's sorry. He said he was a different man back then, and he regrets what he did."

She rests her forehead on his chest, and he kisses the top of her head.

Then he looks across at Joanna. She's standing there, still white-faced. "Are you okay, sweetheart?" He holds out a hand. "I'm so sorry I lied to you."

"Oh, Daddy," she squeaks, and she runs up next to her mother and wraps her arms around him.

I stand there awkwardly, my heart racing, as he comforts them both.

"You know I love you, right?" he says to Joanna, his voice husky.

"I love you too, Daddy."

"So Mum told you what happened?"

She nods. "She said she got pregnant by your brother, and he left her and went away, so you said you'd pretend to be my father and that you'd look after us both."

"I *am* your father," he says firmly. "I was there when you were born, and I've been there for every major event of your life. I'll be there when you graduate from university, and I'll give you away when you get married. I'm your dad, and nothing's going to change that, do you hear me?" He's clearly emotional.

She nods.

"You should have told me that you knew," he says more gently. "I want you always to be able to talk to me about anything, okay?"

"Yes, Daddy."

He sighs, and for the first time his gaze comes over to me. I'm so full of emotion that all I can do is blink at him.

He clears his throat, and Brandy looks up, then moves back. He kisses the top of his daughter's head, and then releases her.

"Let's go to your room," Brandy says to Joanna, "and hang your clothes up in the wardrobe."

"Okay." Joanna picks up her bag, and the two of them go through to the spare room and close the door behind them.

I watch them go, then turn to face Huxley. He's slid his hands into his pockets, and he's watching me cautiously. His face is pale—this has come as quite a shock to him.

Nymph lies down and puts her snout on her paws, as if she can feel the tension in the room.

"Are you mad at me?" he asks softly.

I shake my head, and he exhales with relief.

We look at each other for a moment. It feels as if there's so much to say, I don't know where to start.

Eventually I swallow hard. "Brandy said that you and she... that you never slept together."

"Nope. There's never been anything romantic between us."

"It never made sense to me," I whisper. "You and she had this connection that I knew would always be bigger than anything we could have, but you never had any chemistry."

He gives a small smile. "She's not my type." He tips his head to the side. "You know who is my type?"

Emotion rushes through me. I don't know why, but the fact that he's never slept with Brandy fills me with joy.

"I can't believe you did that," I say. "You took on your brother's child, even though you knew everyone would look down on you for getting Brandy pregnant. Oh my God, Hux, the way your father ripped into you." I've witnessed several of Peter's explosions toward his son.

"Yeah." He looks at his feet. "That's been tough at times." He looks back up at me. "I wanted to tell you. So many times. But I promised Brandy I'd never tell anyone, and I didn't want to jeopardize Joanna's safety and happiness."

"What about Mack and Victoria? Both of them told me that what happened back then wasn't what I thought."

"I've never discussed it with them. They must have guessed."

Again, I feel a swell of pleasure. He didn't tell everyone else but keep it from me. I haven't been excluded from his confidence.

"I'm so sorry," he says, moving a few feet closer to me before stopping. "When I came across Brandy sitting outside Guy's old house, crying, I felt a sense of duty to provide for her."

"Of course you did." Anyone else might have offered to look after her financially without making the incredible lifetime commitment, but the honorable, principled Huxley would have done everything in his power to protect the vulnerable pregnant girl.

"I was nineteen," he says. "I thought about it for weeks, and I thought I'd gone through everything and planned for every eventuality. I decided I'd wait until the baby was six months old, because that seemed a decent amount of time, and then I'd ask you out again, and we'd start over, and everything would be fine. I was incredibly naïve. I honestly didn't expect you to say no. It completely floored me."

"But you still didn't tell me."

"I promised her. I'd made that commitment, and I knew I'd never be able to go back on it."

"Oh, Hux…" I press my fingers to my mouth.

He sighs, closes the distance between us, puts his arms around me, and I bury my face in his T-shirt.

"I've made all the three women in my life cry this morning," he says. "Wow, I'm doing well."

I move back, wiping my face, and look up at him. "I'm so sorry."

He cups my face and smiles as he wipes away my tears with his thumbs. "You've nothing to be sorry about."

"I am, though, for saying no to you. All these years I've convinced myself you were a playboy. And you're not. You're the best man I know."

He brushes his thumb over my lips. "I lost you, though," he murmurs, his voice so low I can barely hear it. "I love Joanna with all my heart, but if I had my time again…" His voice breaks, and he pulls me into his arms.

We stand there like that for a while, both fighting with our emotion. I bury my nose in his T-shirt. He smells so familiar, and his strong arms are holding me so tightly it's as if he never wants to let me go.

I clear my throat, put my hands on his chest, and move back. "You should spend some time with Brandy and your daughter," I say softly.

He studies my face, then bends his head and kisses me. I close my eyes and let him, enjoying the way he kisses softly from one corner of my mouth to the other before returning to the center. I open my mouth to him, lifting my arms around his neck, and we deepen the kiss for a while before I finally draw back, pressing my lips together.

"I'll see you later," I tell him.

He nods. "Can I call you?"

I smile. "Yes, Hux, you can call me."

He hesitates, and I wonder whether he's going to ask me what happens next. But in the end he just smiles back.

I collect my bag, clip Nymph's lead onto her collar, give him one last look, then leave, letting the door close behind me.

He needs time to be with his daughter, to talk about what happened and make sure she's okay. And I need time to think about what I discovered here today, and what it means going forward.

I love Joanna with all my heart, but if I had my time again… The last thing I'd want is for him to wish he hadn't had his daughter. His implication that he half-wishes he'd chosen me makes me both unbearably happy, and unutterably sad.

As Nymph and I go down in the elevator, I rest my hand on my tummy. I don't want whether I'm pregnant or not to influence my decision. That wouldn't be fair on Huxley or the baby, if there were to be one. They're two separate things. I still have another week before I can take a test. Before next weekend, I need to decide what I'm going to do about England. And what I'm going to do about the man who brought bolt cutters to the padlock around my heart, and stole it from right under my nose.

*

Monday

Huxley

Around midday, I'm inspecting one of the boardrooms in the club with Victoria, trying to decide whether it's worth getting a new set of chairs, when she glances over at the doorway and says, "Oh, hey."

I turn and see Mack leaning against the door jamb, hands in his pockets, watching us.

"Hello," I say. "You're back." He and Sidnie have been in Fiji for their honeymoon. Sidnie told him she didn't expect him to take time off to go away with her, but he insisted. I thought he might only make a few days before he flew back, but he lasted the whole week, and now he looks tanned and relaxed. "Have a good time?"

"Fabulous," he says, and smiles.

"Lots of sex?" Victoria asks.

"Hardly got out of bed the whole time. Sidnie said she's walking like John Wayne when he gets off his horse." He chuckles, and we both laugh.

He pushes off the post and comes into the room. "I've just spoken to Elizabeth."

I meet his eyes and my lips curve up slowly. "Ah."

He shakes his head slowly. "I knew it."

"Knew what?" Victoria asks. She looks from Mack to me, and says, "Oh... You told her you're not Joanna's birth father."

"Guy turned up at his apartment," Mack says. "Brandy, Joanna, and Elizabeth were all there."

"Fuck," Victoria says.

"Yeah," I reply. "It wasn't the easiest morning I've ever had."

"Guy twigged it?" she asks, gesturing for us to sit at the table.

We all pull out chairs and sit as I continue, "He put two and two together, yeah. But it turns out Brandy had already told Joanna. I didn't know."

Her brow creases. "Aw, that's tough."

I sigh. "Maybe it was better that she had told her. It would have been tougher if she hadn't, and then she'd met Guy."

"How was Joanna about it?"

"Brandy and I sat down with her for a while. I said she could ask me anything she wanted. But she didn't seem interested in Guy at all. She said I was her dad, and she didn't need to know anything else." I shrug. "I said she might feel differently as she grows older, and that she could ask me whatever she wanted at any time. And that was it, really. I took her to the cinema, and then we went home and made pizza and played a board game, and she didn't mention it again."

"I'm so glad," Victoria says. "She's such a lovely girl. So… what happened with Elizabeth?"

"We didn't get much chance to talk about it. She was shocked, obviously. You know what she's like; she needs time to think about it. We've texted a couple of times, but I haven't seen her since."

"So you don't know what's happening with England?" Mack asks. "Whether she's still going to go?"

I shake my head. "Her career is important to her, and she has this great opportunity, and I don't want to be the one standing in her way. I think maybe she's starting to believe I'm serious about her. And if it wasn't for the relationships she's had since then, she might have come around. But I think she's been too badly scarred. I don't know if she'll ever be able to trust a man fully, and I can't blame her, after how she's been treated."

Mack purses his lips. Then he says, "There is one thing you could do."

"What?"

"Make a grand gesture."

"I tried that, remember? I'm not jumping off another fucking building."

"Actually," he says, "I was thinking of something a little different…"

*

The next day, I arrive at Albert Park in the early afternoon. The warm autumn sun is flooding the park with a buttery yellow light, and although the city is busy, the park is relatively quiet. The kids are still at school, and there are only a few dog walkers and one or two couples strolling through, enjoying the sunshine.

I pass the statue of Queen Victoria and arrive at the fountain. When I called Elizabeth's office and they told me she'd taken Nymph for a walk, I was convinced this was where she'd come, as I know it's her favorite place to walk the dog. Sure enough, she's sitting on one of the benches, her eyes closed, with Nymph stretched out on the grass, dozing.

I lean against the lamppost, watching Elizabeth for a moment, relieved to have found her. She's wearing a light-gray trouser suit with a white shirt, although she's exchanged her high heels for a pair of Converses that must be more comfortable for walking.

She's sitting with her head tipped back, face tilted to the sun, her chocolate-brown hair hanging down past her shoulders, sleek and shiny. She's gorgeous, and I feel a flutter of nerves as I think about why I'm here.

At that moment, Nymph lifts her head and spots me, gets to her feet, and barks. Elizabeth opens her eyes and looks around. Her gaze falls on me, and I feel a rush of pleasure as I see her eyes widen, and she inhales and sits up.

I walk across the path to her and let my backpack drop onto the bench as I fuss Nymph. "Afternoon."

"Hello," she says. "What are you doing here?"

"I was just walking by." I unzip the backpack.

She gives me a wry look. "How did you know I'd be here?"

"Your PA said you'd taken Nymph for a walk. I knew you'd come here." I take out a small speaker and turn it on.

She glances at it. "What are you doing?"

"Just a second."

She looks back up at me and takes a deep breath. "Hux, I've been giving it a lot of thought, and—"

"Nope." In alarm, I shake my head. "Don't. I've prepared a speech," I say. "Please, let me go through with it first, before you say anything."

"But—"

"Elizabeth!"

She stops. "Okay."

I take out my phone, pull up Spotify, and press play, and The Beatles' *Don't Let Me Down* begins playing—one of her favorite songs that we danced to on the yacht. Leaving the phone on the seat, I hold out a hand.

Elizabeth lifts an eyebrow. I flick my fingers toward me. She glances around. A man is walking his red setter on the other side of the fountain, and a couple is just exiting the circle around the fountain, but otherwise it's quiet. Her lips twitch, and she slides her hand into mine and lets me pull her to her feet.

I hold her right hand with my left, and slide my right into the dip of her back. She rests her left hand on my shoulder. And slowly, we begin to move to the music.

"What's this about?" she asks softly.

I clear my throat. "I've been thinking about you a lot. Almost non-stop, actually."

"Me too." She brushes my shoulder with her thumb. "How's Joanna?"

"She's fine."

"No ill effects from Guy's visit?"

"No, not at all. We had a lovely day on Sunday, actually. If anything, I think it's brought us closer together."

"I'm glad."

I pull her toward me a bit more as John sings that nobody has ever loved me like she does. I'm tempted to cross my fingers.

"Here goes," I say. "Let me get through it before you say anything, okay?"

"Okay."

I take a deep breath. "I've been in love with you since the day we first met. Now you know the truth about what happened, and hopefully you understand how hard it was to make the decisions that I did. Like I said, if I had my time again, maybe I'd choose differently, be more selfish, I don't know. I love my daughter with all my heart, but in gaining her, I lost you, and that has been hard to bear."

Her eyes glisten. "I want to—"

"Elizabeth, please. Over the years, I tried to move on as it became clear that we weren't going to work out, but I just couldn't. I'm still in love with you—ten times, maybe a hundred times—more than I was when we were young. I thought that if I could just get you into bed, you'd realize how right we were for each other. I was so arrogant, I realize that now. I know how important your career is to you, and I'm so proud of you for what you've achieved. I know you're going to go on and do amazing things, and stopping you achieving those goals is the last thing I want. But I do want you."

She presses her lips together, her brown eyes wide as they look up at me.

As Lennon tells her that I'm in love for the first time, and that it's going to last, I slide a hand into the pocket of my trousers and take out the small velvet box I bought this morning. Cracking it open, I release her, then sink onto one knee.

"Elizabeth Tremblay," I say, "I'm asking you to marry me, but that's not all. I want us to be engaged when you go to England. That way, I hope you can trust me when I tell you that I want to wait for you. I want you to go and be amazing over there, and achieve all the things you want to achieve. I'll come over and see you as often as I can. And then when you're done, and you come back to New Zealand, we'll get married."

She stares at me for a long, long time. The warm autumn wind brushes across us, and Nymph sneezes.

"You'd wait two years for me?" Elizabeth asks eventually.

"It's not so long. I've waited ten years already, haven't I?" I waggle the box at her.

She looks at the ring properly for the first time. Her eyes widen even more. "Holy fuck."

I glance at it. It's six-point-eight excellent cut round diamond. Over half a million dollars fitted into a tiny band.

"Hux," she says in an awed voice. "That must have cost you a fortune." She meets my eyes. "You crazy fucker."

"Not quite the romantic endearment I was hoping for."

"Get up, for God's sake."

"You haven't answered me yet," I tell her. I try to sound firm, but I think it might come across as slightly pathetic. I want this girl so much. She's spent so long running away from me, and I'm still crazy about her. Even Lennon knows it's a love that's going to last forever. Surely, she's not going to turn me down?

Chapter Twenty-Four

Elizabeth

I haven't replied, because I'm completely in shock.

Huxley's asking me to marry him?

He'd wait for me? For two years?

I can't believe it. After all this time... after I've turned him down every month for ten years... He still wants me?

I look down at him, and all at once the floodgates open and emotion bursts through me like water through a crack in a dam. "Oh my God, of course I'll marry you, you idiot."

His eyes light up, and he rises slowly to his feet. "Seriously?"

"And pass up the chance to wear this ring?" I tease. "You've got to be kidding me." I stare at it. The diamond is absolutely huge. I've never seen one so big. Jesus, I'm almost too frightened to touch it.

Gently, he removes it from the box, picks up my hand, and slides it onto my fourth finger. It fits perfectly, and it glitters in the autumn sun.

"It's so beautiful," I say breathlessly.

"I'm glad you like it."

I look up at him then and laugh. "Of course I like it." I throw my arms around him, and he hugs me, lifting me off my feet.

"I don't believe it," he whispers in my ear. "You're really going to marry me?" He lowers me down to look at me.

My arms still around him, I look up at him and nod. "I love you so much. I always have. I'm sorry I've taken so long to open my heart to you. I was so afraid of getting hurt again." I hesitate, then tell him the decision I made just minutes ago, when I came to the park to think. "Huxley... I've decided to stay."

"I thought that maybe you might... Wait, what?"

"I'm not going to England," I say softly.

He stares at me. "But… I said I'd wait for you…"

"I know, and I'm so incredibly touched by that, I want to bawl my eyes out. But I'd already decided, Hux. I've been thinking about nothing else for days. I came here today to make the decision, and when I sat down in this beautiful park in the autumn sunshine, and thought about what I wanted to do, and not what I thought I *should* do, the answer was blindingly obvious. I want to stay, and I want to be with you."

"You're absolutely sure? The fact that I'd wait for you, it doesn't change your mind?"

"No, if anything it strengthens my decision." I cup his face in my hands. "I can't believe you'd wait for me."

"I would."

"I know you would. I absolutely know it now. I trust you with all my heart."

"But I know how much the project means to you. What will you do?"

"I'll talk to Titus. He did say he would consider going if I didn't want to. And if he doesn't, well, we'll talk to Acheron and work something out. I'm not going to be blackmailed into it just to get the funding."

The ring glitters in the sun, blindingly beautiful. I lift up onto my tiptoes and kiss him, sliding my hands into his hair, filled with such happiness that I think I might burst.

When I eventually move back, his eyes are filled with wonder. "You're really going to stay?"

I nod and tease, "Well that way we can try to make a baby as much as is humanly possible."

He slides his gaze down me to rest on my belly. "So you're not pregnant?"

"Oh, I don't know yet. Another week or so. I'm just saying, if I stay, we can practice as often as we like."

He chuckles and hugs me. "I'd like that. I'm excited to watch our baby grow inside you. I can't imagine how amazing that's going to be."

Of course, all along I've thought that he's been through it all before, but although he was with Brandy when she was pregnant, he hadn't fathered the child inside her. It's a revelation to me, and it fills me with joy.

I slide my arms around his waist, and we stand there like that for a while, just enjoying being close, in the late afternoon sun.

"I love you," he says.

I bury my face in his shirt. "I love you too, Huxley. So, so much." I can't believe how wonderful it feels to say that. It's as if there have been tight metal bands around my chest, and they've finally snapped. I've been so afraid to say how I feel, to tell him what's in my heart.

"Let's get married soon," he says. "I don't want to wait."

"Okay."

"Will you take my name or keep yours?"

"Elizabeth Huxley," I whisper. "I like the sound of that. I suppose I'll have to start calling you Oliver now, will I?"

He snorts. "Not unless you want me to be permanently grumpy."

"I don't know why you don't like your name. I think it's elegant. Oliver."

"Actually, although I don't like Ollie, I don't mind Oliver. It wasn't my decision not to use it. It was Mack—he started calling me Huxley and everyone else just followed suit."

"I think he'll be pleased we're getting married," I say.

He laughs. "Yeah. He'll be over the moon."

I rest my left hand on his chest. "I can't believe this ring. It's so incredibly beautiful."

"Not as beautiful as you," he says simply. "You outshine it, Elizabeth. You're a hundred times more precious to me than any diamond. I'm just crazy about you, and I always will be. I can't wait to promise to love you forever in front of everyone we know."

And as the tears finally spill over my lashes, he kisses me, while Nymph sniffs around us in the grass, and the warm autumn breeze ruffles our hair.

*

Friday

Huxley

When I turn up for our usual Friday meeting, Titus, Mack, and Victoria all cheer when I walk into the boardroom. Although Elizabeth and I have told them all that she's agreed to marry me, it's the first time we've had a chance to celebrate together. Victoria has organized a slightly more luxurious lunch for us all today, with hot food brought in from the nearby Chinese restaurant. A bottle of champagne is chilling in an ice bucket by the table. We don't usually drink alcohol at lunch, but Titus pops the cork now, and fills our glasses with a splash of the champagne.

"This looks nice," I say, taking a seat.

"We were just admiring the ring," Victoria says. "It's so beautiful."

"I know." Elizabeth looks at it, "I'm almost too afraid to wear it."

She smiles, but her face is pale, and I feel a twinge of concern. I know she, Mack, and Titus had a conference call with Alan Woodridge from Acheron Pharmaceuticals this morning, and they were going to tell him that she wouldn't be going to England. I don't know how it went. Was it bad news?

"We're all absolutely thrilled for you both," Mack says. "Have you set a date?"

"We don't want to wait," I reply, "like you and Sidnie. We're thinking about August, actually, because Heidi will be home then."

"Will it be here?" Mack asks.

"Maybe Queenstown," Elizabeth says. "We're still thinking."

"That would be amazing," Victoria states. "In the snow! How romantic."

"Let's have a toast," Titus says, "to Huxley and Elizabeth."

We all lift our glasses and have a sip of the champagne. I meet Elizabeth's eyes. She gives me a tentative smile, but I know I was right—something's upset her.

"Tuck in," Victoria says afterward, "before it gets cold."

We all help ourselves to the delicious-smelling containers of dim sum, Sichuan beef, chicken in black bean sauce, and the various vegetarian dishes including rice with cashew nuts and a stir-fried vegetable selection.

Elizabeth puts some on her plate, then sits back. Something's definitely bothering her. She meets my eyes, and I open my mouth to ask, but she gives a little shake of her head, and I close my mouth again.

"So what's the news with Acheron?" Victoria asks, biting into a dim sum.

"It went well enough," Titus says. "He was disappointed, but he understood."

I feel a rush of relief, because Elizabeth was really worried that she'd ruined the project. "Oh, I'm so glad."

Titus nods, tucking into his lunch. "It was a relief to know he was happy to discuss other options."

"So what did you decide? Are you going instead?"

"Not sure yet. I'll probably fly over there and discuss it with him. I don't particularly want to go for two years, but I will if I have to."

I glance at Elizabeth. She's not eating. Mack frowns and gestures with his head toward her. I give a slight shrug.

"You all right?" I ask her. "You look very pale."

She nods and swallows. "I…" She presses her lips together. Then she puts down her serviette and hurriedly gets to her feet. "I'm so sorry, I think I'm going to be sick." She turns and rushes from the room, her heels tapping as she runs down the corridor to the Ladies'.

I stare after her, then look at the others.

As one, the other three start to smile. "Holy fuck," Mack says softly.

My jaw drops, but no words come out.

"Is she late?" Victoria asks me.

"I don't think so," I say, my voice husky. "Her period is due tomorrow, I think."

"Can she get symptoms this early?" Titus asks.

"I don't know." Victoria pulls out her phone and Googles it, while I watch her, my head spinning. She reads quickly, then smiles and lowers her phone. "Yeah, apparently some women can feel nauseous a week after conception."

"It could just be a stomach bug," I say, my voice a squeak.

Mack chuckles. "Yeah, keep telling yourself that, *Daddy*."

"Jesus. I feel dizzy."

"You're hyperventilating," Victoria says, "put your head between your knees."

At that moment, though, the door opens, and Elizabeth comes back in.

I get to my feet and go around the table to her. "Are you all right?"

She nods, but I can see the excitement in her eyes.

"Do you think…" I begin.

"I don't know." She moistens her lips with the tip of her tongue. "I'm not late yet."

"Victoria looked it up. Some women apparently feel nauseous a week after conception."

Our gazes lock, and we both start smiling.

"I'm going to buy a test," she says.

"I'll come with you." I turn back to the guys. "You don't mind?"

"Go," they all call. "Just come back and let us know!"

Together, Elizabeth and I leave the club and walk the short distance to the nearest pharmacy. My heart hammers as we scan the shelf of pregnancy tests. "Look at this," I say, picking one up, "it says it can detect the pregnancy hormones five days before you miss your period."

"Oh my God, really?" She gets two packs. "Come on."

She takes them to the counter and pays for them, and then we go back outside. "I might go to my apartment," she says.

"Can I come with you?"

She nods. "I'd like that."

Holding hands, we walk the short distance to her apartment.

She drops Nymph off with her brother on Friday mornings, so the apartment is empty and quiet. I pace up and down the living room as she goes into the bathroom, then turn when she comes out holding the test.

"Three minutes," she says breathlessly. "Apparently it's nearly ninety-nine percent accurate, even this early."

She puts the test on the kitchen counter face down. I stand in front of her and hold her hands.

"How are you feeling?" I ask softly.

"Okay." She looks up at me with her big brown eyes. "You?"

I chuckle. "I'm okay."

"Are you nervous?"

I pull her into my arms and kiss the top of her head. "No. Excited."

"It might be negative. Maybe I've just got a stomach bug."

"If it is, we'll try again."

She buries her face in my shirt. "I don't want to have to go through IVF. I've seen what it's done to Pen and Paul…"

I hug her tightly. "Hey, whatever happens, we'll face it together. I'm not arrogant enough anymore to think I can make it happen by sheer force of will. But I do think it will happen for us. I just have a feeling."

She moves back a little and looks up at me. "I love you."

"I love you, too. So much."

I lower my lips to hers, and we exchange a long kiss, until her phone emits a merry jangle.

She stops the alarm and reaches for the test. "One line for negative, two for positive," she says. She takes a deep breath. And turns it over.

It contains two lines.

"Oh my God!" She squeals and claps a hand over her mouth.

"It's positive?"

She nods, tears brimming in her eyes.

I feel a rush of hot emotion. She's not staying because she's pregnant. She chose to stay, and to accept my proposal, before she found out.

We're going to get married. And we're going to have a baby.

Her tears spill down her cheeks, and I pull her into my arms once again and kiss her, overcome with joy.

*

Elizabeth

Huxley calls Mack and tells him, then says we're going to be late back, and they should finish lunch without us. Mack just laughs and replies that he's not surprised, and they're all absolutely thrilled for us.

Then the two of us go to bed and make love, and Huxley is so sweet and tender that it makes me ache.

Afterward, I curl up in the bed, looking out at the harbor, and Huxley puts his arms around me and kisses my ear.

"I love you," he murmurs, nuzzling the spot behind the lobe.

I give a happy sigh. "I love you too."

"I still can't believe it." He rests his hand on my tummy. "You have a baby growing inside you. How amazing is that?"

I rest my hand on top of his, thinking of how extraordinary the process is. "How is it that two people can make another person?"

"I know. A little piece of me, and a little piece of you. It's a miracle."

"Thank you so much," I whisper.

"It was my pleasure. Literally." He nips my earlobe.

"Ow." I chuckle. "I'm so happy right now."

"Me too." He strokes my arm and yawns. "Let's have a snooze."

"We should get back to work."

"Half an hour won't hurt anyone."

"True." I nestle back into his arms, watching the clouds scud across the sky, and feel his breathing grow deep and even behind me as he dozes, worn out by all the emotion.

I'm tired, too, and now I know why. My stomach flutters—far too early to be the baby, more a swell of butterflies at the thought of what's to come.

I've watched Pen go through all kinds of problems, and I know I mustn't get too excited. One in four pregnancies end in miscarriage, and that's one issue with testing so early.

But equally, Hux is right, and it is a miracle. Right here, right now, I'm pregnant, and I'm not going to scold myself for feeling so much joy.

The clouds outside are drifting away, and the sky is a brilliant blue. I hold up my hands and move each finger as I calculate my dates. I'm going to be due in December. Oh, wait until I tell him. It's going to be the best Christmas present ever.

My heart floating with happiness, with Huxley's warm body pressed against my back, I close my eyes and slowly drift off to sleep.

Newsletter

If you'd like to be informed when my next book is available,
you can sign up for my mailing list on my website,
http://www.serenitywoodsromance.com

About the Author

USA Today bestselling author Serenity Woods writes sexy contemporary romances, most of which are set in the sub-tropical Northland of New Zealand, where she lives with her wonderful husband.

Website: http://www.serenitywoodsromance.com
Facebook: http://www.facebook.com/serenitywoodsromance